C000080390

AT
NIGHT
YOU
SLEEP
ALONE

AT NIGHT YOU SLEEP ALONE

PARKASH SOHAL

Copyright © 2016 Parkash Sohal
First Published in 2015

The moral right of the author has been asserted.

Apart from any fair dealing for the purposes of research or private study,
or criticism or review, as permitted under the Copyright, Designs and Patents
Act 1988, this publication may only be reproduced, stored or transmitted, in
any form or by any means, with the prior permission in writing of the
publishers, or in the case of reprographic reproduction in accordance with
the terms of licences issued by the Copyright Licensing Agency. Enquiries
concerning reproduction outside those terms should be sent to the publishers.

This is a work of fiction. Names, characters, businesses, places, events
and incidents are either the products of the author's imagination
or used in a fictitious manner. Any resemblance to actual persons,
living or dead, or actual events is purely coincidental.

Matador
9 Priory Business Park,
Wistow Road, Kibworth Beauchamp,
Leicestershire. LE8 0RX
Tel: 0116 279 2299
Email: books@troubador.co.uk
Web: www.troubador.co.uk/matador
Twitter: @matadorbooks

ISBN 978 1785891 809

British Library Cataloguing in Publication Data.
A catalogue record for this book is available from the British Library.

Printed and bound by CPI Group (UK) Ltd, Croydon, CR0 4YY
Typeset in 11pt Adobe Garamond Pro by Troubador Publishing Ltd, Leicester, UK

Matador is an imprint of Troubador Publishing Ltd

MIX
Paper from
responsible sources
FSC® C013604

To Jinder

'Though in the busy daylight hours
Our dark thoughts we disown,
When darkness falls, they will return
At night, you sleep alone...'

DIANE PERRY

PART ONE

1.1

—w—

TWENTY YEARS LATER...

22 AUGUST 1989

It is around two thirty on a Tuesday afternoon when the telephone in my factory rings. Gurjit, who works on the factory floor, always picks up.

I own a clothing factory in East London, Aldgate to be precise, where over fifty people work. They are mostly Asian immigrants who come to the UK in search of a better future. Gurjit, despite being the youngest, is the brightest of the workers. She was born here, so English is her first language. It is her duty to pick up the phone, deal with customers and visitors.

'Uncle, a lady on the phone is asking for you,' she shouts.

'Who is it, what's her name?'

'Dr Simran.'

Do I know a Dr Simran? I pick up the phone in the office.

'Hello, can I help you?'

To my surprise, the caller speaks in confident Punjabi. 'Sat Siri Akaal, Uncle Ji. I'm Dr Simran Ahluwalia. My mum Sharnjit thinks of you so much, it's true, Uncle Ji.'

'Beta Ji, you must be mistaken; I'm not familiar with anyone by the name of Sharnjit.' 'Your name is Parkash Sohal? Is that right, Uncle Ji?' she asks.

'Yes, but I still cannot recall anyone by your mum's name.'

'Okay, I'll ring back in half an hour.' She sounds disappointed. Is it possible she got the wrong number? But then, how did she know my name? Unable to come up with an answer, I get busy with work.

Half an hour later, the telephone rings again, making me jump.

'Uncle, the same lady again; she wants you.'

'Sat Siri Akaal, Uncle Ji. I am Simran Ahluwalia daughter of Nirmal.' This time, she speaks with certainty and determination as if to say, *'You are the right person.'*

The ground moves from under my feet. I am speechless and shaken for a moment.

'Nir...mal, Nir...mal.' *Oh my God.* I don't believe what I'm hearing. My legs are shaking. Twenty years ago, I lost hope of ever finding her again. I take a deep breath and try to control my emotions. 'Yes... yes, my dear Beta Ji. Now I know who you are. Where is Nirmal? How is she? Is she here in the UK?'

'We have lived in Hayes, Uncle Ji, for the past twenty years. Mom remembered you every single day with every breath. She is not too well,' she says and bursts into tears. 'Be strong, Beta Ji, she'll be fine.' Although I say all this to keep control of the situation, I am far from being okay myself.

'She is not well and is not going to be, if she carries on the way she does. She is so stubborn, Uncle Ji. She does not listen. I've tried.'

'Sorry, Beta Ji, I don't get it. What are you asking her to do?'

'Oh, Uncle Ji, she refuses to go to the hospital for treatment and keeps saying, "Once I see my Sardar Parkash, I will die in peace."'

Simran starts to sob again and pleads, 'Uncle Ji, save my mum... please.'

'Beta Ji, please control yourself. Rest assured, I will come to see Nirmal. Please give me your address. In fact I'll come right now.' My whole body has gone cold and there is an air of despair and emptiness within me. *What could be so wrong with her…? Why is she refusing treatment…?* I am so overwhelmed with emotion that I have forgotten to ask her about her father and so many other questions. Perhaps it is not the right time for details.

After a pause, she says, 'No, Uncle Ji, not today, come tomorrow and stays with us all day. I'm sure you can spare one day of your life for your Nirmal. She has waited for you for over twenty years.'

'Tell her to dress up nicely,' I say, trying to lighten the mood.

'Yes, Uncle Ji, Mum hasn't forgotten what your choices were.' There is happiness in her voice this time.

I'm completely lost in thought when I put the phone down. Simran must be very close to her mother to know what my choices were in those days.

'Yes I will… I will be with you, Nirmal,' I murmur. Simran speaks exactly like her mother and the reassurance in her voice has taken me back twenty years.

On a day in January, Nirmal and I were having tea at our favourite dhaba in Gali No. 2. The large pots of marigolds were in full bloom, basking in the sun in one corner. She had pointed at them saying, 'Oh, aren't they lovely? What's your favourite colour?'

'All flowers in bloom look beautiful but I love light yellow, fresh cotton flowers. Especially in the morning when they have tiny droplets of dew on them, bathed in the early morning rays of sun. They dry up and become a little limp when the day gets hotter. I love their journey from first kiss of the sun's rays to the giving in to the heat of the mid-day sun. Infancy to old – a journey of life indeed,' I said.

'You have the art of finding the hidden meaning of life in the minutest of details,' she said, holding my hand in her beautiful soft hands. I remember their softness and warmth even today. On our first date, she wore my favourite colour: a lemon yellow dress.

My mind is going round in circles. I never thought I would find Nirmal in this situation. I come out of the office puzzled. Well,

I am hiding something. My wife, Jinder, has a habit of asking, "Who was on the phone?" Regardless of whether it concerns her or not, she will ask anyway.

'Umm... from the bank...'

'Oh, Gurjit was saying it was some doctor?' She has probably seen through my lies already.

'So why can't a doctor be a banker?' I raise my voice.

It is normal for a person to raise their voice when they are trying to hide something. Well, it is a big part of human nature; we are all guilty of lying from time to time.

Jinder manages the factory with Gurjit and my job is to deal with customers. Our routine is such that Jinder leaves at five and I lock up around half past six.

I find myself in a real dilemma. Ever since we got married, we made a pact not to lie to each other. Ours is a strong relationship built on trust. There are those rare occasions when I do not tell her everything. Especially when I think that things don't concern her, I don't share everything. However, this would be of real concern to her. I'm going to see another woman – my first love. How would she react if she found out? There is no doubt she will find out eventually. Whatever the circumstances, a lie is a lie. In my childhood, my mother used to tell us a story about the oldest Pandava, Yudhisthira, who never lied. He was well known for his honesty and his friends and enemies respected him. He lied only once, but was punished and not forgiven by God. With such stories, she instilled in us the virtue of always being honest.

Under normal circumstances, Jinder accepts what I tell her without question. It has worked well for us thus far. Now I am lying to her about the phone call and tomorrow I would be lying again.

Help me, God! I plead my helplessness. We, Indians have this habit of calling upon God on anything and everything as if He has nothing better to do.

A debate is raging in my head.

'*Hypocrite!*' a voice keeps telling me. '*What if the roles were reversed? What if she told you she's going to see her first love? You'd never tolerate it. The mutual trust will be shattered. Your relationship will be broken.*'

'*She wouldn't understand.*'

'*She may.*'

'*I can't risk it.*'

'*You've already risked it.*'

I don't know what's wrong and what's right. I cannot let Nirmal down. She needs me. I'm just going to visit her after all those years. It is my duty as a friend. Do they not say… a friend in need is a friend indeed? Still feeling uneasy, I console myself with various words of wisdom.

1.2

WE MEET AGAIN

This morning, I'm all set to go.

'Jinder, I will be out for most of the day. Will you please, lock the factory up if I do not come back on time?' I hurry out of the door before she can ask me any more questions. My excitement is mixed with apprehension and some grief too.

I arrive at the house around 10 a.m. I see the doorbell button right in front of me but I cannot seem to muster the courage to press it. My whole being is frozen. My hands get clammy. I'm scared and do not know what I'm scared of. The little button in front of my eyes seems to turn into a huge red ball of fire. If I touch, it will melt everything that I have so far managed to keep intact. 'O God, please help me... I can't face Nirmal.' Twenty long years have passed and here I am, turning back to the first chapter again.

A woman I guess to be Simran opens the door. She looks so much like her mother did.

'Parkash Sohal,' I introduce myself.

'No, Uncle Ji, Sardar Parkash,' she whispers.

'Simran...?' I ask.

She greets me with a broad smile and asks me to come in. The house looks neat and clean. As I enter the lounge...Oh my God!

There she is! Nirmal is standing near the fireplace, draped in a light yellow Punjabi suit, looking like a princess, waiting with her hands folded. My heart almost misses a beat or two. We look at each other; I walk towards her and after a pause, without saying a word, I take her hands. I hold both hands as I did many years ago on the banks of Yamuna under the half-shady tree; as I did sitting in the dhaba listening to her speak. Her hands are still as soft and warm. We've lost control over the tears falling over our cheeks. The special fragrance that has been lingering in my mind for years is here – right in front of me. Simran and I escort Nirmal to her bedroom. Simran sits beside her, 'Where did you get all this strength from, Mum? You should ask us to give you support.'

'You both have a chat while I make tea.' Simran goes into kitchen, leaving us alone.

Those tears, buried in our eyes for years, come flooding out and the silent question comes back to haunt us, *'Why did it happen?'*

We both have no answer. O God! Twenty-two years to account for and nothing to say. Words do not come out.

A tsunami of emotions has engulfed us. Somehow, I gather strength and try to calm down as I sit on the chair next to Nirmal, caressing her hands. I call Simran back from the kitchen.

'Tea can wait. Please tell me about your mum first.'

Simran starts sobbing again as she sits on the other side of the bed.

'I can deal with patients and control my emotions but not when it comes to Mum. I just can't. She gives me lots of stress by not listening. We found her cancer at too late a stage. The damn disease has damaged her left breast completely now. She hid it from everyone for a long time. Now she says she will not die piecemeal.'

'I can understand. It must be very difficult for her to tell you all this,' I sympathise.

I cannot take it anymore and feel as if my head is going to burst open. When I left home this morning, never in my wildest dreams had I imagined that I would be confronted with this situation. Nirmal suffers so much and still takes it on with such courage.

'What are the doctors saying?'

'They told us that left breast should be removed and chemotherapy will need to start at once.'

Simran starts to sob again. 'The answer I get from Mum is "I do not wish to lose my hair. How will I face Sardar Parkash, who adored my hair? No. I can't have my breast removed either." '

"She is not even scared of dying."

Simran's sobbing does not stop and I'm finding it difficult to hold back my tears. 'There must be some cure, somewhere? There has to be something we can do to get rid of this terrible disease. From a doctor's point of view, tell me what we need to do.'

'The cancer has now spread to both sides, Uncle Ji, but the big problem is Mum. She doesn't want to seek any cure. All she wants to do is to see you and then go in peace.'

'I understand the dilemma – On the one hand, a loving daughter wants to try everything to save her mum and feels helpless. On the other hand, her mother knows her own fate but still tries her best to hide her pain. She loves her daughter far too much to give her any grief. I understand it fully well,' I say to myself.

'What you are doing is not right, Nirmal. Our children have rights over us. You cannot take Simran's mother away from her. She needs you, Nirmal.' I plead.

The phone rings. Simran has to go the hospital to cover an emergency.

'I'll be back in a couple of hours, Uncle Ji. Please look after Mum. The nurse will be here any minute,' she says assured that I will be staying the day with them. She treats me as if I was already a part of her family. Look after Mum she said without hesitation.

1.3

A STORY OF TWENTY TWO YEARS...

'Sardar Parkash, tell me all about your twenty odd years. How has life been?' Nirmal gazes deep into my eyes.

God's special creation, I murmur. Age has made a very little difference... that special sparkle is still there in her beautiful eyes. They drove me crazy those days; they still do today.

'First tell me—what do I call you? Nirmal or Sharnjit?' I ask.

'It used to make a difference once upon a time, but not anymore. Nirmal means "pure" as you used to tell me. It was a struggle to keep myself Nirmal in the environment I was living in. I took up the challenge and succeeded, I believe. Whoever came to Ammi Jaan, has to change her name to a new name. Odd, I thought but followed suit just for the fun of it. It was those mad old days when taking chances and standing on the edge felt exhilarating. Also, I was living there as a tenant; not like others who found sanctuary.' She takes a sip of water as she loses her breath, and then continues.

'Now you can call me by whatever name you like. Simran has been keeping me informed about you but I want to hear from you.'

'Nirmal, the truth is that my life has kept me so occupied that twenty years have gone past without me really noticing. My wife and I have a very good understanding. She's well versed in how to run the home life. In fact, she's the one who manages everything. I make many mistakes but she is always there to forgive and guide me. I'm the father of three lovely daughters and an intelligent son.'

But it has not really been that easy. Those twenty-two long years, in which I haven't been able to keep Nirmal from my mind for even one second. My mind has been stuck in the *'what if'* syndrome for a long time. But no, whatever turbulences I had in my life, I must not discuss them now. She has more than enough to deal with.

'Tell me, Nirmal, how did it go for you all these years? Remember your promise? "See you tomorrow!" became twenty two years.'

Nirmal lay motionless and quiet with a blank look in her eyes. Perhaps she is also seeking an answer. Some questions do not have answers. Not appropriate ones. Perhaps it's better that they remain questions without answers.

She stares straight ahead and says, 'I cannot tell you in brief even if I try. So much has happened... so much. I will complete it in instalments with your permission, Sardar Parkash.' She smirks at the name. I see the mischievousness return to her big eyes.

This sparkling of her eyes used to drive me crazy and still does so. I do not know where my new fearlessness comes from and I find myself saying 'Of course. I'll come to see you every day.'

'So, my illness has worked. At least you will come and see me as you promised!'

'Now that I've found you, I won't make the mistake of losing you again.'

'No sir, you did not find us. Simran found you,' she says.

There is long a silence while I sit next to her, caressing her hands.

'I haven't measured up to your expectations. I'm so sorry. It was entirely my fault. Sardar Parkash, I take the blame. I'm so sorry.' She suddenly bursts out crying, breaking the calm silence that has descended between us.

She holds my hands even more tightly now. The atmosphere has changed. Warm tears come gushing down from our eyes and land on our clasped hands. The words have dried up. A lot is being said in the tear-tossed silence.

'One thing you need to do is make a promise. Promise that you will let us find a solution for your illness. You will not refuse treatment. Every problem has a solution,' I say, trying to change the subject.

'Secondly, I've loved you with all my heart and soul. Therefore, I do have the right to know everything about you, Nirmal. I lived with many questions; you must answer them now.' I gather some control as I continue. 'I know why you changed your name but why were you living at a Twaif's house?

'What forced you to stay in oblivion? You had my address; why didn't you contact me or anyone else? Every time I think of you, I confront the question – *Why?*

'Please Nirmal, please tell me…'

There is a long pause again as she looks up at the ceiling. 'Now that we have met, I wish to live again. I want you to find a cure for me. But please, I don't want anyone to cut any part of my body. I don't want to lose anything. You loved me as I am. Remember how you used to call me "Princess"?' There was nothing left in me that was mine. I gave you everything I had, twenty years ago on the banks of the Yamuna. The meeting of our minds mattered, nothing else… You'll get your answers when your time comes.' The smirk returns to her face when she gives me that trademark answer of hers.

'Okay, whenever you're ready. But one thing – you are always in my heart as Nirmal. I do not wish to call you anything else,' I say.

'I will always be your Nirmal' she says, looking deep into my eyes.

1.4

AFTERNOON TEA

It is four in the evening, and all of sudden, Nirmal wakes up. 'Simran Beta, time for your Uncle Ji's tea,' she says.

I smile and say with pretend astonishment, 'So you haven't forgotten that I take tea at four, come what may.'

Poor Simran has to do so much work. She just came back from the hospital and has straightaway set to doing the house chores, and she still has a smile on her face.

'Can I help you in any way?' I ask as I go in the kitchen.

'No, Uncle Ji. You just sit with Mum, keep her busy with conversation. You both have a lot to tell to each other, I'm sure.'

'Sardar Parkash, please come and sit with me,' Nirmal calls. 'Tell me, what made you come to England?'

I sit beside Nirmal. Simran brings tea and biscuits. 'Uncle Ji, now tell us the whole story, I want to know. Can I sit with you, Mum?' she asks.

Nirmal nods. Simran pulls up a chair, sits beside me and asks as she pours teas in the cups, 'We both, Mum and I, have wondered: what made you come to the UK?'

'I remember everything as if it happened yesterday, especially our last meeting at the Natraj Cinema. In those days, holding hands in public was considered daring, but we did a lot more on that day. It was a phenomenal feeling. I was overwhelmed with emotions as this was the first time someone had come that close to me. I completely forgot about asking you to stay. By the time I realised, you'd already gone, Nirmal. I didn't get the chance to ask for your address. Even if I'd asked, your answer was always, "Your turn to ask questions hasn't come yet." Still, I managed to find out where you lived. I remembered dropping you and Mittal at the end of GB Road. After the initial hiccups I found Shamim who told me all about you and gave me the letter you left for me. But I didn't understand one thing: your best friend didn't remember your real name.'

There is an uncomfortable, emotional silence, until Simran breaks the ice and asks, 'Uncle Ji, please tell me all. I want to know why you both did not get together.'

For a moment, I completely forget that Simran is there too. I began to address Nirmal as though no one else were in the room. I hold her hands and experience the old cosiness. It gives me strength and reassurance.

'I've never been able to either understand or forgive myself for not asking you to stay, Nirmal. After you went, I wanted to take an auto to come after you, but had no knowledge of where you lived.

'However, I was, after reading your letter, a bit relieved. At least you were safe, wherever you were. I took your advice and dedicated myself to my studies. My mind was not fully consumed though, so I went to my village and told Sokhi the whole story. His first reaction was "Bhabi couldn't do this, Bhaji. She just can't do this." He blamed me for everything, which was right I suppose.'

I hear Nirmal sobbing. Voice shaking, she speaks.

'I loved it when he called me Bhabi. It meant a lot at that time, but alas, I couldn't fulfil my promise. I didn't have the good fortune of becoming his bhabi. Oh God! It was entirely my fault,' she says and starts sobbing uncontrollably. A warm tear falls onto my hands.

'No, Nirmal, it wasn't your fault. It simply wasn't meant to be. Do you remember Simon Sahib? He helped me a lot in finding you. Mittal and I had a proper falling out.'

Simran is listening intently. 'What stopped you from giving him your address, Mum? You loved him so much; why not tell him everything about yourself? I wouldn't have done what you did if I were in your place, Mum. This was not fair to Uncle Ji.'

'Oh, it was never my intention to not tell Sardar Parkash. We just didn't come round to it,' Nirmal says 'Sokhi, forever the optimist said, "We will definitely find Bhabi Ji, please don't worry". He came up with a master plan to find you. Remember,you took him on a sightseeing trip and told him that it takes about forty minutes from Ludhiana to get to your village? So we made a list of all the villages that were fifty minutes away, but then we didn't know whether it was calculated by scooter, cycle or on foot.'

'Oh, we always took a bus from Ludhiana to the nearby village and then cycled home. You couldn't have guessed it,' Nirmal says.

'In every village, you will find people who have nothing better to do than play cards. You normally find them at the entrance or just outside the village, sitting under big, shady trees. When we went around, a few people were helpful and said they did not know anyone by the name of Nirmal. However, there were some nasty ones as well, who enjoyed making fun of us. One stupid old man kept us waiting for an hour and gave us hints, telling us that he knew who we were looking for. Finally he asked, "What was her name, Nirmal? No, we don't have anybody with that name." We were so annoyed; Sokhi was furious. I said to Sokhi, "Let us forget the whole thing; we are not going to find your bhabi. She probably doesn't want us to find her. She couldn't go back to Delhi, I understand, but she knows where you live and she could've easily contacted you if she wanted."

'Sokhi was hopeful that we would eventually find you. Then something strange happened. We went to this village and just outside, there was a big Haveli of well-to-do person. It looked impressive. The huge gates were wide open. We saw a few people sitting there, so we went in and asked the same question—"We are looking for a girl, her name is Nirmal and she has been studying in Delhi for the past three years."

'A smart, middle-aged woman was nice to us and kindly offered us a glass of water. She said to the other much older man who was busy with the newspaper, "Our Sharn also studied in Delhi." The older man interrupted before she could finish what she was saying. He became abrupt and shooed us away saying, "No we don't know anybody by that name."'

'So near and yet so far away...the gods have been so cruel to us," Nirmal sighs. 'Please do go on. I want to know it all.'

'I do not remember a time when Sokhi and I had nothing to say to each other. We could never stay quiet. However, for the whole bus journey back to our village, we didn't utter a single word to each other. I found it difficult to cope with the "No we don't know anybody by that name".

'It didn't look right, Sokhi said. "There is something fishy here, Bhaji."

'"Yes, you may be right, but if the person does not want to tell you, then there is nothing much we can do."

'"People are not helpful, Bhaji," he said with resignation.

'I thought we were never going to see each other. My eyes were wet for a long time. I almost cried. I prayed that a miracle would happen.

'Sokhi, the brave one, couldn't control his emotions anymore. "You will not be lost forever, Bhabi, I'll find you," he said so loud that everyone on the bus turned and stared at us.'

'Please, Sardar Parkash. Please, I can't take any more of this.' Nirmal holds tight to my hands and tears come gushing down her cheeks. She sobs and says, 'Please forgive me for pulling both you and Santokh into this. In my heart, I knew you would try your best to find me, but you couldn't have. I made it almost impossible for you. I gave you no address and a false name. You still tried to find a needle in a haystack. I'm really and truly sorry.'

Another sip of water and a long breather she needs to continue. There was a time when this girl did not know what getting tired meant. However, here I am, making it more difficult for her. I must keep hold of my emotions and sadness.

'It may sound crazy now but in those days, it was magical to be called bhabi by Sokhi. It meant a lot; my whole life was wrapped around that name. But it never happened, I didn't become Sokhi's bhabi.' Her voice is full of sadness and remorse.

'Nirmal, I didn't do anything extraordinary. It certainly was not your fault. I share the blame for giving up on you too soon. I ought to have stayed in India. At that time, I honestly tried to find an escape route. Not being able to complete my education – the very reason I went to Delhi and then to lose you the way I did – was too much to bear. I panicked, I suppose. Nothing seemed to make sense. I made a childish decision. The one thing I did not realize was that memories have a habit of following wherever you go. Leaving India was not an escape. I loved you and needed you more than ever,' I confess.

'Why did you leave India?' she asks, as though still not satisfied by my answer.

'When you start thinking negatively, everything starts to look dark and bleak. I had a notion – a strange and perhaps stupid notion – that you'd rejected me, that the solitary kiss or my behaviour annoyed you. My not asking you to stay the night – was it a terrible mistake? Perhaps I didn't measure up to your expectations. Even Sokhi wondered why I not asked you to stay. "She came with a suitcase, Bhaji, was that not a hint enough?" he said. It made me feel somewhat inadequate. To be honest, I'd carried that thought for a long time. To add to that, I did not know your real name, or your home address. Shamim said the Nirmal wasn't your real name but she couldn't remember what it was either. It all added up and there was anger building inside me. I was simply getting angrier and angrier –with whom, I didn't know. This was definitely the time when I could easily have joined the Naxalites movement and done something stupid just to get my frustration out.'

I see both sympathy and frustration in Nirmal's eyes. She doesn't say anything but keeps staring at the picture of the rising sun on the wall of her room. I think that what I've said has hurt her, so I try to divert her attention a bit and continue, 'Remember, you used to say every grain meant for us has our name on it. So we go wherever destiny takes us.'

'It is the good old karma...'

'...consolation prize,' I finish.

'So you decided to come to the UK soon after? How did you find life here?'

I can't tell Nirmal that the first five years were the most horrific time of my life. I never came to terms with the thought of never seeing her again. During the day, I would keep staring at the clouds and imagine what it would be like if she were there, wrapped in a yellow dupatta. I tried to find the colour of her dupatta in every rainbow. I couldn't sleep but when I did, all I did was dream about her. She was everywhere, all around me. I tried so hard to form new relationships, but failed because she was always there and my mind could not stop comparing everything and everyone to her. I can't tell her that once, while on the Woolwich Ferry, I got so fed up that I was on the verge of ending it all – forever. I also cannot tell that her Sardar Parkash, who had never touched a drink, started drinking so heavily and was found in drunken state by police and rushed to Wipps Cross Hospital with half functioning lungs and kidneys. But even drinking could not help me forget her even for a tiny second. No. No. No. What would I achieve by telling her all that? Earn her pity, a few brownie points, show my affection for her or make it clear that I had been such a fool? 'I'm here to give her comfort, support and assurance – I must keep control of my emotions and refrain from saying anything that might make her feel bad,' I remind myself.

'Let us call it fate. I promise to tell you everything if you promise to get back to full health quickly... and no more crying please.' I find myself once again caressing her hands. I feel so much closer to Nirmal now than I ever did before.

Our story telling carries on for a while. I tell her about Shamim, how helpful she had been and Simon Sahib, who was very unhappy that I had given up on Delhi.

I spend most of the day with Nirmal – say a lot, learn a lot. It is difficult to say bye to both Nirmal and Simran but I do it with my heart laden with sorrow and mind full of confusion.

'Please don't be too late tomorrow, Uncle Ji. A specialist is coming to see Mum and it will help if you are also present. We can then decide what we should do. Just one more day, Uncle Ji, please.'

'Yes, I'll be here tomorrow.' I make this promise knowing fully well that it may not be possible. After all, I have to tell Jinder where I've been all day.

1.5

TIME TO FACE THE MUSIC

With a thousand stories resonating in my head, I return home. Seeing Nirmal in this state has shaken me to my very core. How does she manage to put on a brave face in spite of all that pain?

I know that what I'm doing might be seen as wrong. Love affairs are for the young. But then the thought of letting Nirmal down enters my mind and I know that I can't just be a bystander to her pain. She is very ill, and it is my moral duty as her friend to help her recover. I'll leave no stone unturned to get her back on her feet.

I've been a faithful husband to my wife and good father to my children for the past twenty years. Jinder has given me her full support through thick and thin. I have barely kept anything from her, and never lied to her about the big things. I haven't had to. I have always tried to be a good husband and a good friend.

When I come home, Jinder asks me, 'How was your meeting with the Manager?'

I sense an extra emphasis on the man's title, but that may just be my own guilt making me a little uneasy.

'Yes… it was good… okay.'

'But your face does not say that. What's wrong?'

'Please give me half an hour; I've something important to say to you.'

She is used to my habit of not coming to the point straightaway. I'm good at beating around the bush.

'Yes, all right.' She leaves me and goes back to her work in the kitchen.

After a lot of thought, I finally tell Jinder about Nirmal.

'So sorry to hear about Nirmal's health. Poor thing,' she says calmly.

Where is the major volcanic eruption? I wonder.

I'll go with you tomorrow,' she says.

I'm stunned. She's behaving as though nothing major has happened and here I am, pulling my hair out with worry. Jinder's reaction is most uncharacteristic. I expected her to be annoyed, to sulk and not speak to me for days as she does when she is upset with me.

The next day, we hand over the factory keys to the manager and both Jinder and I make our way to Nirmal's house. Throughout the hour-long journey, we talk about everything but Nirmal. I wonder if she isn't really bothered about Nirmal at all.

Simran opens the door immediately. 'Good morning. Aunty Ji, thank you so much for coming. Mum will be very happy to see you.'

I felt better staying in the lounge and letting them meet first. Simran and Jinder go straight to Nirmal. They seem to speak hurriedly.

Soon, the consultant enters and Simran leads him to the lounge, leaving Nirmal and Jinder together.

'What can we do to save Nirmal? There must be some cure.' I ask the consultant.

'Uncle Ji, first we have to get her to agree to the treatment. I tried my utmost, but she's so stubborn.'

Doctor Williamson has noticed a change in Nirmal; she seems to have perked up a bit since the last time he saw her. We discuss various options and agree to take her to a specialist's clinic in New York. Both Simran and I decide to go with her.

'Uncle Ji, it won't take me more than three days to organise everything – travel documents and all the other things,' Simran says.

'I think we should talk to Nirmal first. She needs to have the desire to live. The doctor can give her medication for her illness but not the desire to live,' Dr. Williamson says philosophically.

When we enter the bedroom, we are staggered to see quite a moving scene. Jinder is clutching onto Nirmal's hands, their eyes seem to be full of tears. It looks as though they have known each other for years. *Well, they do have someone in common*, I say to myself.

When Jinder sees us, she demands of me, 'You are always busy doing things for others, can't you do something for Nirmal Behn now? You must do whatever it takes to get her better.' Alas! I wish this cure were in my hands! Jinder's request has made the last of my uncertainty melt away—I feel as though we are all one family, connected in the desire to see Nirmal live.

'Nirmal Behan, we don't want you to say no. Just listen and let them find a cure. They're intelligent; they have to make you healthy. My husband knows a lot of good people.'

Jinder doesn't take no for an answer. Nirmal smiles as she says, 'Yes, Behn Ji, whatever you think best. You have rekindled in me a desire to live. I wish we'd met a long time ago.' She caresses Jinder's hands warmly.

Nirmal is wearing the same light yellow headscarf she left with me some twenty years ago. How did it get to her? When I see it, those memories resurface.

I used to love seeing Nirmal wrapped in this dupatta and would make comments like, 'you look like an angel', 'this is your colour' and many more. At our last meeting at my place in Delhi, she intentionally left this dupatta in my room. It was drenched with her unique fragrance, I managed to bring it here with me and hid it among my own clothes for many years. In fact, this dupatta was the only token of Nirmal that I had had left. Touching and getting lost in its fragrance kept me going. Whenever I wished to be close to Nirmal, I held the dupatta. This was my only well-kept secret from Jinder. Yes, it does sound crazy.

Then one day, it was not there. I looked everywhere for it. Jinder had come in and said abruptly, 'Are you looking for the yellow dupatta?' and before I could say anything she said, 'It was too old and smelly, so I threw it in the bin.'

What could I say? She probably saw the disgust on my face. It hurt me so much that I couldn't utter a word. I felt sorry for myself but at the same time, I understood her rationale. No wife will ever tolerate her husband's keeping the past alive. This was the first promise she had made me make when we got married.

Years have passed since then and I'd completely forgotten about it. Seeing Nirmal in it now is so wonderful. She looks as beautiful as she did at our first meeting.

Jinder and Nirmal both smirk at my astonished face.

Just as you do, I do have a heart. How could I throw away something so precious to you? I knew that Nirmal lived somewhere in your heart and I'd never ask you to forget her. I'm your present and you have always made me feel very proud and happy. I'll be even happier if you do everything you can for Nirmal,' she says, looking directly at my face. For once, I'm unable to confront her stare.

Everything she is doing and saying today is surprising me. I'd always assumed her to be narrow-minded, to be unforgiving of any discretions on my part. 'Jinder, I salute your thinking!' I say to her.

'The past is a part of us; we cannot run away from ourselves. I suggest you leave everything aside and take Nirmal to New York at once. I'll look after the business and everything else here. I've already invited Behan Ji to our house as soon as she gets better,' Jinder says with assurance in her voice.

Nirmal clasps Jinder's hands. 'Jinder, you are my younger sister. I really appreciate what you're doing for me. I will never forget it. I'm ready to do whatever you want me to do… I want to live now. I really do… but you have to make a promise to me.'

'Yes, Behn Ji. If I can do whatever you ask of me, I will do it. I promise.'

'Please make sure that Sardar Parkash would write a book about my life. I've already chosen the title. I know he can write well,' Nirmal says.

I can't keep myself from interrupting here. 'I'm not capable of writing stories or novels. Writing a book is an extreme meditation and I do not have that ability.'

'I understand, but you have the real story in front of you. Fiction writing may be difficult but a true story does not need you to make up a plot. You do not need to add spice to make it interesting.'

'Yes, what Nirmal says is very true,' Jinder says with authority as if she were an experienced writer herself.

With the help of the nurse, Nirmal slowly gets up and makes her way to the wardrobe. She carefully takes out three diaries and a notebook and hands them over to Jinder. 'In these is my account of those years – when I was just at the door of my youth, when my mind was completely free from the sorrows of this world, when everything, all my surroundings, were in full bloom. Those years as well – when all of sudden I fell from the sky with a single jolt, flat on my face, when my desire to become a fragrant flower was quickly dashed. They also record the lovely days I spent close to Sardar Parkash and a lot more.'

On the one hand, I'm curious to know about her life, the years that have passed. On the other, I'm terrified. I look at her diaries, and feel as though I'm already trespassing.

It's nearly four o'clock when we come back home. Jinder and I haven't uttered a word to each other over the long journey.

We sit down and look at each other now, questions brimming between us.

'Nirmal Behan Ji is such a nice person. I can't believe fate has been so unkind to her. Every person needs a partner, women more than men do, probably. The man provides security and comfort where the woman provides love and warmth,' she says.

'Don't worry about work, I'll manage. You should take her to New York before it gets too late. Do you think she'll be okay? I'm sure she is going to be fine. America has the best doctors.'

Later that evening, Simran calls. 'Mum's very happy with what we are doing, and everything has changed. Pass on her thanks to Aunty Ji, please. We'll leave in about three days' time and I'll let you know the details later, Uncle Ji.'

The yellow dupatta has come back home and Jinder has wrapped the diaries in it as if they were religious books. For the next couple of days we visit Nirmal in turns. Now there's a ray of hope to sustain us. Maybe Nirmal will recover soon.

PART TWO

PART TWO

2.1

---m---

My Childhood Days – Village Life

In 1966/67, my village, Sohal Jagir, like most villages in Punjab, had no electricity. The villages had no chance of getting electricity until the demand from the main cities was fully satisfied. It was the same for tarmac roads. We had mud roads, which in the summer became intolerably dusty and in the monsoon season gave us the opportunity to practice our circus skills as we jumped for the rare dry space to avoid puddles.

We had very basic sanitary facilities and no toilets in our homes; instead, we did our deeds in the open fields every morning. No one complained as everyone in the village had to do the same. Open sewage called 'Kachian Galiaan' ran, right through the middle of the village end to end. It ended up in massive big ponds on both sides of our village. These ponds filled with access water from the village's daily use and from the Monsoons rains. They never dried out and our buffalos had their daily dip and wash in them. A few of us who were not very hygiene conscious sometimes had a dip in the big ponds too. Only the shopkeeper cum moneylender 'Banian' had 'Puckian Galiaan' made up of cement instead of just mud. Opposite the front of the shop, there were two wooden benches placed to cover the Galiaan underneath, where idle bones played cards all day long.

What I have described above has very little to do with Nirmal's story. I am merely attempting to set the scene and take your mind back to that period when life in our villages was very basic.

But there was beauty in the simplicity. We felt very close to nature and the daily routine, the basic amenities or the lack of it, made us extract enjoyment from small things. Most evenings, we played kabaddi in the fields and received our share of injuries, which we expertly hid from our mothers for fear of getting a telling off.

I belonged to a well-known family of landowners and my father was Lambardar and Sarpanch of the village. My childhood had been very comfortable and my parents had put a lot of emphasis on giving me a good education. My mother always taught her children the value of leading a good life. Both my parents were well – known for their truthfulness and belief in fair play. They tried to instil the same qualities in us.

I'd passed my higher secondary exams from Shahkot Higher Secondary School, obtaining very high marks. In fact, I achieved the second highest marks in my school. A tiny Bania girl beat me. Thanks to this, I was very distraught for some time. Some of my friends said that I was lucky but luck had nothing to do with it. They spent so much of their time watching Hindi movies and chasing girls around the trees like those heroes. They blamed the examiner for being too harsh and not letting them copy the answers from the books.

DAV College was the best one in Jalandhar. Punjabi Jat students believed that the admission criteria for DAV was very tough. To get in, you either, had to score very high marks or belong to the Hindu middle class. The 'HMC', as we called them, despite living in Punjab for decades and speaking Punjabi for generations, still answered 'Hindi' as their first language in surveys. They had no problem getting into DAV College.

I was pleasantly surprised when I was offered a place in the college. For a little while, I felt proud and satisfied by my efforts and showed off to my friends.

Although I was proud that I'd achieved admission at the DAV, it did not feel right. I felt out of place, like a villager lost at a rich man's party in town. It seemed that everyone at DAV was only interested in studying. That was not what I had imagined college life to be. I had looked forward to a bit of studying, a bit of mischief and the possibility of striking up a friendship with a young girl or two. Mingling freely with girls was very high up on my agenda.

All my friends who wanted to study further sought admission at Khalsa College, so I went along with them. Oh! There was such a difference! This college matched my dreams. Smart, Punjabi speaking girls and boys mingled with each other. One of my friends already had a request from a girl to help her fill her admission form. This was the first time a girl had asked him for anything and he was very excited. I too began to fantasise about having the opportunity to have a proper talk with a girl, maybe even finding a girlfriend! I thought it might be easy for me because I was quite good at my studies and good-looking too. Just the thought of it made me feel so good. How nice it would be, to have a beautiful girlfriend sitting in front of me and sipping a cup of tea, looking into my eyes with love and affection All my friends would be envious. Just thinking about it made me very happy.

I made up my mind to tell my dad that I wished to join Khalsa College and not DAV. Knowing full well that he might not agree, I figured there was no harm in trying anyway. If you don't ask, you don't get, after all.

My happiness, however, was short lived. Dad had already asked his learned friends for their advice on the best college for me. It certainly was not Khalsa College. They said I'd done so well in my exams, why should I not think of going to the capital? The idea of studying in Delhi appealed to me as well. I felt excited at the prospect of exploring the unknown, and pride too. It wasn't everyone who got to study in Delhi.

My mother made the expected protest: 'I won't see him every

day. Who is going to cook for him and wash his clothes? He doesn't even know how to make a cup of tea,' and so on. But even she knew that for us Punjabis, Delhi was the second best place to study, right after England. In the end, I got my way.

2.2

~~~

HELLO, DELHI!

I was quite apprehensive and nervous because I'd never lived away from home. It was going to be difficult, I knew. But being in Delhi was exciting enough to overcome my trepidation.

I asked Santokh, my childhood friend, to come with me to Delhi. Though he was a year younger than me, I considered him mentally much tougher. He had always been my strength. Together, we could do anything.

Anyhow, after our nine-hour train journey, we stood at the New Delhi Railway Station, looking at everyone going about the daily work. It already felt so different from Punjab. Everyone seemed to be in a bit of hurry; there was a lot of pushing, people constantly trying to get in front of each other. For a moment, everyone seemed to turn into rats, even me! I saw myself waiting anxiously to join the rat race and be a contender too.

We took an auto to Doctor Sahib's house, and it was quite an unnerving experience. In Punjab, we were used to the smell of fresh air, of open fields, and traffic was not that bad. To be fair, we were village people who had hardly ever visited the big cities in Punjab. The traffic in Delhi was new for us.

Finally, we arrived at our destination after an hour and half of travel. Doctor Sahib's whole family was very kind and seemed glad to see us. We brought with us fresh vegetables, desi ghee and sweets.

We were allotted a room on the rooftop, a 'barsati'. It was just a little shed used to store unused items. Sokhi and I looked at each other and exclaimed in unison, *'Delhi Hai Piaray'* – meaning, 'This is Delhi for you!' It didn't take long for us to realise that we should consider ourselves lucky to have a roof over our heads. Indeed, the barsati suited us well, for it was an independent setup, and private.

Our first night there was horrendous. Both of us stayed awake most of the night and I had started to realise what a stupid mistake I'd made. Delhi did not feel like a welcoming place.

On our second day, we learned that people from Punjab had much bigger appetites than those who lived in Delhi. Things were very expensive here, so people did not eat a lot, nor did they waste any food. We took the hint. From then on, we ate very little. It bothered me, mostly for Sokhi's sake. I was not a big eater, but he really loved food.

After staying for a day and half in the Barsati, we ventured out to the bazaar just to pass the time. It was so hectic, we felt as if we were in a different country altogether. We did however manage to find a very cheap dhaba. A couple of fluorescent tubes hung from the ceiling, looking like they had never been cleaned, but still giving enough light that the customers could just about see what they were eating. There were a few rusted steel chairs around the wooden tables but the food was good and plentiful. You paid for chapattis and got a plate of curry free. It suited us fine. 'Beggars can't be choosers,' I said.

Two weeks later, the time had come for Sokhi to go back to Punjab. The realisation that I was going to be on my own made me feel very low. Just seeing him getting on the train was no easy, and I wondered if I shouldn't just get on the train with him. But somehow, I managed to control my emotions and put up with it. Sokhi had fifty-five rupees in his pocket. He handed it to me and said, 'I'll bring more soon; make sure you eat properly'. I hugged him and watched as the train left the station.

2.3

—∿∿—

GET REAL TIME...

Soon, I realized that sulking and feeling sorry for myself wasn't going to achieve anything. Doctor Sahib arranged work for me. 'You'll be going to a Chartered Accountant's office and learning book keeping and accounts,' he said. 'Once your training is done, we'll find you work as a bookkeeper. This will give you an income to support yourself.' My main purpose for coming to Delhi for study seemed to have become less important.

My office was at Sarai Rouhela. It did not take me long to learn about trial balance, P&L and the balance sheet. I believed that I was now ready to do book keeping and enter the world of commerce.

But I was also getting bored of keep doing the same thing again and again. It might have been different if I was earning money. As my money was running out, I was becoming desperate for work that would pay. Whenever I asked about this, the CA Sahib would just tell me that he was looking out for opportunities, but I knew this was against his best interests and therefore probably only half the truth. I was putting in so much work free..., why would they want to lose such a good worker bee?

It was well past nine when I left work that day. Every day, CA Sahib would leave so much work on my table that it was getting difficult for me to finish even by nine o'clock. One question that kept popping up in my head was why I was here in Delhi. If I came here to study, I'd wasted over four months and done nothing. On the other hand, if I was here to become a Munim I could've done it in Punjab. This uncertainty and helplessness was killing me.

It was ten by the time I got home, and everyone had assumed that I'd eaten already, so there was no food left for me. I threw myself on my bed, and was trying to ignore the hard wood beneath me. There was no one there to stop me from sobbing like a child.

I simply had to decide what I was going to do. I couldn't go on like this; my finances were messed up, and after paying for my food and transport every day, my cash was dwindling fast.

I'd my usual cup of tea in the morning. I was in strange state of mind when I took the usual bus. It was overcrowded; I just managed to grab hold of the outer bar.

My total capital was about seventy rupees. I always kept thirty rupees apart for the fare to Jalandhar, just in case I had to return.

The DTU bus stopped near my office on Old Rohtak Road but I did not feel like going in to work that day. I began to walk in the opposite direction without any clear aim in mind.

Where was I going?

What was I doing?

I walked until I reached Gali No 2. It resembled an industrial estate with many small sheds and factory buildings. Right at the end of the street, I saw a clean dhaba. The smell of the freshly cooked *kachori* and *choley* set me drooling. I entered and placed my order, but when I reached into my pocket for the money to pay, I very nearly had a heart attack. My wallet was gone! I managed to pay the bill with the money that I'd set aside for that Jalandhar fare. At least I was able to save myself from humiliation.

One of the other customers had witnessed the drama, and having guessed what had happened, he came to my table and sat with me. He put his hand on my shoulder, and I truly appreciated his sympathy. Never in my eighteen years of life had I felt so low and vulnerable. Mr. Simon—as I later found out his name, offered me the chance to be his book – keeper for a salary of sixty rupees per month.

That's how I got my first client.

2.4

~~~

A LESSON FOR GOOD LIFE

The incident I'm about to relate now is a source of great shame to me. I once saw Arvind, the eldest son of Doctor Sahib, being chased by his wife and mother with a spoon full of cream. He refused to eat it. It reminded me of my mother; she always used to add cream before she gave me a glass of milk. Seeing this also reminded me that I hadn't had a drop of milk since I had arrived in Delhi.

On my way back from work that day, I rushed to my usual *halwai* and asked for a plate of cream. Even the hefty portion I received for ten rupees wasn't enough to satiate my craving. I needed proper food, but I had only ten rupees left to me!

Doctor Sahib used to bring the day's earnings from the shop and leave it in the cloth cupboard to be deposited in the bank the next day. I stole twenty rupees from that stash. Nobody noticed and I did it again the next day. But later, my guilt was triggered off and I was disgusted by my behaviour.

I ran to Doctor Sahib's shop and, my head bowed, placed the twenty rupee note before him. He understood, but he gave me another twenty Rupee note and said, 'I'm so sorry we haven't been able to look after you as we should've. I feel like I must give you some advice now. The real world is cruel. Always try to tell the truth and take nothing that is not yours.'

I listened to him and took an oath – I would never take anything that did not belong to me. I've lived by that ever since.

Within two weeks, I'd learnt how to survive on one good meal a day. On the work front, things were progressing well; I had three firms' accounts to do. CA Sahib was quite happy that I'd brought in four more accounts for him. My accommodation problem had also been resolved. I would do the book keeping for Marwaha Ji and in return he would give me a room in his kothi for no price.

A month later, I moved out of the barsati. My new room was also in Rajouri Garden, just twenty minutes away from the old one. Marwaha Ji had also provided a blanket, pillow and wooden charpoy as gesture of goodwill. He was an intelligent, well-read, God-fearing man and had been very generous. I loved listening to him recite poetry. I'd started to borrow books by prominent Punjabi writers from him. He was perhaps twice my age but always called me his best friend.

One evening, when I opened my door, I found the lights on. I was confused—had I not switched off the lights when I left? But then I saw Sokhi sitting there! I rushed to hug him tight.

'When did you come? How did you get in?'

'O, Bhaji, I just came, I haven't seen you for so long! I couldn't stop myself and Beeji also asked me to bring all these things to you,' he said, as calm and collected as ever.

He opened his metal suitcase and took out the contents, one by one.

'I've already left the vegetables and sweets in Doctor Sahib's house. Jitender dropped me here. Your landlady was superb; she served me tea and opened the room for me.'

He took out a brown envelope, which he hid in the sweet box and extracted some money.

'Here is 250 rupees from Beeji and I've also saved one hundred,' he said with pride in his voice.

My heart was filled with love for both of them.

'You keep it for now. I'm financially stable for the moment, Santokh. I'm earning enough to keep me going,' I said.

Sokhi stayed with me for about a month. He made me promise that I would come back to village for a break soon.

It had been a year since I'd left Punjab, and I'd changed. I was no longer the innocent, soft Parkash. Delhi had made me hard headed. I'd realised that I couldn't be an outsider; I had to join the rat race. I'd grown with experience through my deals with clients and was managing the books for twelve small firms, and now earning more than enough money for my day-to-day needs. My room was full of expensive perfumes, shaving sets and new clothes. Indeed, I'd now become a proper Delhi-wala, but one thing I hadn't learnt was *hera feri* (cheating). I was always truthful and didn't double-cross my client for the sake of earning more money. This got me into fights with CA Sahib.

At last, I decided to visit Shahkot after a whole year away. Nothing seemed to have changed there. People moved about as lazily and leisurely as before, a total shock to me after Delhi! It hit me then how I'd changed.

My friends came to see me. They asked about my college life in Delhi. I couldn't tell them that I hadn't been to a college yet. I felt ashamed and made excuses, threw them off the topic. Just to get out of situation I made up one lie after another. I finally only told my parents about the whole situation. I knew they would understand, and even though they were disappointed, they didn't show it. Babuji asked me not to go back to Delhi but to stay on and study at home. He consoled me as much he could. I knew that all he wanted was to see me happy.

I assured him I would complete my education in Delhi and that it was intention to join college the moment I went back.

After staying for a week in Shahkot, I went back to Delhi. I started book keeping work for Mittal just a few weeks after I joined Simon Sahib. Mittal's factory was next door to his. In fact, Simon Sahib introduced us. Mittal was a manufacturer of spare parts for a famous motorcycle company. His was a cottage size business, employing around twelve people. For the first few months, he paid my accountancy fees regularly. We developed a good relationship. But thanks to the free help I extended to him, I became sucked deeper and deeper into the running of his factory.

Most of the raw material for Mittal's factory came from Marwaha Sahib. One day whilst I was sitting in Marwaha Sahib's office writing his accounts, Mittal rang and asked me if I could pay Marwaha four hundred rupees on his behalf and he will pay me back when I got back. Reason was that Marwaha Sahib had difficulty in the past getting Mittal to pay on time. Now he was holding the raw material until he was paid. Reluctantly, therefore, I parted with the money.

Over six months had gone, so far I haven't asked, and Mittal hasn't bothered to pay me back.

I confided in Simon Sahib about the problem. He gave me a friendly telling off. Why did I let it build so much? *'Mother doesn't give milk till the baby cries.'* Punjabi saying and his words of wisdom have stuck cord with me.

I asked him nicely for my money, a couple of months ago, but he just laughed it off. I also thought about leaving his work but then there the dilemma. 'If I leave, he is definitely not going to pay… and if I carry on working he may. But then he may not.' Small loss now or big loss later… that was the question. Only thing that had kept me going was that *'may'.*

Since I asked him to pay, his attitude towards me had changed completely. He no longer talked to me freely… in fact he tried to avoid me. On my part, I'd also stopped doing any extra work and visited him only every Tuesday just for a couple of hours to do his accounts. Bored… that's what I was just bored.

It was around eleven o'clock on a Tuesday when my life changed. I walked into Mittal's factory, said Namaste to everyone and went straight to the office. The place was empty, and I sat down to my work.

I'd been looking through the books for about half an hour when someone knocked at the door.

'Do come in,' I said. Normally one of the junior worker brings tea for me, this time it was a beautiful well-dressed young woman. 'I'm Nirmal,' she said hesitantly.

'Oh, I'm Parkash... Parkash Sohal... from Punjab.' I was so nervous. I had never spoken to such a beautiful girl before.

Nirmal was very fair, tall and slim with long brown hair and big brown eyes. I noticed she had long fingers and her nails were painted a light pink.. She was wearing a pure white salwar-kameez and a baby pink dupatta. I was speechless. If there was such thing as *love at first sight* then this was it. I was simply blown away by her beauty. We said nothing else to each other, but the look in her eyes conveyed everything.

On the way back from work, all I could think about was Nirmal. I longed to see her again. I rehearsed what I would say when I meet her the next time and tried to think of excuses to bump into her.

When Tuesday finally arrived, I was sitting in my usual place in the Dhaba, reading a newspaper. I couldn't believe my eyes when I saw her sitting right in front of me. All my rehearsal of what I was going to say went out the window.

'Where are you from in Punjab?' She smirked, opening the conversation.

I told her what she asked for and much more. I knew that once I got over my apprehension I wouldn't stop talking. All she told me was she was a Punjabi who had come to Delhi to study. On my part, I got carried away telling her everything about myself and forgot to ask anything about her. She didn't try to stop me either. I was over the moon.

Nirmal spoke gently but firmly, and when I called her Nirmala, she stopped me mid-sentence and corrected me. There was so much in common between us. We were both Punjabi and from the same caste. Both of us loved Punjabi literature, especially poetry.

At our first meeting, she asked, 'who is your favourite poet?'

'From the past, I love the one and only great poet Warish Shah for his Heer. No one has ever written like him. I call the William Shakespeare of the Punjabi literature, I said.

'Yes, he is my favourite too – there was so much pain and love in every line he wrote.' She said.

'Do you write…?' I asked.

'No, but you have made me a writer,' she said and recited the very first poem she had written about us.

'Such beautiful words can only come from a beautiful person,' I said.

I'd fallen deeply in love with her and wanted to be with her all the time, barely being able to wait for Tuesday. My week was spent counting the days and hours until finally, the moment arrived. We would meet at the Dhaba for lunch. Sabah, Nirmal and I sat at the same table. Sabah and she were sisters, and they lived together at Ammi's house.

One of those Tuesdays, Mittal spotted the three of us joking and laughing. We could see from his face that he didn't like it one bit. In fact, he made some obnoxious remarks. Sabah told me, 'Mittal is not their relation as he keeps telling people. We are not his girls. We are his employees like everyone else and nothing more.'

I'd reached a point where I really didn't care about Mittal anymore. Hell with him, I thought. I was happy that I'd talked to Nirmal and discovered that we had so much in common. I knew she was in love with me as much as I was, but as Indian tradition goes, we did not say a single word about love in our conversation.

Something did bother me though. I was unable to understand how Sabah and Nirmal were sisters, as one was a Punjabi Jat and the other a Muslim from Gujrat. I had no idea who Ammi Jaan was. Sikhs do not call their mothers Ammi. But I was so overwhelmed with the affection Nirmal showered on me that nothing else mattered for the time being.

Thursday was also usually quite an enjoyable day for me. I tended to spend about half the day with Marwaha Sahib. '

As soon as I'd finished with the books, Marwaha Sahib would walk in, sit in front of me like a schoolmaster, and order milky tea. Though he always asked me what I wanted to eat, he never waited for my answer and ordered anyway. There was no refusal with Marwaha Sahib. He was a father figure and always treated me well.

'You look a little thoughtful today, Parkash Ji,' he said one day.

Before I could answer, he recited a verse from the Guru Granth Sahib. *Those who love Him are loved by Him.*

'I'm more concerned with earthly love at the moment,' I told him. 'How do you know if you are in love with someone?'

'When your hands are busy writing accounts but your mind is somewhere else: these are the first signs. Who is the lucky girl?'

'She works at Mittal's as a packer but is still a student.'

'And how long you have known her?'

'Just a few weeks.'

'And you want someone else to tell you whether you are in love?'

'I'm sure about myself, Marwaha Sahib, but I do not know if she feels the same way,'

'Have you asked her?'

'No. What if she says no? I cannot take that chance.'

'Well, you have to initiate it. A girl is never going to ask you first.'

'But, what if she says no? How do I find out if she loves me as much as I do?'

'O Parkash Ji, you will know. You'll know for sure. She may not utter a single word but the look in her eyes will convey the message, all right. However, my advice at the moment is– you can't hurry love.'

Dear Reader,

Many thanks for buying my Novel, in doing so you have helped to provide **free eye care** to underprivileged people in Punjab, India. All proceeds from the sale of this book will go to the Karnail Singh Memorial trust, which has been set up to continue my late father's legacy of organising free eye care treatment camps every year for over twenty years (a cause very close to his heart whilst he was alive). I, along with my family wish to continue playing my part. Now you have become a partner in that program.

It is very much appreciated. I hope you enjoy the read, and please do not forget to register your review on Amazon – every comment goes a long way.

Yours truly
Parkash Sohal
Author - At Night You Sleep Alone

2.5

—₥—

YOU CAN'T HURRY LOVE...

My long wait was over and Tuesday had finally come again. I was going to tell Nirmal that I was deeply in love with her but I would not push her for an answer. She could let me know her emotions at any time.

I also made the decision to stop working for Mittal. First, I would bring the books up to date and then ask him to pay me within the next two weeks. I would be firm.

The morning was spent with Simon Sahib, completing his books. I told him about Nirmal and my decision regarding Mittal.

'You two will make a lovely couple,' he said.

I needed that reassurance. It felt so sweet, as if it were a voice from Heaven.

I was at Mittal's at about eleven and said my usual hello to everybody. I went to the office.

I must have been working for an hour when Mittal told everyone to stop work and summoned me as well. 'I've an important announcement to make,' he said. 'I'm gonna marry Nirmal.'

There was dead silence and a look of utter disbelief on everyone's faces. Both Sabah and Nirmal looked at each other in astonishment and did not utter a single word. My whole world came tumbling down in a second. I put the books away and walked out in disgust without uttering a word or acknowledging anyone. My throat dried up and I would've stopped breathing if I'd stayed in the factory.

Mittal's announcement kept ringing in my ears. I was seething with anger. I felt the urge to go back in and bash him up, but then a part of me spoke up and asked why no one, even Sabah, who was friendly with him, had spoken up and called out his lies. I wondered whether both she and Nirmal had in fact known exactly what was going to happen.

I'd never been this upset my whole life. I wandered aimlessly in the bazaar and had a cup of tea. I didn't feel like eating, but still ordered food at a dhaba. I had just one bite, and couldn't eat after that.

Was this how love stories began and ended? I went straight to the roof of my house and lay down on the bed, looking at the stars as if my answer were there in the sky. I couldn't face the questions that kept popping up in my head. When I couldn't go to sleep, I would start counting stars. Tonight was different though.

I spent most of the week wondering about the situation. In the end, I decided to meet Jitender and go to the cinema with him to take my mind off things. He'd been a very good friend and I'd always found comfort in sharing whatever was on my mind with him. We went to the cinema together almost every week. He was aware of my feelings for Nirmal and actively encouraged our relationship.

The Sunday that we met, he leapt into conversation straight away. 'What's the matter with you today? You are unusually quiet,' he said.

'No… nothing really,' I replied.

'Nothing really… eh?' he quizzed

'Mittal announced that he's marrying Nirmal. It doesn't make any sense.' It hurt me to repeat those words.

'But he is already married,' he laughed.

'How do you know?'

'I'm sure he is married and has children as well. My father knows his father. I guess he must have said that to annoy you or something. I told you many times; he is not a good man, be careful of him. But as usual, you didn't listen.'

We watched the movie and had coffee afterward. I didn't enjoy the film one bit. All I could think about was Mittal and Nirmal. It simply did not add up.

Later that night, I tried to make a list, to write down all the things about the situation that was troubling me.

'Is there a match between Nirmal and Mittal? He is a short, dark skinned man with glasses. He is wiry and with oily hair. Nirmal is so beautiful and much taller than he is.

'Sabah is usually the one who keeps close company with him. You might think they have something going between them. Nirmal hardly talks to him. Therefore, he ought to be proposing to Sabha. How does this make any sense?

'How can they be sisters? They share no resemblance at all. Who is Ammi Jaan and what relationship do they have with her?

'Why did Mittal made the announcement in his workshop? We are workers, not his relatives!

'Why didn't Nirmal or Sabah rebuke him there and then? Why keep quiet?

'Is Mittal so jealous of us that he just said that to upset me? Why did he not say in private?

'Mittal and I have worked together for over a year and we were good friends. I've always tried to help him, even begged Marwaha Sahib to loan him raw material and lent him money myself. I'm not a factory worker but still I have helped him with packing and labelling. Why does he suddenly hate me so much?

'If he has children, why does he lie about it?'

My eyes seemed to be stuck on a star that shone brighter than the others. As I stared, it sparkled and gave out plenty of light before it burned away. Was this what would happen to my love? Would hopes always rise to extreme heights before they got broken?

When I woke the next morning, I saw that someone had put a blanket over me, put my notebook and pen away and switched off the light. Who else could do that be, except my generous landlady, who always treated me like her younger brother? 'This world is full of good people as well,' I said to myself.

The next Tuesday, I was still very upset but I needed to put on a brave face and work normally. Imagine my surprise when I entered Simon Sahib's office to find Nirmal there!

'Where have you been? We looked for you everywhere! Nobody knew where you lived. How were we supposed to contact you?' Simon Sahib said to me. 'Nirmal has been coming here every day since you left Mittal's office. Look at her, poor girl, look what you've done to her. I thought you were a responsible person.'

'I come here every Tuesday, as agreed,' I said politely but sheepishly too. I knew they were right. There was no way anyone could contact me in an emergency.

'You two talk while I get some coffee for us.' Simon Sahib deliberately left us alone.

I looked at Nirmal's pensive face and saw that her eyes were full of tears. She stared at my face a moment longer as if to say, *Love is trust, where is yours?* Her look sent a million messages. 'Meet me for lunch,' she said, finally.

Without waiting for my answer, she got up and walked out. I held my head in my hands and squeezed hard as though trying to make sense of all this. *Why do I always think negatively? Why am I always wrong? Why?*

Simon Sahib entered a few minutes later, followed by the Dhaba boy with the coffee tray.

'Where's Nirmal?' He asked.

'She's left soon after you did.'

'Why did you let her go?'

Without waiting for my answer, he carried on lecturing.

'Where have your manners gone, Parkash? You have acted so naively today. She was our guest. Is this how we treat our guests? How could you let her go without giving her a cup of coffee? You need to learn the value of a good relationship. As soon as I accepted you as my brother, my responsibilities towards you increased. Now, it is my duty to tell you that you must understand what is important in a relationship.'

He took large sip of coffee, cleared his throat and got ready to lecture like a schoolteacher.

'Before we consider the value of the relationship, we must first know what kind of relationship we share with someone. Then and only then can we appreciate their value and importance. Until you and Nirmal give a name or realise what relationship you share, you won't be able give it the respect it deserves. Don't get me wrong: every relationship is important, but all of them have different expectations. For example, what Nirmal is to you and you to her, until that is decided you will both not know what to expect. Try not to waste time either, thinking about petty things. Sometimes we do not realise the importance of someone until it's too late.'

Heaving a big sigh, he continued, 'If I'd realised the importance of my relationship and that I was in love with Liz, we would've been together today. It doesn't mean that I'm not happy with what I have now, but *if it had happened,* that big *if* always stays with you.

'Nirmal is very genuine, beautiful, well-spoken and intelligent girl. You make a lovely couple. She knows the value of your relationship, a lot more than you do, Parkash. She's been coming here for the past three days looking for you. She has also been to your college but you've been missing from there as well. Do not waste time. Go meet with her and apologise for your behaviour.'

'What about this marriage to Mittal?' I asked.

'It will be best if you ask her. I'm sure you will get your answers,' Simon Sahib said with confidence.

I was overwhelmed; my thought process stopped for a moment. 'How could I be so wrong, she wouldn't be here, if she did not care. May be, she would say that she has to marry Mittal for this reason or other. She is helpless. This word *helpless* is used quite often when someone wishes to say *no* gently.' Oh! I could not bear the thought of this, what will I do. Simon Sahib's words of wisdom were ringing in my ears.

Reading the emotions on my face perhaps, Simon Sahib continued with the conversation. 'It is man's DNA, and all men are the same. We want our women to be so *pure*, live in isolation. We even object to the touch of wind and water on their bodies. We forget, conveniently, that the woman has to live in the jungle filled with wild animals just like us.

I took my leave and went for a walk to clear my mind. There was an hour to go for lunch.

Finally, I went slightly early and sat in our usual place at the dhaba. I didn't feel like eating. I wanted answers, not food.

Nirmal came on time, looking self – assured. She sat down next to me, took my cup of tea and began to sip from it as though nothing had happened.

'Aren't you having lunch?' She asked.

'No, no…yes, yes,' that was all that I was able to say. She called the waiter ordered two more cups of tea and our usual lunch of samosa chana for her and bread chana for me.

'Why are you looking so tense and sad? You didn't come to the factory either… why?'

'No… I was… I was…'

A few minutes later the waiter brought us our food and tea. She took my hand, squeezed it in her warm soft hands, and looked at me straight in the eye. 'I can't bear to see you this sad. It hurts me. I feel your sadness because our hearts have made a connection.'

There was a silence of just few seconds but it felt like an eternity. But so much was being said by our eyes alone.

'You call me your soul mate, a friend, and then it seems you are going to be married to Mittal. Is that true?'

She smirked. 'Yes… it must be true for him. I didn't say I'm marrying him. That's the difference. He can say whatever he likes. I was very angry, and I wanted to slap him, but Sabah stopped me. It was the right thing to do. Let him bark. If you throw dirt up, it is going to fall on your face too.

'Barking dogs don't bite. The little ones are always loud in their own backyard. He is harmless but least keeps the other dogs away. He will probably announce tomorrow that he is marrying the Queen of England.' We both laughed.

Nirmal had become very emotional and her grip on my hands was tightening as she spoke.

'Your Nirmal has a learnt a lot from you – honesty and integrity. I will always be *pure* and yours, regardless of whatever comes.'

Long after she'd gone, I felt her presence. I looked at my hands. They had touched hers. I was over the moon as I travelled back to my house. I felt God was on my side.

2.6

~~~

THE TIDE HAS TURNED...

It had been well over seven months since I joined the private college in Moti Nagar. My desire to join SR College will remain unfulfilled. I do not have the resources for full time education, so this Imperial College a private institute is the best I could afford. Flexibility of lesson timing and evening study in fact suits me fine. How hard you study is up to the individual, this principle, embedded in me from my growing up days. Love, misunderstanding, making up, so much has happened in the past few months. However, I'd managed to strike a balance between study and work. It is very hard but I'd no choice but to manage.

I needed to get back to my studies; the exams were just round the corner. My brain needed a little rest, so I decided to go with Jitender to watch a movie. I always enjoyed his company and especially watching Hindi Film with him. We decided to meet up at the Natraj cinema, to watch *'Baharein Phir Bi Ayengi'*. There was news twist attached to this film. Rumours had it that Guru Dutt a famous Actor/ Director wrote a song for this film and committed suicide soon after because of failure in love. He loved Wahida Rahman, but she loved someone else. How true the story was, we'll never know, but it made us pay double the money on black market because it was running *Full House* from weeks. It also made me think about the heavy price love demands.

At the interval, we had our usual coffee, Jitender lit a cigarette, and after having a big puff, he made a proclamation like a king. I met Jitender sometime later for our usual movie date. Afterwards, as we sipped our coffee, he gave me some welcome news. 'Your dear Mittal's secret has come out. The bastard is married and has children as well, two lovely girls. I told you not to trust what he says.'

He'd warned me countless times to be wary of Mittal, but I never paid much attention. If Mittal was indeed a married man why was he so upset about my friendship with Nirmal? I will, throw this on his face. *Marrying Nirmal, eh... My foot.'*

'I hope you are telling me the truth. Do you have any proof?'

'Well, why don't you see it with your own eyes?'

'How?'

'Let's buy presents for his kids and deliver them to the house and pretend that Mittal sent them. I can easily find out where he lives. Honestly, Parkash, I think he is controlling your brain. What is wrong with you? Can't you see that he is a coward and untrustworthy? He is doing all these stunts just to annoy you.'

'But Jitender, I don't deserve this. I've done nothing but helped him. Anyway, I'm going to be tough and straight with him. If he does not pay me, I will have to show him my bad side.' Frustration showed on my face.

2.7

LET US GET BACK ...

Time was passing quickly. Over a month had passed since my discussion with Nirmal. My exams had gone well. I didn't have any time for wasteful thoughts. Both Sabah and Nirmal took leave from Mittal's factory to prepare for their exams as well. It felt strange, because I had lost a year of study, Nirmal was my senior!

I'd been going to Simon Sahib on a regular basis. Just being in his company and talking to him gave me comfort and reassurance.

One day, I asked him, 'Did you know Mittal was married?'

'Yes, I remember seeing his wife a couple of years ago, and I believe he has two daughters as well. Whether he is still married, I don't know.'

'Nirmal has no clue why he said he was going to marry her,' I said.

Simon Sahib took another big sip of his tea. This usually meant he was getting ready for a major lecture.

'You know, Parkash, every woman's weakness is marriage, especially in India. She wishes to have a loving husband, children and a house. This is what our society expects of her and sees as normal. Indian women programmed to think that way. Crooked men like our friend Mittal will always take advantage of this. He has probably promised this to many others too.'

Simon Sahib did not wait for my reply. I think something had touched his nerve.

'There are stray dogs, wandering from door to door that get turned away. They can never change their habit; they will always be on the loose, prowling. Then there are those who belong to their master and are loved.'

He then started to recite the famous lines of the Sufi poet Baba Buley Shah, *'dar dar de phirne nalo'n ek dar da ho k behja'* (Do not stray from door to door, stick to one master).

When I went to Mittal's, I realized that his attitude seemed to have changed. He spoke to me in an apologetic manner. I told him that for me to carry on doing his accounts he needed to start paying me. He smirked and went out. Half an hour later, he came and sat in front me.

'I can buy a dozen girls tomorrow, but she is a bit special, probably worth a bit more,' he said.

I wondered what had brought this out in him. He said some horrendous things about women and seemed to have no respect for them. I was especially disturbed by what he'd said about Nirmal. What the hell was he insinuating about her?

'You may look fine, but your mind is definitely sick, Mittal.' I said as I walked out.

2.8

—〰—

LIFE GOES ON...

By now Nirmal had begun visiting Simon Sahib's office either to see me or leave a message for me without any hesitation. He gave her lots of respect and never let her go without having a cup of tea.

Things had quietened down a bit, and the three of us once again resumed our lunches at the Dhaba. There seemed to be some change in Mittal's attitude. Perhaps it was because of Sabah, since she'd become very friendly with him He still kept filling her with poison about me. 'Tell Nirmal that Parkash is a Jat from Punjab and not a businessman. He is just a book keeper. Don't trust him. He is an opportunist.' A lot more filth would come out of his mouth. Nirmal didn't care, so it didn't bother me either. Mittal also promised to start paying what he owed me, but nothing had materialised yet..

This was the first time in my life that I was so busy with study and work. There was hardly any time left for romance.

Six weeks had gone and exams were now over, so we all heaved a sigh of relief. We started to meet up again for lunch again.

Our results came through and we were over the moon at the grades that we'd managed to achieve. 'I will now be able to boast to my friends back in Punjab,' I thought. Nirmal's interest in me increased. She kept asking questions about my routine and my life at home. Whenever I asked about her, there was always the same answer: 'Your turn for asking questions has not come yet'. I never really pushed for answers any way; I figured there was plenty of time for that.

I saw so much love and affection in Nirmal's eyes these days. Whenever Sabah was not around, our conversation became very personal. However, we did not confess our feelings to each other.

One day, Sabah came back from placing our order and announced, 'Let's celebrate our results. Party is on you, Parkash Ji'

'He's very tight when it comes to money. This Dhaba is probably the best he can afford,' Nirmal smirked.

'Let's go to some good restaurant, we must celebrate,' I smiled.

'Nirula's?' It was decided to meet there the next Tuesday for lunch.

'Who's going to ask Mittal for a day off? It has to be Sabah. She's getting very close to him these days,' Nirmal said mischievously.

'Why me?' Sabah queried.

'Well, you seem to be stuck to him most of the time, presumably talking rubbish all day long! Just tell him we want to take a day off to celebrate. We are his employees, not his slaves,' Nirmal said.

'He thinks he's clever, I'm going to teach him a lesson or two. I'll make him dance on my fingertips, you just watch,' declared Sabah.

'You're weaving a web of love around him, but what if you get caught in it yourself? What then?' Nirmal said.

'Don't worry, I handle it and if get caught than I'll be Mrs. Sabah Mittal, a businessman's wife with lots of money, a big house, servants, cars, expensive jewellery and the lot,' Sabah said cheekily, and burst out laughing.

'Let me know when you both finish so I can have a say as well?' I interrupted.

'Sorry, Sardar Parkash, we just got carried away,' Nirmal apologised.

'I agree with Nirmal, just tell him the truth. Why do you care what he thinks? Anyway, I'll be there on time and you girls can decide what to do with him,' I said.

2.9

LET THE PARTY BEGIN...

I was very excited when the day finally arrived, as I had been looking forward to meeting the girls in a different setting. 'I may even get the chance to talk to Nirmal alone,' I thought. 'I must gather courage and let her know of my feelings and how I see our relationship. As Simon Sahib said, we must define our relationship. It becomes easier that way.'

Everyone seemed very excited and eager, and so we all got to Nirula's about half an hour before time. It was too early for lunch so we decided to sit in Central Park in the middle of Connaught Place and watch the crowd. Nirmal looked stunning in her light blue salwar kameez and dark blue, printed dupatta. She seemed to have made a conscious effort to look very Punjabi. She knew I would love that. I couldn't take my eyes off of her. She was laughing and giggling without any care in the world. I hadn't seen her this happy before. She was not letting anyone else say a word either.

Oh no! The mood suddenly changed when we saw Mittal coming towards us.

'What the hell is he doing here?' Nirmal asked.

'You are useless, Sabah! Can't you do anything right? Why did you invite him?'

I had to calm her down. 'It's okay, Nirmal. Let's not ruin our celebration. Welcome him as a friend, please.'

'I did not invite him at all. I just said we are going to celebrate at Nirula's. He asked if he could come. I said yes, but it was not an invitation! I'm so sorry. I really am,' Sabah said.

'Hey, Sabah, don't be silly. It's not your fault he's so bloody shameless, but please let us behave normally,' I said. Nirmal liked my attitude and these small things did help to create a respectable image, I knew.

We welcomed Mittal and thanked him for coming. He told us his filmy jokes and laughed at them himself. Sabah played a clever trick and invited him on a walk. He seemed in two minds; on the one hand, , he probably wanted to walk with Sabah but on the other, he didn't want to leave Nirmal and me alone. Anyway, Sabah succeeded in dragging him away.

So finally, Nirmal and I were alone. Words completely dried up when she looked at me with so much care, love and affection in her eyes. All my rehearsals had been in vain and my brain just froze. Our eyes met; a million questions were asked and answered without a word being spoken.

Nirmal carefully plucked a white flower and placed it in her notebook.

'Its connection with the main has been broken forever, it will die now,' I said.

'It's grown in a public park, its luck is to be crushed by the foot, and at least I will look after it.'

'Well, beauty lies in the living.'

'No, beauty lies in the eyes of beholder, not in the flowers.'

'Well, the fragrance will surely die.'

'No, no, fragrance never dies, it is in our hearts.'

'There is difference between the living and the dead. Don't you agree?'

'The difference comes from how you feel. Freshness is a feeling.'

'Can these feelings last till the end?' I asked, looking deep into her eyes as if to say, *you are right – if we can hold on to these precious feelings.*

'Why not?'

The assurance in her voice said it all. There was a strength of conviction, calmness and self-belief in her eyes. I slipped once again into the world of dreams as I watched her plucking the second flower with utmost care and placing it beside the first one.

'Why did you take the second?' I asked.

'It is necessary to have companion. Only then can the journey of life goes smoothly.'

The journey of our *Love* began thus.

'I hope you don't mind, Nirmal. I wish to say something to you. Promise me you'll tell me if I'm wrong or if you dislike what I say.'

She listened attentively but seemed to be in deep thought, as though lost in her own world. I was having difficulty saying my bit. The air was certainly filled with love and affection. Her beautiful fingers were playing with the grass. I believe she knew fully well what was on my mind but was waiting for those beautiful words from me, and here I was, dithering, beating around the bush, saying everything in a roundabout way.

I took a deep breath.

'Nirmal, I really… your happiness matters a lot to me… I… I am…' and before I could finish, I felt the pressure of a hand on my shoulder and saw Mittal standing over us. My dream shattered and I came crashing down from the seventh heaven.

I was annoyed and sorry for myself at the same time. What would Nirmal think of me? *She probably thinks I'm hopeless.*

If loving someone was no sin, then why I was being so hesitant in expressing myself to her? I was aware that these important decisions need to be taken in a timely manner. I didn't want to leave it for too late.

So many new questions kept creeping in my mind. 'Am I capable yet…? What will my parents say? What will my social circle, society, my friends and relative say? Can I handle love and the responsibilities that come with it? I am still very young. Is it true love or infatuation?'

Our mind has the capacity to wander, from one place to million miles away. Then the other questions; 'Nirmal was a Punjabi Jat, why she calls someone Ammi Jaan? They are friends and not sisters. Where does she lives, who with? I know nothing about her except her name. Why is she so reluctant to tell me about herself and her family?' I, however, was busy telling her stories about myself and never really given her the chance… that's why.

'Will we get married soon and where? Will it be Delhi or Punjab? I cannot take an unmarried girl to my parents. It has to be done in the proper way. My parents need to go to her parents and ask for her hand. That's how it is done. Will I be able to handle the responsibilities that marriage brings?' I did not have enough income to support us both. 'Must I wait?' I'd just entered in my prime years. Love might be enough to keep the soul going but body would need food to survive. Brain says *'think and wait,'* and heart says, *'can't wait.'* Even the thought of not being with Nirmal filled me with emptiness. I adored the beauty and the beautiful person she was.

I believed in not making false promises. Foundation of any lasting relationship couldn't be built upon falsehood. 'Relationship based on trust lasts. If you promise then you must fulfil, once you start on a journey, you must not look back, defend your honour with pride and life' this was in my DNA. This was what my family is made of. I heard my parents reminding me of these virtues.

'Love is not a business; it's not a balance sheet either. You cannot measure love, how much someone or you love someone.' All I could say that as soon as her name *Nirmal* came in my mind, it gave me warmth, I felt surrounded by a fragrance that was hers – unique. I felt the luckiest, the happiest person in the world. Her philosophical conversation left me a feeling of sweetness in my mind. I remembered her smile and a smirk came on my lips automatically.

The food at Nirula's was very good and everyone enjoyed it. Mittal looked quite happy with his trick of touching the girls' feet under the table and then laughing about it. He was succeeding in winding us up, especially Nirmal who was trying her best to keep calm. Sabah was trying to control the situation.

And then something went wrong. Mittal must have done something under the table. I could see Nirmal getting annoyed and Sabah trying her best to divert attention.

'I will have a coffee, anyone else…?' Sabah threw the question in air.

'You can always include me, I never say *no* to coffee or tea,' I said to Sabah.

Mittal looked at Nirmal from the corner of his eyes and said, 'Coffee for me as well.'

Nirmal had had enough of his annoying antics. She got up, and declared that she was going to get an ice cream and walks towards the counter.

Mittal sheepishly said, 'I think I'll have ice cream as well,' and went and stood beside Nirmal. I didn't really know what happened but Mittal came back with two plates of strawberry ice cream. Nirmal seemed to change her mind and had coffee instead. From her face, we could tell that she was angry and frustrated with Mittal.

When the party ended, we got ready to go and Nirmal announced, 'Sardar Parkash, you will spend the whole day with me, next Tuesday.'

How daring of her! She didn't wait for my response. We were all taken back by her courage. The real Nirmal was back with a bang.

Sabah wished us good luck with a mischievous smile.

I was feeling very lucky already. It had become clear to me that we were both deeply in love. My whole body shivered with excitement and fear at the same time. 'Alone all day, no one to disturb us!' I repeated it so many times.

There were still four days to go for that day though, and the wait was becoming unbearable. I counted minutes. As the day of meeting came closer, I certainly got a little worried. Nirmal had asked that we meet at my place. I wondered why she hadn't picked another spot.

'What am I going to tell my landlady?' We were not in the West. Simon Sahib, who had been to England and Scotland a few times, had told us. 'Once you are an adult, you are free to go, do what you like, with whom you like and no one bothers. It is nobody else's business. That is a truly free country, but here we are so nosy and spend most of time worrying about others'.

'A beautiful young girl alone with a young man, no ...no ... no. Definitely a no-go area,' I expected my landlady to say this but then the thought of 'why should I bother?' entered my brain.

I would tell her Nirmal was my cousin. No, that wouldn't work because this excuse was too old. People were neither blind nor were they stupid, they can see love and affection when two eyes meet. I could not let anyone disrespect Nirmal. My landlady had always behaved like an elder sister. I would tell her the truth, I decided.

2.10

AT LAST, THE DAY OF RECKONING...

At last the waiting was over, the day of hope, happiness and apprehension had finally arrived. I usually rose at five in the morning, but today, it was four, and I was already out of bed.

'Good Morning behan ji' I said to my landlady.

'Shall I make you a cup of tea or will you wait?' she replied.

'No, thank you Behan Ji, I'll make it myself.' She didn't usually offer me tea. I wondered what the 'will you wait' was supposed to signify. Did she know about Nirmal? I quickly brushed my teeth and washed my face. I made myself a cup of tea and opened up the newspaper.

At exactly 6.30, I heard an auto stop outside the front door. A minute later, Behan Ji was welcoming Nirmal. 'What is happening?' I asked myself in astonishment. 'Do they know each other?'

I carried Nirmal's little suitcase and some other luggage to my room. I was feeling quite shy because I normally wear a kurta and pyjama at night. Nirmal had never seen me in this kind of get up. She was also wearing her jogging suit and hadn't put on any make up. I didn't think she needed to anyway. She was so beautiful already.

'Have you had your tea? Why didn't you wait for me? This

driver was late in the first place and then he drove so slowly,' she said, without looking at me.

'You didn't have to come so early! Or you could have asked me to pick you up.' I just said this; the truth was that I was very pleased that she was here. Her presence filled my surroundings with a lovely fragrance that was unique to her.

'Did I not say I want your whole day? My day starts when I wake and finishes when I'm asleep.'

'All women are perhaps experts at multitasking.' She was talking to me while putting everything in my room in the right place – my clothes and old newspapers. It seemed that she'd taken over my house and my life for the day. After having a quick cup of tea which Behan Ji made for us, she said, 'Come, it is seven o'clock. Let's go for a walk and we'll have breakfast when we get back.'

'Yes, ma'am…' I said, and happily followed her command. Tri Nagar, where I live, was at the edge of the urban area and there were only a couple of houses before the agricultural land began. Just about 200-300 yards away, there was a small irrigation canal. We walked along the channel for about half a mile, Nirmal was busy throwing small stones in the water like a young child. She opened both her arms, looked up at the sky, inhaled deeply and exclaimed, 'Oh, it is so beautiful and serene here!'

Right in front of us was the farm owned by Sardar Jaswant Singh. After graduating from college, he had worked at the farm, taking it on after the death of his father. He had adopted the modern technique of farming, which was quite successful. I'd been coming here for some time now and we had become very good friends. My spare time was spent at the farm.

I often told him he was very lucky as he had the benefit of both worlds. He was living on the farm and also enjoyed the benefits of the city. Jaswant's wife, my dear Bhabi Ji Satwinder Kaur, whom he called *Sati,* was a gem of a person. She treated me like a younger brother and cooked tasty Punjabi food just like my mother would whenever I visited the farm. Their children clung on to me whenever they saw me; I brought chocolates and little toys for them, especially for their birthdays or other festivals – Diwali, Lohri and so on.

As we passed the main entrance, their little dog Billu came running towards us. This really scared Nirmal and she clung onto my shoulder. 'Please, Billu, carry on for a little longer,' I thought.

'Animals know who their friends and foes are, Nirmal.' I played with Billu and he quietened down.

'This dog is your friend too,' Nirmal remarked.

Jaswant came towards us and said, 'I haven't seen you for so many days, where have you been?' He looked at Nirmal and asked, 'Who is this beautiful young lady?'

'Oh… Nirmal… she is my fiancée… my best friend,' I said without hesitation. Nirmal's eyes lit up, full of love and affection. I could not think of any other word and 'fiancée' came unintentionally. I wanted this to be true though. Nirmal respectfully said, 'Sat Sri Akal, Bhaji' as we walked together to his farmhouse.

'Would you like your tea made with raw or refined sugar? If you want refined sugar then you have to wait about five minutes for Sati.'

'We'll wait for Bhabi Ji,' Nirmal decided.

One thing I noticed about Nirmal was that she never dithered. She made a firm decision and stuck to it while I did the opposite. It would have taken me time to decide whether I wanted raw or refined sugar.

'Here she comes!' When I was on my own, I didn't get this treatment because I was never treated like a guest.

'Sat Siri Akaal, everyone,' Sati said with her hands clasped together. Nirmal and Bhabi Ji both went into kitchen to make tea. I could hear them both gossiping and laughing together as if they'd known each other for years. I marvelled at how easily women could become friendly, so unlike us men.

Jaswant insisted that we have breakfast with them, but it was nearly ten o'clock and we were already late, so we took our leave and headed back to my house.

On the way back, I repeated the word 'fiancée' to myself several times. It really felt good. Nirmal must have been thinking the same as we walked back, both deeply immersed in our dreams.

'I will have a quick shower first and then while I get the breakfast ready, you can get ready.' She was issuing orders like a housewife and I meekly followed them.

She came out of the shower room, drying her wet hair with a towel and wearing my white shirt. She looked stunning.

'Now get up, you have the rest of your life to look at me. Go have your bath now and don't spend whole day there, we've other things to do.' She said this firmly but with a smile.

The bathroom and kitchen were next to each other in my house, so I could hear Nirmal and the landlady talking nonstop but couldn't make sense of it.

When I came out of the bathroom, the amazing smell of *parathas* hit my nostrils. It was so good that I immediately felt hungry. Now I knew the reason behind not having breakfast with Jaswant.

At last, the food was ready and all three of us, Nirmal, my landlady and I, sat around the table. The stuffed *parathas* reminded me off my mother. This was how she cooked back home. The food was tasty and genuinely Punjabi.

It is nearly noon when we headed towards Okhla in an auto. As we reached Okhla, Nirmal saw a Gol Gappa vendor and ran towards him in pure excitement. She indulged herself before walking towards the Yamuna River.

I'd never been to Okhla before. It seemed a very peaceful and beautiful place. On one side, we saw a couple of families with children, enjoying their picnic on the banks. There were several colourful benches dotted around and a play area as well. Further along, a few children seemed to be busy building sand castles.

However, that was not the side for people like us. We wanted to go somewhere where no one could see us. We walked in the opposite direction, where there was no picnic area.

Any river looks beautiful when full, and the Yamuna looked stunning that day because Nirmal was walking barefoot along the beautiful, sandy banks with me. Without a bit of hesitation, she took my hand, kissed and held it in her soft warm palms. I stopped in the shade of a tree, but Nirmal breezed on by.

'Come on! Why did you stop?' She shouted.

'Where are you going?' I asked.

'As far as the river takes me!'

'We've already come too far,' I said.

'Not far enough… my heart,' she said, and smirked.

She was picking up small stones like a child and throwing them into the water.

'What a way to have fun!' I said.

'Water brings out the child in us all.'

She'd gone quite far. I could see her sitting and writing something in the sand with a small stick. She stood up and admired her artwork before the river washed it away. Then she came running back to me.

She was completely out of breath as she fell into my lap like a little child. Feeling secure, she clung on, and held my hands tight.

Not a single word spoken. My fingers automatically caressed her beautiful long hair. All I could hear was the washing of the waves against the riverbank. My whole being was heavy with the intoxication of love. Our eyes closed slowly and we fell into a deep sleep.

However, dreams do have a cruel way of ending. A whiff of hot, cruel air blew, enough to wake us up, and reality returned.

Nirmal kissed my hands with affection and sat beside me, hugging my shoulders.

'When I'm near you, I feel intoxicated by your love. I forget where I am and what to do. My mind wishes that this dream would continue forever, Nirmal. I wish to spend my life with you, forever and forever…' I said. She came even closer to me, holding on to my hand as if worried about letting it go.

'God! Look at the time… we have to go home. Where are you taking me now?' I asked.

'Why do you look so worried? It's my day, I can take you wherever I want. Are you scared?'

'Yes, I am. You are not normal; you do not behave like other girls. You have taken over my life and it seems as if you've been with me for years. On the other hand, you were lying in my lap just like a child, oblivious to the surroundings. There are so many colours to your personality.'

'There is so much I want to know about you. I want to keep talking about you.'

'Is there anything that you don't know about me? You know about my parents, my village, my likes and dislikes. Even a wife might not know this much!'

'The truth is that I don't get bored talking about you. In fact, all I want to do is talk about you.'

'Are these signs of true love or is it sheer madness?' I asked with smirk.

'You may call it madness; it makes no difference, Sardar Parkash.'

In such a short time, we'd come so close to each other. One reason for this was the compatibility of our thoughts. She was so deep into everything and there was always logic in what she said. Secondly, she was also very emotional, like me. I agreed with most of what she said but sometimes just to carry the conversation forward, I deliberately disagreed, and this got her going. I enjoyed the debates we would have.

'Nirmal, don't you think that love renders a person helpless and dependant on the other one for happiness? It makes one weak, doesn't it?'

'No, I don't think so. I believe love gives a person strength and teaches them the true meaning of life. Without love, life is incomplete... completely wasted... obsolete.' She smiled her assurance.

'I was just joking with you, my friend. You took it so seriously. What you said about love is right. There is nothing more powerful than love.' I smiled, but abruptly became serious again. 'There is something I must talk to you about, Nirmal.'

I told her my whole story, from my childhood to the present in Delhi. She listened to everything intently.

'...and lastly, my mother has her wishes too, she would want her son to have a proper wedding. The whole village will join the celebrations and the marriage party with *Band-Baja* will come to your village to take you to mine. I cannot get married in a registry office in Delhi.'

Nirmal listened to my speech without interrupting and then there was a long silence. That worried me. I wondered if I had said too much.

'If you've anything else to say, please say it now, because, you're not going have the chance again And stop feeling sorry for yourself. You've done enough, achieved enough. So what if you didn't go to college for a year? You needed time to settle anyway... we all do.'

She kissed my hands again and held them close to her heart.

After a long pause she continued. 'I accept you as you are, and am not disappointed at all. In fact, I'm very proud of you. You've done well and managed to settle yourself. At least you're not burden on anyone. I appreciate and admire your honesty. You're different from anyone else and that's what is good about you. Your sincerity is your best virtue and I love it. A person makes his own fortune.

'Nirmal is forever yours. Whatever comes in our way, we will deal with it together,' she said. She became very emotional and I could see a tear just about to fall from her eyes. To keep her from crying, I tried to change the subject. 'Look, we have come very far. We should go back...'

'Who wants to go back? I don't,' she said.

'Enough with the philosophy anyway. When can we eat, madam? I am starving.' Reluctantly, she led me back along the riverbank. This time the stones she threw in seemed to reek of disappointment rather than fun.

'I have one more thing to say, please listen…' she said, finally. 'You have to make adjustments and sacrifices. Studying is never easy, especially part time. Why don't you study full time this year?'

'And how exactly do you expect me to survive? You need money and lots of it here.'

'That is exactly what I'm trying to say. I'll work and support you while you finish your studies. I do have the capacity to work hard. Trust me. I can do it,' she said.

'I have lots of respect for what you are offering, but the man I am would not allow me to accept your offer. I simply couldn't. In fact, I should be the one supporting you,'

'You Indian men! If a woman helps then it affects your big ego, but we women are always practical. Working hard will not affect my health, will it? And I only have to work while you are not working. Once you finish your education then I will be on permanent holiday anyway.'

'Permanent holidays? What do you mean?'

'After marriage, I'll have plenty of children, that many…' and she stretched her arms wide.

I could not stop myself from bursting into a laugh.

'We have to get married first!'

'Sabah and I have decided not to work for Mittal any more. We will resign next week. We've been offered a very good job as trainee managers with starting salaries of 1100 rupees per month in a fashion shop in Karol Bagh.'

'That is fantastic news; I always wondered why two educated girls were doing packing jobs in Mittal's factory at such a low wage!' I said. 'But, Nirmal, can you tell me what kind of life you are expecting with me? What do you see me doing and what are your ambitions and aspirations?'

'Well, it doesn't make any difference to me. I'll be happy so long as we are together. We won't have any problem earning a living. I'm not hoping to be mega rich or anything – just being comfortable will be fine for me.' Her voice was full of satisfaction and contentment.

'Still, you must have some preferences?' I asked.

'Not really. A wife is expected to do what the husband wants in our society, isn't that so?'

'You are an educated girl. Do you want to be the wife of a farmer, Munim ji?' I teased.

'You say *Munim Ji* as if it is a derogatory word. There is nothing wrong being a Munim Ji. It is all about earning a living.'

'You are right. I may have been too harsh on myself.'

'We won't be poor. We'll find a way.' She smiled.

'However many arguments you put to me, I do not want to remain an accountant for the rest of my life. I am not a desk person; I'm doing it because I have to. I want to run my own business,' I said.

We went to the famous *Roshan Di Kulfi* in the middle of Karol Bagh for lunch. The shop's speciality was ice cream but the other food was also quite good and affordable. We ate in a rush because Nirmal had bought tickets for *Do Badan,* the six to nine show at the Natraj Cinema in Moti Nagar. She'd chosen this because the hero Manoj Kumar and heroine Asha Parekh were my favourite stars.

We arrived at the show with barely two minutes to spare. Nirmal grasped my hand as we sat in those comfortable leather seats. Her grasp became looser or tighter according to what was happening on screen.

During the interval, I felt as though everyone were staring at us, envying me for having coffee with the most beautiful girl. Nirmal had become very involved in the story of the film and said,

'Why is our society always against people who love each other? Why are people bent on creating obstacles in the path of love? I want them to be together and live happily. Yep… that's what I want,' and then she became very emotional.

'Oh come, Nirmal, it is only a film, they have to have these highs and lows to make it interesting. It is a strange world anyway. People enjoy tragedy and they laugh at other persons' misfortune. However, you don't have to worry; our story will not be like this. As long as we love each other, nothing will keep us from being together,' I said.

I noticed a change in Nirmal. She didn't hesitate to take my hand in front of people, as though she were trying to say, *I don't care.* 'Indian society doesn't mind two grown up men holding hands in public but will not tolerate any show of affection between a man and woman. It is considered vulgar and cheap. The fact is that in India, women are not considered equal. Equal rights may have been written in the Constitution, but in practice, it's totally the opposite.' Nirmal's courage was remarkable and made me blush a little. I was a very shy person, especially when it came to these things.

We'd come out of the cinema but hadn't decided what we were going to do. It was getting quite dark and I was worried about how Nirmal was going to get home.

Suddenly, her warm lips touched mine, and we were on cloud nine. All my other concerns melted away as I indulged myself in that moment.

It was half past nine and quite dark by now. 'Shall I take you home?' I said half-heartedly. I didn't want her to go. She said nothing and slowly walked towards the auto stand. The people seemed in a rush to get home. Nirmal's turn came, and she sat in the auto with a plea in her eyes. They seemed to say, 'Don't let me go away from you. Take me home.'

'Where to?' the driver asked.

'Chandni Chowk,' she said half-heartedly.

Was it my sense of morality that was keeping me silent? I tried to speak but couldn't. My words dried up completely. I managed to ask, finally, as if woken from deep sleep. 'Nirmal… Suitcase…?'

'Don't worry, it's safe with you,' she said and her auto roared away, leaving me staring into the dust and smoke it left behind. I tried to run after it, asking her to stop, but it was too late and she was gone. People were looking at me in amazement, probably wondering if I had gone mad.

I could not understand my own feelings. She'd gone but her fragrance lingered on as if she were still present.

I wandered aimlessly for about half an hour. I realized that I should have asked her to stay. Why else would she have brought a suitcase if she weren't planning to stay? I hadn't behaved responsibly either. It was so late; I should've dropped her home at least.

By the time I got home, it was nearly eleven o'clock. I was confronted by my landlady's voice coming from the kitchen. 'Come on you two, food is ready now'.

'Where is Nirmal?' she asked, when she entered my room.

'Oh, she didn't come; she's gone to her house,' I said.

'But why? She was supposed to stay with us for a few days as our guest. She told me to get the food ready and we'll all eat together. This girl is…'

A little pause and then she continued, 'Okay, at least you can have dinner with us. I made your favourite kheer. Nirmal told me you are fond of it. She knows so much about you already. I think you two will make a lovely couple.'

'I've already eaten, Behan Ji, thank you very much'. I went straight to the barsati and lay down, looking at the stars. I don't remember when I dozed off.

In the morning, the landlady confronted me when I had my tea. 'Did you ask Nirmal to come?'

'No, Behn Ji, how could she stay with me?'

'She was not supposed to stay with you… what was wrong in staying with her sister? That's what the programme was,' she said

'What about her parents?' I asked.

'She doesn't live with her parents; they are in Ludhiana. She shares a room with one of her friends. I'd already cleared a room for her. She was going to move here with us.' She paused, then continued. 'She is a wonderful girl, Parkash. Don't miss the chance to marry her.'

'Yes, Behan Ji, she is unique.' It always made me very happy when someone praised Nirmal.

The next day, I had a sudden urge to go to my village and meet Santokh. We were very close, whenever I was happy or sad, I'd to share it him. This time I was so overjoyed that Nirmal accepted my friendship, I felt like shouting from the roof tops. I'd to go... I'd to tell Santokh every single word that she said and see his reaction. I told the landlady I was going to Punjab for ten days, and if Nirmal were to ask, she should let her know.

2.11

Home sweet Home

The train was moving very quickly towards Ludhiana and so were my thoughts. Many questions kept coming to my mind, the most important being, 'why do I take so long to make decisions?' This had certainly been a weakness for a long time. In the past, I had suffered because of this habit, and good opportunities had left me behind due to my taking too long to decide. Nirmal was completely the opposite. She did not dither when it came to taking tough decisions and this was what I liked about her. I wished that one day, she would just come up to me and tell me that our marriage had been arranged for such and such date and all I had to do was to make sure to be there.

When I reached the village, I went to Sokhi's haveli. I told him everything about Nirmal but he still kept asking me what happened next.

'Bhaji, you should've brought Bhabi Ji with you,' Sokhi said.

'But how? We haven't even discussed about marriage and you're already calling her Bhabi Ji,' I said.

'But you said that you spent the whole day with her. You did not discuss marriage at all? I thought she was ready?'

'Yes, but, it is not that simple, Sokhi.'

'Why don't we let Biji know? I'll talk to her. She'll be alright. In fact, she would be very happy.'

'No, no, we can't tell Biji yet. It can go wrong.'

'What you mean? What can go wrong?'

'What if she says no? Then what?'

'Why would she say no? Nirmal is beautiful, educated and from same caste as us. She must belong to a good family, not everyone can send their children to Delhi to study. I don't see any problem.'

'If Babuji says *no* then it's *no*. The very first thing he is going say is complete your studies first; right now, you're too young to get married. I don't think their generation understands love.'

'But, Bhaji, he can say yes as well. What will you do if they find someone of their own choice for you? What if Bhabhi's parents find a suitable boy for her, now that she is about to complete her degree? Parents are always on the hunt. It will be very difficult to change their minds then. Tell me honestly, Bhaji, do you really want to get married to her or is this just a time pass affair?'

'Now that's a very silly question. Of course, I love her. I want to marry her. I can't think of my life without her but I am scared of failure... scared of getting a no from Babuji. I'm also worried that I will lose their trust. You know how parents react to love. They will think that I've gone off the rails. They might say, don't go back to Delhi, study here. I'm very confused brother... very confused.'

'I agree with most of what you said, Bhaji, but I think she is perfect in their eyes. What else would they want?'

'You know, Santokh, when we prepare a trial balance, both the debit and credit side has to match. If there is a small difference, we leave it in suspense account so that we can come back to it later or lose it somewhere. Now parents do exactly the same when it comes matchmaking.'

'Then let's do a trial balance in our case, Bhaji – Parkash and Nirmal.'

Caste: Jat, same in this case

Sub caste: 'It must be different – you can't marry another Sohal,' Sokhi said. 'We don't know her sub caste because you haven't yet asked her.'

'Neither did you, Santokh. You spent a whole day with her, why did you not ask?' I asked.

'You know, come to think of it we only talked about you the whole day. She kept asking me questions, and I told her everything. Bhabi Ji is very clever; she knows how to make you talk. Spending a day was such a wonderful experience. I thought that Gujarati girl… what was her name? Oh Sabah, she was a bit dry. So, she is not a Sohal – tick – yes.'

Religion: 'Sikh – same.'

Looks: 'She definitely looks nicer than you. Tall, slim and very fair too. You're not bad looking but she has the edge, Bhaji,' Sokhi said with a mischievous smirk.

'Men do not have to look that nice,' I said.

Status: 'Very important – rich and poor don't go together. In our case, very high plus… we don't know about Bhabi Ji but I presume her status must be good.'

Education: 'She is more educated. Hmmm… that can be overlooked but her parents would want you to complete your degree so that they can boast about it to their relatives.'

Profession or Job: 'Will you be able to support her? In this, you may not like your job but at least you're earning good money, so yes – tick.'

Love: 'No, Bhaji, love doesn't come into the equation! This will be your suspense account.'

'You are right Santokh, love has no place in matchmaking. You get married to a person your parents have met, and love supposed to grow after marriage.'

'But that is just a compromise. What if you do not like each other? You just have to live with it for the rest of your life,' Sokhi said.

'That's why so many people are unhappy with their partners. Sometimes they have nothing in common. Especially girls; they hardly have a say when their parents tell them whom they are getting married to. This is arranged marriage, my friend. A love marriage is treated as a curse – an abnormality. Just look at our village! There is not a single love marriage. Mine will be the first one. God forbid, if there is even even the smallest of disagreements between me and Nirmal, we will be reminded: didn't we tell you so? It's a love marriage, therefore, you deal with it yourself. Let's get back to our test. Do we match?' And we had a hearty laugh.

'Parkash Bhaji, I've got an idea – we should tell Biji about Nirmal and ask permission for you two to get engaged now and get married after a couple of years from now. People do that all the time. That way everything will be easier and I can call her Bhabi Ji openly.'

I considered what he'd said. I'd never lied to my parents, especially Biji. I would've to tell her some day any way. But I also knew that I hadn't spoken about any of this to Nirmal. She might not be ready for this step. But she had, after all, made a promise to spend her life with me, come what may!

'Sokhi brother, I like your plan. I think it is workable, but let's keep quiet about it, just for a while. Let me ask Nirmal once more whether she wants me tell my parents. When I come next time we'll definitely disclose this to Biji and Baoji.

'Now tell me what you know about Nirmal. How did you find her? Do you think she will make a good daughter in law for Biji?'

'Let me tell you honestly what I think, Bhaji,' Sokhi began. 'I think she's better looking than you. She's more educated than you are and talks intelligently. She's very courageous as well. I remember how she gave a good telling off to a rickshaw driver. I think she'll definitely fit into in our family. Biji will love her. Don't you lose this chance, Bhaji.'

'Okay, when you come to Delhi this time, we'll have a proper discussion,' I said before I left.

2.12

―᠊ᢦᢠᢥ᠊―

RETURNING TO DELHI...

I had figured out my programme for the week, and had decided to work very hard for a few days before going to see Nirmal. I was dying to meet her again. Behan Ji told me that she had come home but had been in a hurry and did not leave any message.

This time, I was very clear on what I needed to do. I kept telling myself the plan. I would propose to her, officially. Then I would meet her parents. And finally, I would stop working for Mittal altogether.

When Tuesday finally came, I spent extra time getting dressed and wore the blue striped shirt and the trouser with a belt that Nirmal had gifted me. I knew the smile on her face would be enough to justify my effort.

With great excitement, I rang the doorbell of Mittal's factory. I knew that either Sabah or Nirmal would come to door. They normally did so because their packing table was nearby. However, today Ratnu, the foreman, opened the door. He looked a bit agitated when he saw me and kept gazing at floor.

'What's the matter, Ratnu? What's happened? Where is everybody?'

'Babuji, everything has gone wrong, there is nothing right here!' he said.

'Where's Mittal?'

'Ji, I think he's gone to Marwaha to get raw material. We have had no work for the past two days. There's no material.'

'And Nirmal and Sabah, where are they?' I asked.

'Babuji, they both have left work. There was a big upheaval here.'

I slumped on the chair and asked him anxiously, 'Now tell me slowly, what exactly happened?'

'Babuji, on Wednesday, the material from Marwaha came a little late, but we all worked very hard and got the order ready by Thursday. Everything seemed to be fine. Mittal sir came in late and for a while he did not come out of his office. I think it was lunchtime when both Sabah and Nirmal went into the office. I saw a piece of paper in their hands. I believe it was their resignation. Mittal Sahib sent Sabah out and kept Nirmal behind. Soon, we heard a loud argument; it sounded as if they were fighting. We could see a little through the darkened glass. It looked as though Mittal Sahib were trying to hold her and she was struggling to escape. Then they both came out arguing and Mittal got angry and slapped her. That was it Babuji. Nirmal gave him two slaps back and pushed him with force. He fell down, hit his face on the corner of the table, and started bleeding. She was shouting, *Wants to buy me... bastard.*'

'Where were you? Why did you not stop them?'

'Babuji, I know Mittal was wrong, so I let him get beat up. Nirmal is a Punjaban and can look after herself.' He sobbed as he relived what had happened. There was a pause for minute or two. He took a sip of water before he continued.

'Sabah and I separated them and made Mittal sit in the office. Sabah, I believe, ran to Simon Sahib who came straightaway and told Mittal off. He sent Sabah and Nirmal to his office. Mittal was obviously very angry and insisted on calling the police. He kept on shouting, *bloody prostitute, I will teach you a lesson* and much more slander. Simon Sahib managed to put some sense in his head. He made him apologise to them and pay their wages right up to the last day.'

I couldn't believe that so much had happened while I was away. Controlling my anger, I asked him what happened next.

'…Babuji, things are not the same anymore. Marwaha does not give material and I don't know why. We are anxious, Babuji. How we going to feed our children if we do not work?'

'Where is your Mittal Sahib now?' I asked.

'We don't know where he is. He hasn't come for the last two days, Babuji.'

There wasn't much left to say. I was fuming with anger and frustration that I had not been there when Nirmal needed me. How dare Mittal humiliate her? I took a paper and wrote, 'I cannot work for a disgraceful person like you. You have thrown mud at our friendship. You are a mentally sick and cowardly person.' I placed my resignation on his desk. I left in disgust.

With my mind full of anger, I went to see Simon Sahib. 'So much has happened in the past week and you haven't even told me any of it!' I said to Simon Sahib.

'Come on, Parkash… please calm down and listen. I was very upset and still am. Mittal has behaved so badly with the girls. I've told him off as much as I can but he is really a brainless bastard. Anyway, Nirmal was fine; in fact, she gave him very good beating. She is a Punjabi Jatti capable of looking after herself. Not the type who gets frightened very quickly. Please cool down and don't worry about her too much. She'll be alright.' 'How can I contact her? She hasn't left her address with me,' I said, worried.

'What do mean by *how?* You must know where she lives, surely?' he asked, looking surprised.

'Simon Sahib, all I know is that her name is Nirmal. I don't know where she lives. I hadn't had the chance to ask her yet. One day I was going to Marwaha to collect material for Mittal. Nirmal was feeling unwell and there wasn't much work. She wanted to go home early and asked me if she could get lift in my auto as I was going in the same direction. Mittal heard me saying that she could, and he came along too, saying he had some urgent work to do. I remember dropping them off at the far end of GB Road and saw them crossing the road while my driver whisked me away. That is all I can recall,' I said.

'Hmmm…' Simon Sahib said, and went into deep thought.

'Simon Sahib, the truth is that I do not have a detective's brain. I'm always too deeply involved in my own problems. The only thing on my mind before I left for Punjab was how to ask Marwaha Sahib for more material for Mittal even though he has not paid for the previous three invoices.' I was disgusted with myself for not having listened to Jatinder's advice. How could I have formed a friendship with such a revolting man?

Simon Sahib got up from his chair and put his hand on my shoulder and said, 'I'm your elder brother, your problems are mine too. We'll find Nirmal. I'm sure we will.'

My head was aching with the worry when I got home. I didn't feel like eating, so I went straight to the barsati and lay down. 'Nirmal knows where I live,' I thought, 'why hasn't she come to see me? Maybe she doesn't know that I'm back from Punjab. Could it be that she is now giving me the cold shoulder because of my behaviour? She may be angry and disappointed that I did not ask to her stay that day. Maybe she has taken my apprehensiveness as unwillingness to pursue our relationship. God forbid something has happened to her, and she is in trouble. Why did Mittal say, *I could buy any girl? Is she for sale?* And the most disturbing question of all – why did he call her a *prostitute?* It's a very degrading word to use for any woman.

'She couldn't be living on GB Road. No… no… not on GB Road. That road was well known for its mister minas. *Mujra* and flesh selling take place openly every night and if you walk on that road, you can hear the beat of music coming from the windows where scantily dressed women are standing, giving customers a glimpse of what is happening inside. You meet with pimps on every corner, enticing you to go in. That road is not a respectable address, especially for a young women. She cannot be living there,' I told myself.

It was half past six in the morning and after having a quick shower, I embarked on my mission to find Nirmal. I waved an auto down and the driver asked me, 'Where do want to go, Babu Sahib?'

'GB Road.'

'GB Road?' He asked as if he hadn't heard properly.

'Yes, Bhai, GB Road,' I affirmed.

'Is it not a bit too early for GB Road?' He said with mischievous smirk.

'I've other business at that place, not the one you are thinking of,' I said sternly.

He started his motor, and we were on our way. He still had a smirk on his face as if saying, *don't kid me, no one goes to GB Road for any other business than The Business.*

I asked him to stop exactly at the spot where I had dropped Nirmal and Mittal. The bazaar was like a ghost town, and there was no one around that I could see. All the doors seemed to be shut. If I had gone to any other part of the city there would be buzz around but then this was GB Road, which remained open most of the night and not the day.

I stood there, staring at the building opposite me. 'Is this where she lives? If she lives in a nearby street, then she would've asked the driver to drop her there.' I stared at every single door in the building. Finally, I saw someone coming towards me. He looked me up and down and asked abruptly, 'What you want, Babu?'

I didn't like the tone of his voice one bit but kept my patience.

'I'm looking for a girl... she's my friend... no, my fiancée. Her name is Nirmal. I've lost her address but I know she lives around here. Please help me,' I pleaded.

'Hmmm... Nirmal? Your fiancée?' He laughed – an unfriendly, sarcastic laugh. His mouth was full of betel juice, which he deliberately spat in front of me.

'Yes, brother, I know she lives around here. She is tall, slim with fair skin and she is very good looking. Do you know anyone by that name?' I said to him with a plea in my voice.

'Hmmm... there is Hasina, Shamina, Munni, and Gulabi...' He made up names, seeming to enjoy teasing me. Another gob of spit landed near my feet and I jumped. I knew I had to keep calm, but this man was testing my patience.

'Hmmm... Nirrrrr... mal. No... there is no Nirmal here, they are all used. But come in evening with a pocket full of money than they all will be *Nirmal* hee hee hee...'

I was getting quite worked up. The man's behaviour was tantamount to insult. If this was his sense of humour then it was very mean and degrading.

Somehow, I felt, he knew something but did not want to tell me. I was trying my best to start up a conversation. I'd seen this in the films, how they bribed the doorkeeper. I knew that nothing worked in India unless you greased the palm of the person guarding the door, so I was trying that now. I took out a ten rupee note and gave it to him.

'Please, brother, please help me if you can?' I begged He took the money and put it in his pocket. He spat again and said 'There is no Nirmal – Virmal here, Babu. Go, get lost, and stop wasting my time.'

I walked away disappointed, my head hanging.

I didn't have the courage to knock on any door. I'd a strange feeling that Nirmal would just come walking towards me, asking what was I doing there as if nothing had happened. I walked towards the junction with Chandni Chowk and saw a dhaba some distance away. I hadn't eaten anything since yesterday's lunch and I was very hungry.

It was probably early for the dhaba too; there were only a handful of customers having breakfast. The smell of freshly cooked chana poori was overwhelming.

I'd been sitting there for nearly an hour and had finished my second cup of tea. The restaurant owner obviously knew I was just sitting there to pass time, so he came to me with a polite question, 'Sahib, do you want anything else?' *It meant finish it now... pay and go.*

Ten minutes later, he asked me again: 'Babu Sahib, have you lost something? Can I help you in any way?'

I looked up at him. He seemed a nice person. I felt like trusting him and I had nothing much to lose anyway. 'Yes…, I've lost everything, brother… everythin.,' It was a very big relief to know that someone wanted to help me. I plucked up my courage and began.

'Bhaji, kindly help me. I'd appreciate it very much.'

'Yes, Babuji, certainly. We are all God's children. We must help one another.'

I was so desperate for information that I was prepared to open up to a complete stranger. I began by saying, 'I'm looking for a girl who is going to be my fiancée, God willing. Unfortunately, I've lost her address. I believe she lives around here. She is quite tall and has very fair complexion.' I hadn't even finished giving him the description when he stopped me and said, 'And she is Punjabi and her name is Nirmal?'

'O my God! Yes… yes, yes … she is the one. So, you know Nirmal?' I ask excited.

'Yes… and I know Sabah as well. They are regular customers. They have their breakfast here almost every day. They are very good girls and say little to anyone. I haven't seen them for over a week now,' he said.

'Do you know where they live?'

'No, Babuji, we don't ask our customers where they live, but I think they normally come walking from that area.' He pointed towards the Chandni Chowk and GB Road junction. When he saw my expression he said, 'The whole GB Road is not what you are thinking, Babuji, and those two definitely are not that type.'

I was certainly relieved to hear this. I did not want Nirmal's name to be associated with the twaif business in any way.

'Thank you very much, Bhai Sahib, you really put my mind to rest.' I took my leave of him. *'She is not a Twaif, and she lives around here. I will find her,'* I kept repeating to myself.

This certainly was a strange place; it was well past nine o'clock and still there weren't many people about. I kept walking towards Chandni Chowk and reached the famous Gurdwara Sis Ganj Sahib. I went inside and bowed in front of the Guru Granth Sahib, took prasad, found a spot in a corner and listened to priest reciting from the Holy Book. I closed my eyes and made three wishes; *let Nirmal be fine wherever she is, please keep her under your divine protection and be a little more graceful, and unite us, gracious God!*

After a while, I came out from the Gurdwara and walked towards Central Park. I sat on the non-existent grass and watched people going by. It seemed everybody had a destination in mind and I was the only one who did not see any clear-cut path in front me. Life seemed a bit fuzzy and muddled up.

I was completely exhausted when I reached home. The difference between Delhi and Punjab was quite clear to me. I felt very much on my own here, lonely, depressed and impotent, unable to locate my love. Those twaif businesses, dancing dens, were not my cup of tea. My parents had made every effort that I become a good human being. They went out of their way to give me good education. Little did they know that their son had fallen head over heels in love and was behaving like a lunatic.

It was a little past midnight. There were no clouds, not even the tiny fluffy ones in the sky, just twinkling stars – millions of them – trying to outdo each other. Sleep deserted me, so to keep my mind occupied, I gazed at them and invented stories. It seemed as though some stars were with their loved ones and others who were alone were very lonely. *'Those who shine brighter are extinguished faster,'* Biji used to say. 'Sobbing is only good when someone is there to console you.

I got up early, and after having a cup of tea, I went back to work at Haryana Bus Builders, one of my newer clients. As I began my work Sharma Ji, the owner of HBB, walked into the office and told me that Simon Sahib had been looking for me and I was to see him at the earliest.

I left everything behind and rushed to Simon Sahib. It took me about an hour to get to his office. I told him the whole story of what had happened the previous day. He listened to me attentively.

Simon Sahib has a cup of tea in one hand and a pencil in the other hand, just like a true professional; he listed all the information we had, point by point.

One –we knew that she lived somewhere on GB Road because the dhaba wala had seen her coming from that direction.

Two – both Sabah and Nirmal were connected with Twaif business in some way.

Three – the doorkeeper was not telling the truth; after all, these bastards are hungry for money.

Fourth – this question was most disturbing. Why hadn't Nirmal contacted me? Even if I were absent, she could've left a message with the landlady or Simon Sahib.

Fifth – where was Sabah?

It was nearly half past one when we left for GB Road. About half an hour later, Simon Sahib stopped his Royal Enfield motorcycle right in front of the doorman's post. Simon Sahib, with his tall and imposing frame, cut an impressive figure. The same useless man, who had been making fun of me earlier, came running towards us with his head bowed. Simon Sahib gave him a hundred rupees which he gleefully accepted.

'No rubbish, just tell me what you know,' Simon Sahib said.

'Yes, Sahib Ji,' the man said obediently.

'How many girls live in this kotha?'

'Ji, seven… seven girls live here and Ammi Jaan.'

'Do they all do business?'

'Yes, Sahib Ji, they all do.'

'Is there anyone who doesn't?'

Simon Sahib came back to his motorcycle and lit up a cigarette. Now the doorkeeper was telling us what we wanted to know, and even the things we didn't ask for. He was probably trying to justify the money he had taken from us.

'Sahib Ji, you see that third door? They don't do the Business like us. They are Ammi Jaan's girls; they will be sold to rich people when they are ready. Ammi Jaan looks after them very well and protects them too. They go to college as well and are usually from very poor families.'

This was enough for us. We decided to get back to Simon Sahib's place. I was a bit curious so on our way back I asked Simon Sahib, 'After paying the doorman so much money, why did we not ask about Nirmal?'

'I think that he knew nothing more than he had told us. Had we asked for more, he might have invented stories, just to satisfy us, and we do not want to risk Nirmal's safety by being too inquisitive,' he said. 'Parkash, there is more to it than meets the eye. I think Mittal knows something about this already, hence his boast.'

2.13

—ᴍ—

REALITY CHECK

I was feeling rotten and had very little interest in studying or working. My visits to CA Sahib's office or meetings with Doctor Sahib had almost stopped. I was too busy with the rubbish that rattled around in my head. My life had come to a sudden halt.

The biggest and the most crucial question that kept bothering me was, '*What connection do Sabah and Nirmal have with the Twaif's Kotha?*' Girls from respectable families run miles away from these sorts of places. It didn't make any sense.

Maybe Mittal was right after all, and I'd been taken for a fool. I was beginning to doubt my belief and confidence in people.

However, the next minute, a sensible thought prevailed. '*Nirmal cannot be bad, she is my best friend and remains my best friend. My trust in her is as solid as ever. The warmth in her hands and heart cannot be anything but genuine. Ours is true love.*'

She might have just gone home to her place in Punjab and here I was, sweating and reading too much into it. 'Whatever it takes, I'll find her. I will not be shy to tell the world about our relationship. I will let both sets of parents know too. *It's not a crime to love someone.*' I consoled myself with such positive thoughts.

I worked nonstop even over the weekend and brought most of my accounts right up to date. With determination and vigour, I would resume the search for Nirmal. I would knock on every door on GB Road. 'She can't just vanish…'

It was about eight in the morning and my auto stopped right opposite that doorman's hut. I went straight up to his room and he jumped and greeted me with folded hands. He politely wiped a chair for me. I'd rehearsed what I was going to say. So just as Simon Sahib had, I placed a note on his palm, pretending to look away. He did not pocket the note but placed it on the side table. I thought it might not be enough, so I gave him another one and he placed it on the table again.

'Chhote Sahib Ji, please take a seat. Shall I get you tea?'

'I haven't asked your name yet,' I said.

'Ji, my real name is Imtiaz Hussain but here everyone calls me Khan. Sahib, what shall I get for you? There is a restaurant nearby.'

'Give me a glass of water, please.'

I settled down and waited for him to begin.

'After you left the other day, I went and spoke to Pathan about this. Babu Sahib, you're a nice person and I shouldn't lie to you.'

'Who is this Pathan?'

'He is also a doorman. He looks after Ammi Jaan's other house, where these girls live.'

'Where is he now?'

'His daughter is getting married, so he's gone to his village for two weeks. I'm looking after his patch as well. The Kotha on this side belongs to Ammi Jaan as well. We have proper business here, Mujra and everything, Chhote Babu Sahib. The other house is where Ammi Jaan's special girls live. They are educated. They normally end up as mistresses of rich people. We aren't supposed to know. If Ammi Jaan hears anyone talking about them, she gets very annoyed. She's a very tough woman and has an army of ruthless goons at her disposal. You don't want to get on the wrong side of her. Please, Babu Ji, you're a good man. Don't tell anyone that you were here and secondly keep away from this… this is not for you.'

I kept asking him more, somewhat irrelevant questions. 'So these girls do all this out of their free will? Nobody forces them?'

'Sahib Ji, they are poor. Will or no-will, once they are in, they won't be able to go anywhere else. Also they are normally happy that some rich man can provide them with luxuries they would otherwise only dream of.'

'So Nirmal and Sabah must be the same as the others?'

'No, Babu Sahib, I don't think they are the same, especially Nirmal. She's definitely not one of them. She's proper Punjabi, you know. Why she lives with them, I don't really know, but then you can't tell from the face. To me, they all look respectful.'

He picked up a paper from the table in the corner and started reading from it. 'Last Monday, both came to me about 8 o'clock and said that they needed an auto at 6 am, sharp. When I asked, why so early, Sabah said, Nirmal is going to see someone special. I remember it was for Tri Nagar.' He carefully read his notes again.

'The next morning, the auto driver was about five minutes late… Oh my God, Nirmal was so angry she gave him a proper telling off. She also had a small suitcase and a grey bag with her. When she came back around ten, she looked very happy. She had no bag or suitcase with her. She went straight up and said nothing.'

I did not want to tell him that she had in fact spent the whole day with me.

'On Wednesday, both of them went to work as usual. They usually get back home around eight in the evening, but on that day, both came home around two. I think they were a bit upset but they didn't say anything to me. Then Nirmal went out with Shamim and came back very late. Someone came to collect Sabah in a big white car and she had a suitcase and few other things with her as well. I've not seen Sabah since.'

The whole story was becoming more and more interesting. A question kept leaping in my mind, *has Sabah been sold?* I was sitting in the hub of the flesh trade. Sex was sold here as some kind of commodity. I was disgusted and horrified, but had no choice but to listen to all this. I only hoped that somewhere along the line I would get the information I needed to find Nirmal.

'Sahib Ji, on Thursday I remember Shamim and Nirmal were together around half past eight in the morning. I asked them if they want me get an auto for them but they said no as they were just going to the bazaar. They both looked very pensive that day and said little. I saw them hurrying towards Chandni Chowk but don't remember seeing Nirmal again. I think she went to see her family in Ludhiana.'

Imtiaz was playing the real detective here; he put his notes away and went into deep thought as if evaluating positives and negatives. He then shouted out as if he'd found the missing clue.

'Sahib Ji, something is wrong. I haven't seen Nirmal that quiet before. She always stops by for a minute or two, always asks me about my family and children. Even if she were going on holiday or back home, she would tell me. One more thing, I have seen a dark skinned, short man wearing glasses go upstairs a few times. He doesn't stop or ask anyone; just goes straight up to where Ammi Jaan lives. I think all the deals are made there.'

'Imtiaz Bhai, you can become a good detective.' He enjoyed my praise. One fact was very clear: both Sabah and Nirmal were not here any longer, so the only chance I had of finding them would be to talk to Shamim. She must know where they had gone.

'Nirmal must have told Shamim where she was heading. How can I meet Shamim?'

'Oh, that's easy. She normally leaves at nine, so you can meet her then.'

I looked at my watch. There was still half an hour left for Shamim to come down, so I just continued the random questions, just to pass the time.

'Are you married, Imtiaz?'

'Yes… Babu Sahib, I've got two children, a daughter and a son. My daughter goes to college and son is still at school. He will go to college next year. Both my children are brilliant at their studies. We both husband and wife, are trying our best to give them good education. That's all we both husband and wife live for. Education is must Sahib Ji. We don't want them to end up like us.'

I heard a lot of satisfaction and pride in his voice as he talked about his family. I was beginning to like him now, and could see underneath this tough exterior lived a very sensitive, hardworking proud man, who cared so much for his family.

'Are you from Delhi?'

'No, Sahib Ji, my home is in UP, I visit my family twice a year.'

'Just twice a year, is that enough?' I continued with the conversation although my mind was counting the minutes for Shamim. I'd become hopeful that she might tell me Nirmal's whereabouts.

'Sahib Ji, we poor people do not have much of a choice. I have to earn a living for my family. By God's grace, I earn enough from this job, enough so that I am able to educate my children. Every poor person has a dream that his children get educated so they don't have to do the same what he is doing.'

'Does your wife know that you are working at a Kotha?'

'No, No, Babu Sahib, she thinks I work in a big office as an officer. However, I can't earn that sort of money what I make here. I've got a small house as well. Once my children finish their education, I won't be doing this forever. I'm longing to go back to my village.'

He was an honest man, who was totally committed to his family. I looked at my watch and there were still ten minutes left. Time seems to go slower when you are waiting. So we continued with our conversation.

'You have many girls here? It must be quite nice to keep yourself amused.' I said with a mischief in my voice.

'Yes, Sahib, in our Kotha, there are eight of them there. On our side, we provide the full service, Mujra… the lot, and my answer to your second question, no Sir; I'm doing a job, keeping the unwanted people away. I do not mix work with pleasure, also when you see this every day, you become immune. They get tired like us too they are human beings. No, Babu Ji, what they do is their business, it does not interest me.'

'Imtiaz Bhai, you are a man of high principles, I'm impressed, and how you've given your work the respect and it needed.'

We carried on with our conversation. My knowledge of the twaif's Kotha definitely increased. I was also amused to see a parallel world where things were done so differently. This was the unknown part of Delhi, which I didn't really want to learn about. My eyes were now fixed on the door from which Shamim was supposed to emerge

'Babu Sahib, you want me to knock on the door?'

'No, Imtiaz, let us just wait. Last thing we want is for anyone to get suspicious.'

I got up and shook his hand. 'From today, I'm not your Sahib; you're my friend, my brother. You can call me Bhai Parkash from now on.'

'Thank you, Bhai Parkash Ji. Now that we've become brothers, I cannot take your money. Please put this in your pocket.' He handed over the money lying on the table.

'I haven't earned this money; I did not mind taking money from the Big Babu Sahib. That was my charge for the information provided. You, Parkash Bhai Sahib Ji, are a good person, you have a heart that cares. We'll find Nirmal. Shamim must be knowing but you have to be very careful, these people are very cruel, and Ammi Jaan especially. This is definitely not your world. Respectable people don't come here,' he said, and then we both laughed.

We heard someone coming, so we both stood up, our eyes fixed on the door. There was Shamim. She looked like a very smart girl, and was fully wrapped in shawl. She walked towards Chandni Chowk and I followed her until we were in a very narrow, dingy street. Finally, when I was standing before her, she asked me, 'Are you Sardar Parkash?'

'Yes, I'm Sardar Parkash.'

'I recognised you from Nirmal's descriptions. You shouldn't have come here. Nirmal and Sabah, they're both gone. I accompanied Nirmal to the station. She's gone to see her parents in Punjab. Ammi Jaan was extremely angry when she found out. She made a big fuss. If she ever finds out I helped her then that will be the end of brave Shamim.

Thank Allah that Nirmal got away, but Sabah didn't. You, please go, I'm a little scared right now. Listen, Ammi Jaan will be going away for two, three days next Monday, so please see me on Tuesday at noon at the Roxy Restaurant, in Chandni Chowk.'

I thanked her profusely for and had no choice but to leave.

The whole story was getting out of hand and becoming more confusing every day. There was one question bothering me. What was the relationship this Ammi Jaan had with the girls? Why did they come to her in the first place? I understood that they were poor but life at Kotha as a Twaif... what can be more degrading than that? If they were renting the place from her, then why did they fear her so? Why had Nirmal left in such a hurry?

Simon Sahib had taken the responsibility of being my elder brother and mentor; therefore, it was my duty to share everything with him. When I entered his office, his first question was, 'Parkash Bhai, who the hell is this Ammi Jaan woman? Why are these girls so scared of her? We definitely need to find out.'

'Simon Sahib, that time hasn't come yet. First of all, let me meet Shamim and find out a bit more, then we'll decide what to do. We shouldn't do anything that could harm Shamim.'

'You're right, but I don't understand Nirmal's helplessness. Why would an educated and intelligent person live at the Kotha in the first place? You lose all your respect from any attachment to such a place.'

2.14

KEEP HOPE ALIVE...

I worked very hard over the week, brought all my accounts up to date, and found time to see CA Sahib, who was very pleased to meet me. But the more I tried not to think of Nirmal the more I kept going back to her and millions of silly questions kept entering my head. It was a vicious circle.

When the day finally arrived to meet Shamim, my hopes were touching the sky. All would be revealed in few hours, I thought. I would be able to get answers to all the questions Simon Sahib had raised.

It was very difficult to sit in the restaurant without ordering. I wondered why girls were always late. At last she arrived, breathless.

'Bring us two plates of hot samosa and two teas,' Shamim said to the waiter. Then she turned to me. 'Oh, I'm so sorry for being late. That bloody Ammi Jaan just would not go. As soon as she left I came running. Don't worry, she won't be back for another three or four hours now. Thank God she's gone.'

'Did you not say she was going away for a few days?' I asked.

'Oh, she changed her mind, silly cow. I think she's worried about Nirmal, but we can only guess what's in her mind. She's gone to her other house. Sorry, I've started to speak in Urdu. Nirmal told me to speak to you in Punjabi. She used to teach me Punjabi. I can speak Urdu, Punjabi and English, you know. My mother was from Lahore and could speak Punjabi very well. I learnt from both her and Nirmal. My parents came here during the Partition. My Abbu died when I was ten years old. I've got younger sisters. It was very hard for my mother to bring us up, but she managed, somehow.'

It felt strange to use the past tense to talk about Nirmal. My mind picked up these minute signals, unwittingly. To keep the conversation going, I asked, 'So Ammi Jaan has a second house as well?'

'Ammi Jaan has been the mistress of a very rich Seth for many years. The Seth has bought her a farmhouse where she goes every other day. No one else is allowed there, not even her *goondas*, only the servants who live in the farmhouse. The house where we live also belongs to the seth. Ammi Jaan has the neighbouring *kotha* where girls do *Mujra*. She feeds many goondas, very dangerous men. But it does not matter to us.

Shamim had finished with the samosa, so I asked her politely, 'Shamim Ji, why did Nirmal have to leave ?'

'Okay, now let me tell you the whole story... Nirmal – poor girl, not to blame, not one bit, she got entangled with all this completely by mistake. The week before last, Sabah was sold to a rich Seth. She did a bit of drama but she was actually probably happy to be bought by a rich man. Nirmal tried to talk her out of it, but it didn't have any effect on her.'

I was getting a bit restless. Why did she keep beating around the bush? Why did she not talk about Nirmal?

After a long pause, she cleared her throat and continued with the story.

'Nirmal was very close to me. We had no secrets from each other. In fact, she always treated me like her elder sister. On that day, we were just having our girly chat, when Mittal came to see Ammi Jaan. He was in deep discussion for nearly an hour. We could not hear anything, because Ammi Jaan's sitting room is on the other side and people usually use the door at the far end. We both more or less knew why he was there. Nirmal had already given him a good hiding in his factory. They'd had a big fight. That bastard should have known he didn't stand a chance against the Tigress. He must have come for revenge.'

She took a couple of neatly folded sheets of paper from her purse and laid them down on the table.

'Okay, I wrote the complete conversation as it happened between Ammi Jaan and me. This was meant for Nirmal. I thought if anything happened, and we didn't get the chance to go out, then at least she will know what was happening behind her back. I didn't want to discuss this while other people were in the house. You can't trust everyone blindly. Do you mind if I read from the papers? Do you have time or... some other day, may be? Once Nirmal left, my idea was to get these papers to you somehow. I also added the conversation between me and Nirmal that day as well.'

'No, Shamim, I've plenty of time, you just carry on.' She started reading very carefully again.

'My bedroom is next door to the sitting room and Ammi Jaan's office. We may not enter it without her permission. We call it Ammi Jaan's Darbar. On Thursday, all the girls went out, but I didn't go because I'd the monthly women's headache. I was in my room when I saw three of Ammi Jaan's gangsters come in, talking about Nirmal. I could hear everything because my door was a little open, and they did not know I was in my room. What I heard horrified me.'

Shamim seemed to stretch everything out; all I wanted to know was Nirmal's whereabouts.

'I heard Ammi Jaan saying, *This girl is tough; we won't be able to control her like the others. Mittal is ready to give twenty five thousand for her. He was here yesterday; I told him I need a bit more. She is a virgin, I said...I know I can get more for her. But she is going be very hard to tackle... that much is for sure.*

'*Why don't we cut her wings? Then she won't be able to fly...
that bitch. You can put her in one of your kothas, Ammi Jaan, and
she will earn for you for life. If she still makes a fuss, we will take her
somewhere else and no one will know.*

'*You idiot, use your brain. Who will buy second hand half-chewed
fruit? Hmmm, you are right in one sense. If she agrees and gives her
consent willingly, then that is best, otherwise we'll use your way. I
know a rich seth who would be willing to pay a lot more for her.*' I
heard someone come and join them. I believe it was the Ammi
Jaan's Seth himself. We only saw him occasionally; he was the Big
Boss, who said very little.'

I could see that Shamim was becoming emotional and her
eyes were full of tears. She could not read anymore and gave me
the papers and said, 'You read it yourself.' She left for the powder
room.

She had written: '*Ammi Jaan is a very ruthless woman. I'm
aware of that, but she could be this cruel, I never thought possible.
She is prepared to go to any length to achieve her goal, no matter
how many lives she destroys on the way. She would do anything
for money. I can't fight with Ammi Jaan, so I tried a different
approach, pretending I was on her side . I walked straight into
her room and told her I'd heard her conversation, and that I was
very sorry. Could she please give me a minute as I had something
important to say? She was angry at first but then became a little
calmer and said go on, say what you have to say.*'

'*Ammi Jaan, I've been here with you for the past three years and
never given you any reason to complain. I know you are also happy
with the responsibilities I've taken,*' I said hesitantly to see her
reaction.

'*Is that all you want say?*' she said, chewing and spitting *paan*.

'*No... Ammi Jaan, I have learnt a lot from you. We all know that
you care for us a lot.*' I was a bit apprehensive.

'*Can you stop this beating around the bush? If you have nothing
more to say then go, don't waste my time.*'

'*Your decision regarding Nirmal is not right. She isn't like the other girls. She's come here for an entirely different reason, not like the rest of us. She would say no to you.*'

'*Then?*'

'*First thing: she is a real diamond and you're going sell her for nothing. She's worth more than a lakh.*' I could see that Ammi Jaan's face was turning red.

'*And Ammi Jaan, you know your useless gangsters have no brains. All they know is how to get drunk, kill and rape women. They shouldn't come to our house either,*' I said.

'She was now listening to me intently. *You know Ammi Jaan Ji, both Sabah and Nirmal had a big fall-out with Mittal. He hadn't paid their wages for the past three months. How is he going to afford the amount?*'

'*Hmmm… that's why he was offering me ten thousand as deposit and fifteen thousand later,* Ammi Jaan said.

'I could see that Ammi Jaan had warmed up to me so I continued with the same theme. *I think Nirmal will agree to anyone else but Mittal.*'

'*You are making sense, Shamim, but who will pay one lakh? One lakh is lot of money.*

'*Ammi Jaan Ji, you are stuck on twenty five thousand for the past five years. Everything has gone up, plus there are people who do have lot of money. We're not going get anyone like her again,* I said.

'*That's good, so our Shamim has started to think as well.* She seemed pleased with me.

'*Nirmal wants to study further, so let her. That will give us even more time to market her properly and as far as I know you have stopped no one from studying if they wished,* I said.

'I knew that Ammi Jaan could not go to college and she had always had carried that helplessness in her heart. That was the only soft spot she had.

'*You make sure to keep your mouth shut. Whatever we discussed must stay between us… yes Shamim?* She came back to her normal self and warned me.

'*Ammi Jaan, just one more thing, now that Sabah is gone, we'll have two spare rooms. I'll shift in with Nirmal and try to talk her into our scheme slowly if you allow me.*

'*Yes, I'll send you a couple more girls in the next three to four days.* She lit her cigarette and ordered me to leave.'

Ammi Jaan's character became crystal clear to me, thanks to Shamim's story. She was a ruthless and greedy woman, whose only interest was money. She did not seem to care for her girls.

Once she had gathered herself, Shamim came back and continued her story herself.

'I hoped to get this to you somehow, so you knew why she had to leave so abruptly. Nirmal was quite happy that evening when she got home and I was reluctant to spoil her mood, but I had little choice. The situation could get out of hand very quickly; therefore, I asked her to come with me to the bazaar. We went to Central Park and found a quiet corner. I did not want to give her a shock, so I said, please listen to me very carefully; don't worry too much, I'm with you all the way. We'll find a solution. I gave her the papers to read. She was shocked, very angry and frustrated. We both had a little cry as well. We went back to the house fairly quickly to avoid suspicion.

We were very confused and really didn't know what to do. We spent the whole night worrying. Nirmal kept saying, "*But I'm not for sale, I've been paying my rent since I came here. I'm a lodger*".

We cried through most of the night. In the end, we decided that she had to get out of here quickly. We thought of coming to you first but then decided against it. She did not want to put you in any difficulty. She didn't want Mittal to be involved either—because he knew where you lived.

'We took the decision for her to leave Delhi at the earliest opportunity. It was the easiest and yet the most difficult decision at the same time. It was difficult because she had not been able to contact you, easiest because she had no other choice. So early the next morning, we managed to come out of the house with very little luggage and got to the station. She cried like a baby. I've never seen such a strong person cry like that, and I was moved to tears myself. Her last words as she sat in the train compartment were -*my Sardar Parkash is a very good person and very innocent too. Please God! Look after him. Shamim, my hope of spending my life with him has been not departed. I have faith that we will be together again sometime.*'

Shamim handed me the letter Nirmal had left for me.

'Don't read it now, read it in your own time, when you are on your own. She wanted to see you so much.'

'Did she leave her address with you? Or do you know the name of her village?'

'No. She did not want to tell anyone. I asked her not to tell me because Ammi Jaan could get it from anyone. She tried to keep your name secret, so no harm can come your way. My advice to you is, watch your back for the next few weeks because that Mittal bastard will try his best to stir up trouble. He is no one's friend. If it weren't for him, she could've just carried on with her studies.

'After saying goodbye to Nirmal, I deliberately stayed at home to make sure that Ammi Jaan did not get suspicious. She might even have sent people to meet Nirmal at Ludhiana; these twaifs are very well connected. The next morning, I got up as usual and thought it is best to let Ammi Jaan know in a roundabout way. I knew she would punish me if she suspected I had anything to do with Nirmal getting away.'

'Shamim, you are true friend. No one else would have put themselves at so much risk,' I said.

Shamim smiled at me and continued. 'On that day, I played innocent. Ammi Jaan was crying out, *Nirmal Beta, Oh Nirmal... where are you? Come here I want to talk to you.*'

'*Ammi Jaan Ji, Nirmal is not here, she's gone.* I said.

'*Gone? Where?*

'*She's gone to Punjab to see her parents. I dropped her at the station*, I said calmly, trying to be extra casual.

'*She should have at least told me*, Ammi Jaan shouted.

'My saying that she would probably be back in a couple of days did not satisfy Ammi Jaan. Perhaps she was anxious that this one might have got away.

'*Yes, Ammi Jaan, she should've but then she is unpredictable like that. She makes decisions spontaneously and you have never really stopped her from doing whatever she wants to do. She was actually asking me to go with her.*

'*Are you sure Nirmal will be back? Has she taken her luggage? Have you spoken to her about Mittal? He has given the deposit already.*

'*Nirmal hates Mittal, I think, Ammi Jaan Ji; you should give the deposit back.* Oh no, I had crossed the mark.

'*So, now you will teach me what to do? Let her fly high for a while. How long can she stay away?* I was really feeling very scared for both Nirmal and me.

'After that day, I noticed that Mittal came to see Ammi Jaan a couple of times, but I don't know what they talked about.'

We had spent quite long time in the restaurant, so we decided to go and take a walk in Central Park.

'You think Sabah was sold?' I asked Shamim. 'Will you also get sold some day?' It was probably very insensitive of me to ask her this question, but I was curious, and worried for her.

'I have little left to sell for Ammi Jaan. I've gotten engaged to Yusuf, the younger son of this restaurant owner. Ammi Jaan does not know yet.'

I thanked Shamim for everything she'd done for Nirmal. On the way back, I couldn't stop thinking about the miserable lives of these sex workers and the plight of the girls who were lured by the dream of better life. Do they not know beforehand what they were getting themselves into? Had Nirmal known about this before coming here?

All I could think about now was Nirmal. She had tried to keep me away from this world.

I could not find the courage to open Nirmal's letter. It was lying on the suitcase she had left behind, staring at me. I was scared. 'What if it says thanks *but there is no future for us?* I would not be able to take it. She is my dream and always will be.' I tossed and turned all night.

Early the next morning, I ate my breakfast, said my prayers and readied myself to open the envelope.

My love, Sardar Parkash…

My lips have left a mark on the letter. Please touch me with your lips.

At some point in her life, every girl places someone on a pedestal, higher even than God. I've done just that with you. I've never said this to you before, but my whole world revolves around you. Maybe there wasn't a need to tell you before, but now I have to tell you that your Nirmal is deeply, madly in love with you and wishes to be your life partner.

There's been an unexpected tremor in my life. My world has been turned upside down. Yesterday, my darling Ammi Jaan showed her true colours. I thought she was running a Twaif business next door but in the house where we were living, we were simply her lodgers. Sabah has been sold and I'm shocked that she is now scheming to sell me too. I will not let her succeed. I'm not a coward and have plenty of fight in me. I would rather take my own life than surrender. Your friend Mittal, the slyest person I've met, has initiated all this with that woman.

I so much wanted to come to you, and knew you would take care of me. Then a second thought came in my mind – what would you say to your parents? You would not lie to anyone. I couldn't make things difficult for you. I couldn't take the chance of putting you in harm's way. How would you have explained the fact that their daughter in law has lived at a twaif's house? My foolishness is going to haunt me for the rest of my life. Please forgive me for my blunder. I know you will.

I'm not leaving my address with you. Ammi Jaan is a very cruel woman and if she hears a whisper from any of the girls that you might know where I've gone to, she will make life uncomfortable for you. I can't take that chance.

Nirmal will always be yours. Please don't worry about me; I'm going to be all right. You must ensure that you continue your studies. We are going to be together someday. I have your address, so I will find you.

And another thing: Nirmal is my chosen name, but not my real name. However, it doesn't matter, really. For you, I will always be 'Nirmal'.

I'm a little annoyed with you – why did you not stop me that day? I very much wanted to be in your arms.

Sorry, I must stop writing. I hear someone is coming towards my room.

We will be together one day. I promise.

I love you, forever and ever…

Yours,

Nirmal…

I felt relieved after reading her letter, knowing that she must be safe. Then the thought of not seeing her in the near future hit home. The whole world looked bleak. I felt as if Delhi had been deserted.

I more or less admitted to myself that Nirmal was never going to come back to Delhi. 'There seems to be nothing left for me here. This cruel city has ruined all that I had. My hopes have turned into ashes. No one can change my luck or the circumstances. I'll have to find my own path.' Talking to yourself… those were the very first signs of my madness.

My mind was wandering aimlessly and without any hope. Never before had I felt such helplessness. After a lot of thought and soul searching, I decided that I must finish my studies as soon as possible and say good bye to Delhi for good.

DOWN BUT NOT OUT...

I started going to college five times a week and developed a friendship with my classmate Surinder, son of a Police Sub Inspector, the only Punjabi speaking student in my class. I needed his friendship to fill the massive void left by Nirmal.

Surinder did everything in his own way, one which resembled madness at times. Our college was in Patel Nagar, but he had to follow Anjum, a beautiful student from Ramjas College, in the opposite direction, about 20 miles away, almost on a daily basis. He used to keep his Vespa at my house in Tri Nagar and waited at the bus stand, taking the same bus as she did. Throughout the journey, all they were able to do was sneak a glance and a smile.

'It's all worth it, Parkash. She smiled back today,' he would say. 'You don't understand… it's love… love.' And he would run around like a child who had found his favourite toy.

I smirked and murmured to myself, '*I understand… I understand what a difference just a kind look from the one you love can make. But you have to pay a very heavy price for being in love.*'

2.15

SHE'S GONE...

I had been in Delhi for just over two years. My dream of spending my life with Nirmal seemed to be growing dimmer. My education had not gone as I had envisaged. I had half-heartedly fallen into my occupation of accountancy, just as a way to pass the time and to earn some money. Delhi was not to blame for my mistakes; I hadn't adopted the Delhi ways. Continuous thinking made my brain very tired. This also affected my health and I kept getting bad headaches almost on a daily basis. How long could I carry on like this?

There was this new wave of Naxals doing rounds in the Delhi University and Colleges. Some students were paying more than just a passing look. Surinder had to be at the forefront of everything. We started going to these Naxalite meetings. It resembled more of a semi disorganised military initiation camp. We did our exercises, lot of slogan shouting. '*We'll bring the capitalism down. Snatch from the rich and give it the poor. Down with the Capitalism. You have to fight for your rights. Inklaab Zindabaad* and so on. It all seemed very noble up to a point, but how burning of buses or smashing light bulbs and damaging fan of rail compartment was going to bring the so-called Revolution. I was really having difficulty grasping this concept, but Surinder was all gung – ho about it. He had to be at the forefront of every mischief otherwise it won't be Surinder and being a Police Inspector's son inflated his ego.

I really was not interested but went to the second meeting with Surinder anyway and got enrolled. This time after the Kung Fu body stretching we got to the business of slogans. At question time, I asked the chief, 'if we burn a bus then next time we'll be the one who will have to wait much longer and same goes with train compartment. If we fuse the lights, we will be the one sitting in darkness, because rich man has air-conditioned car, why would they travel by train.' Any way the chief did not like anyone questioning him, so he showed me his displeasure. The result was that Surinder attended the third meeting on his own as I pretended illness.

All my efforts to move away from memories of my time with Nirmal were failing. I could not keep her out of my mind. My hopes of ever seeing her again were dying a slow death.

A few days ago, the story of two buses getting burnt by students had been printed in the newspapers. It was almost impossible for Surinder not to be in thick of it. His dad, as a Police Officer of course also knew. Surinder face turned pale when he told me, 'Parkash, my Papa asked to see you at once at our house'.

'What do you think, he is going ask?' He asked me pleadingly.

'Well, it can't be anything else but our stupid doings. What else do you think?' I said in a bit of anger.

'How many times did I ask you not to get involved? You never listen, Surinder – never … Bloody Revolutionary – my foot. Face the music now.'

'Please do something, Parkash; I'll never do it again. I was so bloody stupid.'

Around six in the evening, Surinder collected me from the bus stop. This was the first time he had not uttered a word to me during forty minutes journey.

As I entered his Kothi type house in a posh area, his Dad, six-foot well-built man, in Police uniform, was standing right in front of us. He scared me but I still managed to say, 'Sat Siri Akaal' Uncle Ji.

He acknowledged with a nod and long hmmm… hmmm… followed. He made a gesture of making both Surinder and I sit in front of him. I had never seen police station from inside but scenes like this in Hindi movie straight away came in my mind. A police station in a posh house.

There was a long silence of probably half a minute but it felt like an eternity. He examined my face with a police type stare – this is special stare which last a moment longer but says a lot, 'Beta Parkash, please give some good advice to your demented friend, if he carries on like this, my Police Uniform will be taken away soon.'

He told us that names of both of us were now in Police files pending investigation. Both Surinder and I realised that his Dad knew all about the bus incident. We had been caught, therefore I decided to admit and beg for forgiveness.

'We've made a big blunder, please forgive us. We both are very sorry, Uncle Ji. We'll never get involved in anything like this again,' I apologised.

'I know you won't do it again but what about now. I'm in-charge of this case.'

'But, Uncle Ji, we didn't do it, we were just there with the hundreds of other students.' I was lying to save Surinder also urging him to say something, but he seemed to have completely lost his voice.

'Let me put you two in Jail for a night or two. You'll soon learn the lesson.'

'Uncle Ji … Jail … me in jail …me.' words like these have got stuck in my throat. My brain was going round in circles. I will be in jail, my Dad will be informed and he'll have to find someone who knows someone in Delhi, to bail me out. We'll have to pay huge bribe. My name will be in the newspapers. This is the end of my study too. So many scenarios keep jumping at me. *'O God please help me this time. Never again – never... Just save me once.'*

Surinder's mum heard it all as she entered behind the servant who was carrying tea and biscuits for us.

She said sternly to Uncle Ji, 'This is my house not your Police Station and stop scaring our boys. They said they haven't done anything, and that's it. Now let them have tea in peace.'

I saw from the corner of my eyes that Uncle Ji had calmed down and his voice was much more conciliatory now. We all sit down and have our tea.

After a while Uncle Ji declared, 'There is a solution, you both need to be out of the country. Go to UK and study there. Yes that way you'll surely keep away from mischief.'

'UK?'... I repeat several times in my mind.

'Jail or UK...?'

'I'll speak to Continental Travel Agents, they are my good friends. Don't worry, Parkash, I know your Dad very well. I was used to be in Punjab Police before,' he said. Now he was talking normally – *me police...you criminal* look disappeared. And he became a normal parent worried about his wayward son.

Surinder looked at me with a plea in his eyes as if to say, *'Parkash, please do not say no.'*

'Okay Uncle Ji, you do not need to ask my Dad, I'll ask myself. I know he will not refuse me.'

This was the first time Surinder had broken his silence, 'I'm very sorry, Papa. We'll study very hard. There's nothing in this country, please send us to UK.'

Suddenly Surinder could see nothing for him in this country. Frankly, I did not know what I was doing or saying. I just wanted to get away from everything. 'Why can't Nirmal just knock on my room door and say here I am... with you forever...?'

He dropped me on his Vespa to the bus stand and there was momentary excitement as we both made programme and started dreaming of UK. Anjum, his true love had already been conveniently forgotten as he talked about the beautiful white English Girls of UK. We all carried this perception that everything is better in the Western World.

On my way back home, all I kept thinking of was our lucky escape, what if another police officer was dealing with this case. The fact, I was tired of Delhi since Nirmal has gone and searching for an excuse to get out of here. There was nothing much left here for me either. My life had become a complete rut. I worked and studied very hard. After so many revisions, nothing seemed to stay in my brain. In accounts, I was making silly mistakes, which I never made before. My account books were always neat and tidy without mistakes. I knew that I could not find Nirmal by sitting here. She was in Punjab and I ought to be there. I'd no desire left to finish my studies and therefore I was seeking an escape route. This seemed to be a good opportunity, so here I was, after saying good-bye to Marwaha Ji, Simon Sahib, CA Sahib, Doctor Sahib and Jitender heading back to Punjab.

2.16

—ᴧᴧ—

Clean Bowled...

As soon as I got back to our village, I rushed to Sokhi's house to let him know of my decision to go to the UK. We normally sat on the grassy bank outside, facing my favourite marigold flowers. Nirmal loved marigolds.

I was expecting him vehemently to oppose my idea but his reaction was totally the opposite.

'Parkash Bhaji, you go first and then bring me there as well. Don't worry about my passport and ticket. I'll get it done here. If we find Bhabi Ji, she can also come.'

'Yes, you can get a student visa without much fuss but the problem is we can't find her. You know, sometimes I feel she didn't really want me. I understand why she ran away from Delhi, but why didn't she contact you? She knows our village... she could've left a message with you. I don't really want to give up but what else can I do?'

'We will find her eventually...we will.'

'But how?'

'Look Bhaji, you go...I'll keep trying...I will go to more villages.'

'What are you going to tell your parents? What about your studies? Going to Ludhiana isn't cheap either. I don't know

Santokh… Now I cannot think of anything… I really miss her, you know.'

Convincing Biji of my decision was a totally different thing. She said everything a mother would say to a son who wanted to go out of country for an indefinite period. *Work on the farm, become a teacher or a police officer, forget about Delhi, study here in Jalandhar,* she said. I was not going to budge and my mind was made up. I couldn't tell that her intelligent son had been rejected in love. Eventually though, she gave in to my stubbornness.

2.17

Snowy Dreamland...

December 29, 1969. It was half past four in the evening and I was standing inside the Heathrow terminal with Surinder, looking out in amazement at the people passing by. Surinder and I had never seen snow before. It was still falling and dim orange lights shone through it, giving it a heavenly effect.

The immigration officer was quite relaxed and did not ask us many questions. We were trained in what to say any way. He stamped our passports, smiled at us and welcomed us to the UK.

'Can you imagine if this were Delhi airport? I can't see anyone saying welcome to India,' Surinder said.

We were waiting for our respective relatives to turn up and collect us. Our first purchase in England was two cups of tea.

'These English people don't know how to make tea. This is just hot water with a spoon of milk in it.' Surinder registered his first complaint in the UK.

We had been waiting for about half an hour when both our sets of relatives arrived. We were going to separate destinations. My Uncle Ji, who sent me the sponsorship, had brought a van instead of a car. He sat with the driver in the front and I was made to sit at the back on some old blankets. The heat did not reach the back. It was so cold. I had never felt this cold before. The clothes I had brought from India were useless in this weather.

The driver had Punjabi music on and was singing completely out of tune for the length of the journey. Before we set off from the terminal, he took a sip of whiskey and gave some to Uncle Ji. He offered me some, but I said, 'I don't drink.'

He laughed and said, 'Woman and whiskey – very important in this weather.' And he laughed. .

2.18

SIX YEARS LATER...

The next six years in England were very difficult. I had done no physical labour in India, so I found it very tough at first. I did, however manage to continue with my studies but was unable to forget Nirmal. So many things reminded me of her. My whole body went numb when I thought of her. I still kept on hatching schemes of how to find her. *I will place an advertisement in the paper for a Lost Person. I will offer prize money. I will ask a pundit or an astrologer.*

On the other hand, I was somewhat resigned to fact that I was never going to see her again. I had not been able to make any friends either, so I was even more lonely.

I had been saving money to buy a car – not just any car but the Ford Cortina Ghia 1.6 in bronze metallic with leather seats – second hand, of course. It was way beyond my means. But somehow, I saved up money and bought it. I used to work in a clothing factory and Kumar, my assistant and best mate those days, and I received the car around five in the evening. There was massive excitement and contentment on our faces.

'Drinks on me today…as you've spent all your money,' Kumar said.

We decided to go the Green Man in Leytonstone. We had a good time and probably one too many lagers. Around ten, we decided to go an Indian restaurant. I was not yet used to the car and found the manoeuvring a little difficult. Kumar stepped out and tried to guide me out of the tight parking space. Suddenly, I felt as though Nirmal were sitting in the passenger seat, holding my hand. I could barely control the car with two hands, let alone one. The back wall escaped damage but my beautiful car was not so beautiful anymore.

On that day, something inside me said. *Where are you going Parkash? What has become of you?* This couldn't be right. My love story had been a disaster, but that did not justify ruining my life.

This was first time I met Surinder since we arrived in England and was extremely surprised to see the change in him. He was no longer a smart turbaned Sikh anymore; instead, he resembled a brown Englishman.

'Hello Parkash, you haven't changed one bit! How are you keeping?' He asked.

We had a lot to catch up on. I was now working for the same company as Surinder. I worked as a helper to the cutter. My time passed more quickly with him around. We gossiped a lot. He worked as a driver for deliveries and if he were on an evening or overnight delivery then I would go with him. I did carry on with my studies by attending evening classes at East Ham College of Technology but Surinder didn't.

Surinder's company had quite an effect on me. Now I started to eat meat and drink heavily too. In fact, on Saturday I would go to clubs or pubs with him where there were plenty of women and alcohol and come home drunk. Surinder had an English girlfriend named Debbie, who called him Indie.

I was having a drink at the Green Man and enjoying the evening with Indie and other English friends. Indie and Debbie were cuddling together. I had one drink too many. Sandra was teaching me the art of kissing when my Uncle walked in to see everything. I was totally unaware of his presence.

Two weeks later, the effects of the viewing were felt. I received a letter from my father. He came straight to the point.

My dear son, Parkash

Hope you are well! It is time you start taking responsibility in your life. Therefore, we have decided to get you married. We've found a very suitable girl. She is very good looking and educated and comes from a very respectable, well to do family of Jat Sikh landowners. Your engagement ceremony took place just a few days ago at the Gurdwara. You should come back to India so that we can fix the date of your marriage.

Love from your Biji and all of us.

Yes, this was it. I was now officially engaged to some very good-looking, educated girl from a respectable family. No, I had not seen any photograph of my bride to be yet but that would follow in due course. I neither had the urge nor the enthusiasm to question my parent's decision. The affair with Nirmal had left me resigned to whatever came next. The desire to find love had certainly dissipated. My despondency pushed me into drinking – beer to start with then the real stuff. In my veins, there was more Bacardi and Coke than the blood. My friends drank Captain Morgan Rum, but I went slightly up market. Indie said Rum was to old fashioned, more suited to uneducated farmers from Punjab.

My heavy drinking also finally bore fruit. Drunk, I fell down the concrete stairs of our factory one day and broke my left ankle. I was hospitalised at the Wipps Cross Hospital for five months. My kidneys, they told me, were ruined. Tuberculosis had eaten up half of my lung but the good thing was that the hospital experience brought me to my senses. Six months later, I was discharged.

I wrote a long letter to my wife to be, telling her about myself. She did not reply.

2.19

A Fresh Start...

My very first conversation with my wife, which took place on our honeymoon night, went something like this.

My friends have told me that NRI boys from the UK are usually of loose character. Can you promise that you will never look outside our marriage? Please make sure your past stays in the past.

I was overwhelmed by her simplistic approach to life. She not only forgave me for my past sins but also extracted a promise from me to make a fresh start on a beautiful life. This certainly showed the quality of her upbringing. Her remarks had woken the good side in me. *No, I will not let her down,* I decided. The trust she had placed in me would be justified.

FIRST YEAR – A RELUCTANT HUSBAND...

Yes, it could've been much better. I'd not been as selfish with Nirmal as I was with Jinder. 'Too much salt… not enough salt… why did you put sugar in my tea… why did you not put sugar in my tea… you don't do this… you always do this.' These complaints carried on for the first year. Then one day, our union really hit home when she became a mother.

Since then, my life had seen many ups and downs. There had been times when I might have gone off the rails but for Jinder, who was always there to lend me a supporting hand and bear with me through the turbulent times.

I had become a successful businessperson. I was blessed with three beautiful daughters and a handsome, intelligent son. They were the four pillars of my being.

I've become very forgetful generally but could never really forget Nirmal. How could I…? There were times when I would talk to her as if she was standing in front of me, especially when I was alone. I felt so lonely even when surrounded by so many of my own people.

There were times when my dear wife questioned, 'Who are you talking to.'

What could I say? The thought of what could've been if Nirmal and I were together, sent shiver down my spine. My whole being shook up. She had occupied her own space in my mind.

However, I'd to carry the duties of a husband and a father with a smile on my face, which I managed to do.

PART THREE

3.1

THE STORY CONTINUES...

I had noticed that something very important always happened in my life after every twenty years interval.. It may well be a superstition but I do sincerely believe that to be the case. The diaries had been handed to me in 1990, and it is now 2010. Jinder had been reminding me of my promise to write about Nirmal, but I hadn't had the courage to read those diaries.

'You know, twenty years have passed since Nirmal gave her diaries to us. And here you are, unable to muster enough courage to open a page,' Jinder said to me.

'You're right, I'm scared to read them, and I may not be able to face what's in them. I'm also worried that if I start writing, my own life will also become an open book. Do you really want me to write? Are you not worried that something could come out which might have an impact on our lives? After all, it will be the story of my love for the other woman in my life.' I said.

'I understand, but we've always been truthful to one another. Every relationship is trust and ours is absolute. If you are going to write then it must be the truth, the whole truth and nothing but the truth,' she said. 'Yes, I know it can't be any other way,' I said.

'Well, then we have her diaries. Just copy what is written in them,' she said. After a pause, I asked, 'Would you read them with me?'

'No, that wouldn't be fair. I will not even read the script, but once it is written you will present me with the very first copy,' Jinder said with such calmness.

Two years after this conversation, I finally took the decision to write a book about Nirmal's life. I would copy as it was in her diaries without a word from me. Her diaries, her voice, her thoughts – as they were.

3.2

NIRMAL'S DIARIES
CARE FREE – CHILDHOOD DAYS

FRIDAY, MARCH 20ᵀᴴ 1964

My tenth class exams have just finished. I've really put a lot of hard work into them this time. I'm very hopeful of getting high marks again. I came first in the school and my father was very happy. As for first prize, I was given two books. My father is very fond of Punjabi and English literature. His room is always full of books.

I have just visited the Gurdwara with my friends. I don't see the point of asking God for help now since the papers are over, and God is not going to write any more in them. You are going to be judged on what you have already written. However, like the others, I prayed to God and make my wish, *Please God, if you help me achieve high marks, I'll donate five rupees to the Golak in the Gurdwara.*

There's nothing much to do now. I'm going to take part in the School's Annual Debate, that's the only interesting thing. The topic chosen this time is *Women's place in Punjabi culture.* I am the girls' team captain as well. We have done a lot of rehearsal. We're fully prepared to take on the boys.

TUESDAY, APRIL 14TH 1964

All our preparation finally paid off! We won a trophy and got the opportunity to shake hands with the head mistress!

My Papa Ji held me in his embrace and said, 'Very proud of you, beta, very proud indeed. My shining star will brighten the name of the family one day. Sharn Beta, let's go to the town, eat, drink and celebrate properly.'

He walked to the kitchen, put his hands around my Bibi's waist, and said, 'Gurmeet, look here, your daughter has won the first prize. Let's go to town and celebrate.'

Biji – 'Have you no shame? Our grown up daughter is looking, take your hands off.' She pushed Papa aside. 'No shame at all. Our lovely daughter doesn't even know how to make a chapatti. Tell her to spend some time in the kitchen with me. What's her mother in law going to do with her medals? Like father like daughter. Always, let us go to town and celebrate.'

Papa Ji – 'Listen Gurmeet; don't be harsh to her, not today. There's plenty of time left for her to learn how to cook. Let her enjoy,' and he put twenty rupees in my palm quietly and winked at me.

Biji – 'You should've included in your debate how a woman graduate is only good for household chores, where's the equal opportunity that's been promised to her since independence? This debating is just a waste of time. Women in Punjab will always be treated as second class citizens.'

Me – 'You're not that badly off Biji, you could've become a school teacher if you wanted. Papa Ji has not stopped you. You're happy with your lot.'

Biji – 'You're just like your Papa. Make sure you work in the kitchen from tomorrow. Look at how much your brother does for me. He helps in the fields first and then helps me when he comes home, but you and your Papa are useless. A woman's place is in the home, my dear.'

Me – 'What! Cooking, cleaning and producing babies? That's not for me!'

I went and sat with Papa Ji and asked him, 'Can I join a Gidda group in these holidays, Papa? All my friends are joining.'

'Okay, Beta, but don't tell your mother yet, let me talk to her.'

FRIDAY, APRIL 24TH 1964

I've joined the Gidda Group. Things have changed a little at home; Biji has mellowed a little and instead of objecting all the time, she joins in and teaches me. She used to be a very good Gidda dancer in her college days.

My dad really loves my mum, and even at this age he's always teasing her. She is always telling him, act your age, we are not in the college canteen, have some shame, you have a grown up daughter in the house.

Biji got married when she was just sixteen and completed her graduation afterwards. She stayed with her parents while studying but used to come and meet Papa in secret.

My Papa Ji's elder brother whom we call Taya Ji is the Sarpanch of the village. Both brothers get on very well and drink together. However, Taya Ji gets drunk sometimes.

Sarpanch Taya Ji's only son, Harnek, is my cousin. I don't like him one bit. His body has grown like an elephant but his brain is as tiny as a mouse. He keeps staring at my breasts. On one occasion, I complained to Biji, but instead of saying anything to him, she told me off saying, 'Why do you wear such tight clothes?'

WEDNESDAY, MARCH 17TH 1965

Another year has gone by and the results have come out again. My brother Satbir and I have both received First Divisions and I'm number one in the school as well. Biji and Papa are over the moon. We are going to town to celebrate, this time with Biji's blessing. But she cannot help saying that I need to learn cooking soon.

We've over twelve acres of land, – we are not rich but not poor either, that's what Papa Ji always tell us. We've made nice pucca rooms at our farm for the farm workers. We're paying the school fees for their children too. I enjoy teaching them.

I've just turned seventeen, and it feels different. I've noticed that the time I spend in front of the mirror is getting longer and longer. I've started looking at filmy magazines as my friends do and learned to do my hair in a fashionable way. My clothes are getting tighter and tighter by the day. Regular questions from Biji are *Where have you been? Why are you late? When are you coming home?* Everything starts with 'W' these days. I've started to knit little lies and make up stories to escape Biji's telling off. I want someone to tell me how beautiful I am, someone to say nice things to me. One of girls in my class has a boyfriend. I want one as well.

Sarpanch's good for nothing son annoys me with his silly antics. I'm his cousin after all. He is really so stupid. However, sometimes I do feel rather sorry for him. There must be something wrong in his brain. Whenever we talk, he is always staring straight at my bust, which I hate.

Biji has started to look for a suitable boy for me. Papa always supports me. He keeps telling Biji, 'It is not the right time, let her complete her education first. There'll be plenty of suitable boys out there for our daughter.'

All Biji can do is to moan, and that she does in plenty. There are two different schools of thought here. Biji wants her grown-up daughter to get married as soon as possible and keeps reminding me that my real house is my in-laws' house. Then the second school of thought, which I like, is that of my Papa, who wants me to carry on with my education as far as I want to go. *Daughters should have equal right to study as sons,* he says with pride

However, life seems so sweet at the moment. Satbir has fallen in love with my best friend Narinder, but is too scared to tell her. '*Please Sharn, you tell her, please… Sharn, give my message. Please Sharn,*' he is always begging me. He is a real chicken when it comes to expressing his love for her.

APRIL 12TH 1965

An urban family, husband and wife and their two children, has arrived from Delhi and is visiting Sarpanch Taya Ji's house. They've come here as special guests to experience village life. Biji ordered me to go to Taya Ji's house and help look after them. This is a tradition our family follows. We help each other when we have extra work or need to look after each other's guests.

Our guest introduced himself and his family to me. 'My name is Rakesh Kumar Bansal and this is my wife, Kamlesh Bansal. That's Priya and her naughty brother Bobby. You are?'

'Ji, I am Sharnjit… Sharnjit Ahluwalia.'

'Aloo like potato!' Bobby burst out laughing.

'She is Aunty Sharn, beta. Don't be naughty,' Kamlesh says.

I've gotten used to both Bobby and Priya very quickly; they are full of questions because they have not seen a farm before, except in pictures. Most of my time is spent with them, answering their queries. 'What is this? What is that, Aunty?' They speak mostly in English and this has given me the chance to sharpen my English as well.

Kamlesh and I have become good friends. I've taken her to see our fields. We sit and discuss various topics while her husband is busy filling himself to the brink with food, fruits and sugarcane from the farm. Kamlesh has told me all about herself and life in New Delhi, which I'm very fascinated by. We've talked about my studies and both Kamlesh and Ramesh have shown a keen interest in it. Rakesh says, '*It's wrong for parents to deny opportunities to their daughters. How far they go should be based on their ability and not on gender.*'

'I fully agree with you. It is very backward to think that a woman's place is only in the home.'

'If our country wishes to make progress like the west, then it is very important for women to get higher education as well. An educated mother can educate her children better.' I like what Rakesh Ji says. 'Why don't you come and study in Delhi? The standard of education is much higher than here in Punjab.'

'But I've never been to Delhi and don't know anyone there!'

'We live in Delhi, you can live with us. We've got a spare room, and you can pay rent to us.'

I look at Kamlesh and wait for her reaction. She has said nothing. She usually ignores our conversations and gets busy with the children who never stop playing, even for a minute.

Later, I do ask Kamlesh about her views and she is very neutral. She just says that it's must for girls to get good education in this day and age.

I'm definitely a strange person; my mind has already started to wander to Delhi. *I'll be independent. I won't have Biji at my back asking what I'm up to all the time.*

FRIDAY, JUNE 18TH 1965

Seems Delhi was nothing but a dream. I've now gotten into our local college. Satbir has made it very clear that I must have my own bicycle; he will not give me rides to the college. I think more than anything his privacy gets disturbed when I'm with him. I tease him, asking what would would happen if Narinder asks for a ride. Then…

(The next page in the Diary has Rakesh Bansal's address and half of the page seems to be badly torn off. After that, the next few pages are completely blank.)

3.3

~~~

LETTER TO GOD...

TUESDAY FEBRUARY 22ND 1966

My hands are trembling, not out of fear but sheer anger. I've been shaken to my roots because of your cruelty, and what you call luck. My entire being is crying with pain. Why am I saying this to you? I know you are deaf, you hear no one's prayers.

Since my childhood, Biji has always said, 'You are kind and considerate. You listen to everyone's prayers. The whole world exists because of your graciousness.' Yes, that is what I was told repeatedly. Whenever human beings find themselves in difficulty, they pray for your help. All seasons, springs, green meadows, new seedlings, everything that is beautiful is your creation. That is what I was led to believe by my elders, my teachers, religious gurus and the like. I worshipped you when I got up, remembered you when I went to sleep.

Whenever I scored high marks in my exams, even though it was all my own effort, I still thanked you. I felt genuinely grateful to you. Well, that was my upbringing, and that was my belief.

Reading the Scriptures, my faith in you grew even deeper. I believed in you and thought you were the Most Gracious.

But now I have given up on you and am no longer yours because you are so cruel, that you cannot be my God. You enjoy throwing people into the mire. What's the ultimate punishment you deliver? Give me death today, I don't wish to live in your horrible, cruel world. But you can't even do that! The day Satbir and my father died, you died for me as well. I no longer care for you. You are dead!

A NOTE FROM PARKASH:

(The following words written in italic are mine and not from Nirmal's diaries.

I am feeling her pain as I write. My heart is crying and a few tears have come rolling down my cheeks. How much pain, how much helplessness the poor girl had to endure. Under those so circumstances, any one would deny His presence and curse Him.

I later found out whilst talking to her that her father and brother both died in an accident while taking a sugar cane trolley to the sugar mill. Her father died on the spot and her brother passed away a day later in the hospital.

When I met her in Delhi as Nirmal, she was a believer and regularly went to the Gurdwara. In her writings, I see a lot of frustration and anger.)

3.4

---~w~---

THE AFTERMATH...

WEDNESDAY, MARCH 2ND 1966

Relatives from far and near come, some to share genuine grief, others for mere show. This is mainly true of the middle-aged women who seem all right up to front door, all laughs and giggles, but as soon as they enter, they go into a frenzy of crying and beating their breasts. Poor Biji has to join in. None of them have any real sympathy; it is all for show and I hate it. They all say, 'Oh, it was God's will, may he give you strength to bear all this.' I wonder why he put us through it in the first place.

MAY 27TH 1966

Three months have gone by since the accident. Biji has done more than enough sobbing and crying. Her tears have completely dried up now. She has taken the bold decision to move on. Nothing is ever going to be the same. I do not cry, there is no use, but there is a time bomb ticking in my head. My helplessness is increasing by the day. All my efforts to take control of my life and emotions end in failure. Nothing seems to interest me anymore.

There are plenty of mad, sick-minded dogs out there, waiting for the first opportunity to pounce on a lonely, single woman. This is not the west, where a single woman can live without fear. This is so called civilised India – where women are never safe and are always treated like second class citizens. My Biji is well aware of that. No matter what colour, race, creed you are, every women on earth has the basic need for comfort and security. Biji is only thirty six and understands her needs very well. She does not wish to be seen as an available woman. Hence, she has taken the decision to take refuge in Sarpanch Taya Ji's haveli, which is just outside the village.

She even has an excuse: she'll be looking after Taya Ji's old mother. *Can you run away from your grief?* I ask myself. Grief is within you and goes where you go. Anyway, she wishes to make a clean break with the past, and I wish her good luck. It is wrong for me to be resentful. However, the truth is that I don't want anyone else to take my Papa's place. It hurts… It hurts like hell.

Taya Ji is happy with the arrangement because he has my young mother in his grasp and might be able to gain control of our land. This accident has worked out well for him. On the face of it, he liked Papa and showed him respect but inside he was always envious of our happy family. He never saw us complaining, and we never asked for his help. He didn't like that because he is so used to people asking for his favours.

'Sharn, I'm your father from now on. Come to me if you need anything. Do not hesitate to ask.' He tells me this whenever he sees me.

Inside, I rage that he cannot ever become my father. I cannot help but despise his double standards. Is he sad that his cousin has died or happy that he got his wife and land so conveniently?

His wife, my Tayi Ji, has made a little fuss over the new arrangements. However, Biji has made an agreement with her, saying that she will never again produce a child. That satisfies Tayi Ji because there will be no one to compete with her only son and all the land will ultimately go to him.

Secondly, she also understands that if a brother dies it is

accepted in our culture that the wife becomes the responsibility of the other brother. What a hopeless and stupid tradition, I say. Time changes, and so should traditions… but it is not so in our village.

THURSDAY, JUNE 2ND 1966

My dear Mother has turned a new page in her life. She has managed to move away from the old memories by moving out of our ancestral house. She's going to spend the rest of her life doing social work, helping those in need and attempt to enter politics. Well, that's how everything starts in India; all politicians start out because of a desire to help the poor and comfort the needy. Yes, that's as true as the fragrance coming from shit.

I am finding it hard to call him Sarpanch Taya Ji; my mind has severed those ties with him of its own accord. From now on, he is simply Sarpanch to me, like he is to everyone else in the village. He keeps calling me Beti this, Beta that. I don't like it at all.

Whether Mum is doing right or wrong, I cannot decide. My inner voice asks me questions and offers advice, "Your Mum has made an intelligent decision. She didn't have any other choice. At least the relatives and people of the village won't be able to say anything. Women, especially Indian women need someone's broad shoulder to protect them from the *always-preying eyes* of the world. Do you want her to sit at home and sob her life away? Life is no life without a companion. You, my dear Sharnjit has to learn to stand on your own two feet too. The time when you are going to need a companion is not that far away. You have no choice but to grow up and face the music, right now. You've to carry your own burden. Let her live life, the way she wants to. Why do we always expect other person to make sacrifices for us? You'll have to be brave now… this endless sobbing, crying and trying to hate everything and everyone isn't going to bring your Papa or Satbir back. They're gone... Dead... RIP." Why do people say Rest in Peace? When you are dead... you are dead...

Our teacher told us that it was originally, 'Come' to Me and 'Rest in Peace.' What an invitation or calling comeback?

Why am I so bitter these days...? Why am I drifting? Truth is I don't want to live anymore and do not have the courage to end my life either. It's better if something happens to me. If God can Rest me in Peace.

Just as I'm being swayed by all these wise thoughts, other voices enter my head, "Why did she have to move out of the house. Papa and Satbir are not there, I live there. Why can't we both mother and daughter face the world together? Does she not care for my wellbeing anymore? Why can't we share the sad moments together? People are people; they are never going to happy." Now they will say bad things behind our backs. However, why care... Why?

THURSDAY, JUNE 9TH 1966

My mother has changed completely. The more I think about it, the more I get angry, frustrated and confused.

I am worried about the way Sarpanch's son looks at me. Our relationship should be even stronger now that my mother has moved into his father's house, but no, he is just stupid and keeps staring at my bust even in college. It's embarrassing to say the least.

I remember Satbir in everything I do. He was a very neat and tidy person. His bicycle was always clean and fully greased. I used to tease him and say, *I'm going to take your bike and you have to give me a lift. If you don't, I'm going tell Biji about you and Narinder.* His face would go red as soon as I mentioned the name of his secret love.

I've taken his bike today; he's not here to stop me. I didn't need to go anywhere; I just wanted to ride his bike. I've just reached the

Shere Punjab dhaba at the bus stop near our village. This dhaba is owned by Uncle Gurnam Ji who is a very good friend of the family. My Papa always stopped here, had his tea and chatted with Gurnam Ji. We always left our bike at his shop and then took the bus to Ludhiana from there. I'm so bored that I've decided to go to Ludhiana today.

I'm wandering from shop to shop in Chaura Bazaar. It is very boring when you don't want to buy anything. However, when I enter Lyallpur Book Store, I feel much happier. I love being surrounded by books. Every book is a virgin until you actually open it. They all look like Indian brides to me, beautifully dressed and waiting for the rightful owner. My fingers do not turn their pages but rather caress them. I buy the epic poetry book, *Waris Shah Di Heer.*

After spending a couple of hours there, I come back from Ludhiana and decided to have tea and samosa at the dhaba. Uncle Gurnam Ji comes and sits in front of me and says, 'Your father was a very good man, Sharn, and I had a lot of time for him. As you probably know, he was a good friend of mine. I want to talk to you about his accident.'

'Yes, Uncle Ji, but now that he's gone, there is nothing left to talk about.'

'No, just come with me; sit in my jeep. I want to show you something. I want to take you where the accident took place; it's only ten minutes away.'

Hesitantly, I go with him.

We inspect the place where the accident took place. All I see is a few torn up branches and the tree, which took the brunt of the impact. Uncle Gurnam Ji is not convinced about the explanation behind the accident. He has various theories as to how and what could've happened, who benefited and so on... but I'm not really listening. What difference does it make? All I know is that my Papa and Satbir are no longer here in this world and my life has completely changed. My whole world has turned upside down.

'Uncle Ji, let us go, I feel suffocated here,' I told him.

SATURDAY, JUNE 18TH 1966

Without telling anyone, I have this morning gone to the gurdwara and made a promise to God that if he leaves me and my family alone, I will not challenge his very existence. *Sorry God Ji, I'm very sorry, there's a lot on my plate right now which needs sorting out.* I need to sort my life out. No one else is going to help me, not even my mother. We have adopted different ways. I do not wish to live in the haveli with her; the old house is my home, and always will be.

I think I will leave Punjab, take up Rakesh Ji's offer, and continue my studies in Delhi. The change will probably benefit me greatly. I'll work, pay rent and study. However, I haven't asked Biji yet. I don't know what her reaction will be.

MONDAY, 20 JUNE 1966

Haven't had an audience with Biji for three days. She has become so busy with her politics lately, and hardly has time for the personal stuff. When you enter politics, personal life takes second place.

I've finally gathered my courage and presented myself in Biji's durbar. I thought that there would be argument and she would say *I forbid you from going to Delhi* and I would revolt. No, nothing of that sort happened. She has given me permission to do what I think best. She has given me five hundred rupees. It will not go very far, so I have to find a job as soon as I get there.

The streets, our fields, village, memories, my friends and that heartbroken Narinder, whose love has withered away before blossoming: all that is holding me back. It is a wrench to leave everything behind and go. Well, that is what brave Sharnjit is going to do: leave and go.

3.5

NEW ENTHUSIASM...

I've worked up some enthusiasm for studying in Delhi but there is a lot of apprehension and the fear of the unknown as well. At the same time, I've confidence in my ability to cope with a tough situation. I've made up my mind that I will stand on my own two feet.

Mum has told me to write to her regularly and come and see her every six months or so.

I'll be leaving tomorrow. Had frank discussion with Mum today, sweet and some sour conversation. I begged forgiveness of her as I have no one else to take my frustration on. She forgives me. 'Parents have to forgive their children' I presume. It felt very satisfying to hear from her that she loved Papa so much and that no one else will replace that love. Papa Ji was her first love, but she also acknowledges that young life has other needs as well which if not satisfied can lead to frustrations and depression. I'm feeling close to her again. She is concerned for me but at the same time cannot ignore her new responsibilities. She will make a good leader for our village.

Sarpanch is an expert in reading the situation well and knows how to play with the public mood. He's going to take advantage of the sympathy people feel towards Biji because of her loss. She's going to become Sarpanch of the village and his eyes are on the

Block Samitee Elections. He always had a desire to move up the scale in the political hierarchy of the area.

Mum no longer wear the fancy suits she loved so much, it's mostly white and Khaadi cloth as worn by most politicians. They do not give much heed to Gandhi's teaching, but one thing they all do, is to wear simple Khaadi cloth like him. It is an absolute hypocrisy, to see them coming out of expensive foreign car dressed as villagers. Oh well that's the Politics in India. Mum is a quick learner and has already changed her look completely.

3.6

⌁

HELLO DELHI... NEW PASTURES

TUESDAY, AUGUST 16TH 1966

This was the first time I travelled alone on a train. My journey from Ludhiana to Delhi has taken just over seven hours. It is very tiring journey, especially when you are alone and a woman. Indian men have not learnt the good manners to give seats to women. The train's compartment is completely bare. To call it third class would be an insult to the class system. It is so crowded that people sit on top of each other.

But here I am now, sitting outside New Delhi Railway Station with a metal trunk and a large, grey canvas bag, no doubt looking like a lost child in a crowded mela.

I thought Rakesh ji would have been here to collect me, but maybe he has not received the letter I sent him. It's also true that people are very busy in Delhi. It's not like Punjab where everyone seems to have a lot of spare time. Here, everyone seems to be in a proper rat race, on the go. I'm a little worried but I know that if I have any difficulty, I'll just take sanctuary for a day or two in a gurdwara.

I gave the Bansals' address to the auto driver, and he has driven me here as if intoxicated. Both Rakesh and Kamlesh Ji have warmly welcomed me to their house and showed me the room where I will be staying. Rakesh Ji has also told me that the driver charged me twice as much as he should have. These drivers take liberties once they know that you are not from Delhi. They can tell this from your dialect and dress.

The room that has been allotted to me is a little away from the main house and in the servant quarters. I think this will suit me better because I won't be in the family's way.

Kamlesh Ji has two servants working for her; one cleans the house, washes clothes and looks after general household duties, the other does all the cooking. He belongs to higher caste so he is allowed in the kitchen. Rakesh Ji has been very business like. He told me that I will be required to pay 100 rupees for rent and another 100 for food per month. I will be provided breakfast and a meal at night but lunch has to be out because everyone works. Some people carry lunch in tiffin carrier, but I will have to buy my own.

I spent the first two days settling in. Both Priya and Bobby are very affectionate towards me. They spend a lot of time in my room, asking all sorts of questions. Most of their conversation is in English. So far, so good.

With Rakesh Ji's help and guidance, I found myself a packing job in a factory, earning 500 rupees per month. This will cover my rent and food comfortably and I will have some money left over to buy sweets for the children. I've started to warm up to Delhi life.

Rakesh Ji even accompanied me to my new college. I have enrolled for evening classes. I work until five in the factory. Life has become very busy.

WEDNESDAY, NOV 16TH 1966

It has been three months since I left home. I do not like the food here very much. People tend to use milk in spoon measures and the curries are cooked in tiny bit of oil. They say it's healthy, I say it is cheapness. Everything in Delhi is rationed – water has to used economically because we only get it at certain times – and there a shortage of electricity, even so more than in Punjab. The capital city should have electricity all day long. One funny thing I have noticed is that it tends to go when we are eating, half way through the meal.

Kamlesh and Rakesh watch a movie or two over the weekends. I look after Priya and Bobby when their parents go to the movies. Kamlesh and I have become good friends; she treats me like her younger sister and confides in me a lot. I am able to speak both Hindi and English fluently now.

3.7

BECOMING DELHITES

THURSDAY, SEPTEMBER 15TH 1966

Two of my classmates, Mohini and Sabah, have become good friends with me. Mohini talks a lot and most of is idle gossip whereas Sabah doesn't say much, but whatever she says has logic and is usually correct. We've shared some of our life stories with each other, although I tend not to say much these days.

I'm getting used to Delhi life and slowly my memories of Punjab are receding. I try to keep myself occupied. It helps me to keep going.

When I look at myself sometimes, it surprises me that I've changed so much and so quickly. My clothes and the way I dress have changed considerably. After paying for my rent and household expenses, I do have some savings for rainy days.

My day goes so quickly and most of it is spent in travel – from Rajouri Garden to work in Sarai Rohela and then college in Patel Nagar. I have decided to patch up my differences with God as well.

So much of my time is spent window-shopping with Sabah now. I'm trying to keep myself busy and my mind occupied. Memories of Satbir keep coming back to me. He was so fond of writing in his diary. Today, I've bought a beautiful, expensive maroon diary. I feel like I have treated myself today. I will start writing in it from tomorrow.

FRIDAY, SEPTEMBER 30TH

I have been tossing and turning in my bed the whole night. I cannot keep lying in bed once awake. After such a long time, I felt like going to the Gurdwara and apologising to God for my tantrums. Priya has accompanied me to the today.

Kamlesh seems to be in a bad mood today and is pretending to have a headache. She does not want to go to the movie with her husband. I try to keep away from their arguments but I can't help overhearing sometimes. They both tend to shout at each other.

It is so hot in my room today. I have put on a sleeveless tee shirt and opened all the windows, but the heat is unbearable. It never feels this hot in Punjab because of the greenery.

I was studying when a hand suddenly appeared on my naked shoulder. I jumped as if I had recevied an electric shock. I could not find anything to cover myself with, so I placed my hands over my chest, trying to cover up. I didn't like Rakesh Ji's behaviour; in fact, I was shocked that he dared to touch me. Where had his manners gone?

'Rakesh Ji, what are doing here? What do you want?'

'Sharnjit, will you go to the cinema with me? I have a spare ticket. Kamlesh doesn't want to go. She's unwell.'

'No, Rakesh Ji, I can't go. You can leave your children with me. I don't mind.'

'Oh, I feel like going with you. Some other time then. If you need anything, just ask me. I'll fulfil all your needs,' he smirked.

I could see that he was trying to prolong the conversation but I didn't want to talk to him. I could see the filth in his eyes as he stared at my breast. His behaviour reminded me of my cousin. It only takes a momentary lapse for someone to fall in your esteem.

MONDAY, OCTOBER 3RD

I have started enjoying Sabah's company immensely. I am hoping that I get a job in the place where she works. Delhi has loads of employment opportunities. There are plenty of small-scale businesses and cottage industries with big name boards.

The argument between the husband and wife continues unabated at home. I have noticed that when Kamlesh gets angry, it is very difficult to cool her down, and she easily gets wound up as well.

What exactly is wrong with Rakesh Ji? He's got this new habit turning up in my room for no reason. I'm trying my best to keep quiet in the hope that it is a short phase and he will see his follies. I do not want to tell Kamlesh. It will only make matters worse.

Oh God, he was very out of order today. When I came out of the bathroom, he banged into me as if he were blind and then smirked rather than saying sorry. This is bizarre behaviour. Kamlesh had seen it. I don't know what is going to happen. He should be a worried man tonight.

TUESDAY, OCTOBER 4TH

My day started in a strange manner. As I got on the bus, a young man just about my age kept staring and smiling at me. When the driver put brakes, he almost fell on me, probably intentionally. I gave him proper lashing. It made me realise that I have to stand up for myself. In Delhi, no one helps you.

FRIDAY, OCTOBER 7TH

Kamlesh has gone to a meeting at school with her children and I was on my own. Sure enough, Rakesh came into my room for no reason.

'Sharn, please listen – you are beautiful, very beautiful… I love you very much… please have a relationship with me… I will give you everything you want… we won't tell anyone… you won't need to pay rent either.'

He latched on to my hand as I tried to move away. 'Please Rakesh Ji… please go… Kamlesh will be here any minute,' I said.

'Please, Sharn, I'll give you a lot of money… we can have a good time… no one will come to know… '

'No… please get out of my room… I'll tell Kamlesh if you don't stop.'

All the respect I had for him has gone down the drain. I'm so confused. Where should I go now?

Whatever the consequences, I have decided to tell Kamlesh.

SATURDAY, OCTOBER 22ND

Every Saturday, Kamlesh goes to the bazar to shop with both her servants. I like to accompany them to enjoy a bit of gossip and coffee. Priya and Bobby both run towards the ice cream parlour. As soon as the shopping finishes, she sends both of them home with the servants and we spend time together, having coffee.

The atmosphere felt a bit tense today. She probably knew half of the story and wanted me to tell her what was happening between me and Rakesh. I've laid myself bare to her and told her of my worries as well. I hope she sees that I'm not at fault, that her husband is the culprit here. Come what may, I have done my duty.

She listened to me very calmly and did not say a single word. The silence was killing me.

'Sharnjit, thank you very much for warning me. I know it's not your fault at all; my dear husband has gone off the rail. Men get tempted very quickly. As soon as they see slightly bigger boobs, their tongue starts dribbling on the ground. Rakesh is no different. Most men think that if they go to other women, their wives can't tell. But women can tell these things so easily. It is a different matter whether we choose to say anything about it or not. Sometimes a woman's silence is taken as acceptance. We are able to look at the bigger picture, but all men interested in is a little fun. Women have to think about their children too.

'Rakesh fell madly in love with me about ten years ago. He was always circling round my Uni, saying things like *I will die if you say no*. I belong to a well to do family and his family was no match for mine. I didn't really like him that much but made a big mistake at a friend's party. I became pregnant, had no choice, and ended up marrying him. This Kothi and car were all given by my Dad. Rakesh loved my sophistication. Look at him now, falling in love with a village girl.

'I'll deal with him later but you have to do me a favour.'

'Yes, Kamlesh, please tell me what you want me to do.'

'Look, Sharnjit, I know you are a very good person and wouldn't wish to see my family disintegrate. My husband's brain is gone and I must put it right before it's too late. If he cannot see you then he cannot do anything. I expect you to help me.'

'I don't understand your riddles; please tell me what you want me to do.'

'Sharnjit, you'll have to find somewhere else to live. You have to move out before next week.'

I was shocked. Kamlesh tried to soften the blow and said, 'You are so beautiful, my darling, even God himself would be tempted.'

WEDNESDAY, NOVEMBER 9TH

I told all my friends that I am in desperate need of a room. Three days have gone by and still there is no news from any of them.

On the fourth day, Mohini has told me about a room, so I went with her. The landlady welcomed us with a smile. She seemed to warm up to me, and my hopes were built up. She asked me why I was moving out of my previous room. Before I could say a word, the chatterbox Mohini opened her big mouth and told her all about Rakesh. This was enough to put the landlady off and she said that she would consult her husband and let me know in few days. In other words, *no thanks*, I don't want trouble in my house. Her initial warmth soon turned into mild hostility and she bid us farewell.

What am I going to do if I cannot find room before Saturday? If I'd kept my mouth shut I wouldn't have been in this situation.

Both Priya and Bobby have not come into my room and seem to be avoiding me. Maybe they are not at home; I've been coming home late almost every night.

SATURDAY, NOVEMBER 12ᵀᴴ

The dreaded day has arrived and I'm extremely worried. I haven't been able to find any alternative accommodation. Although Kamlesh has given me orders to vacate, there is no harm in asking her for one more week. I'm in two minds now so half-heartedly, I start to pack my things again. There is not much to pack, a few clothes and books, one suitcase and a bag. I remember coming here with so much hope…

I've spent most of the day in my room with the door closed. The servant Ramu knocks on the door at six o'clock and tells me, 'Sharnjit, Bibi Ji has asked me help you vacate. Shall I call an auto? Where do you want to go? She has asked me to lock it up once you are gone.'

'Where is Kamlesh?'

'She's gone to her Papa's house with Babu Sahib.'

'Ramu, I'm not going today. Let your Bibi Ji know that I'll go tomorrow instead.'

He's gone but I'm so confused. I don't know what to do. Where I'm going to go?

How do you find a room in Delhi?

SUNDAY, NOVEMBER 13TH

I got up very late this morning. There is no hurry, as I've no plan and the more I think, the more confused I get.

It's just past midday. Kamlesh was supposed to be back by now, but there is still no sign of her. My only hope is that she lets me stay on for another week, but knowing her, that may not be possible. She is very stubborn. Once she's made up her mind and given orders, that is it. I should start crying and look miserable, maybe that will melt her a bit. It hurts me that I haven't done anything wrong but I'm the one who is suffering. Where are you God, when I need your help?

I hadn't had anything to eat, and it's just past six in the evening, so I decided to go to the bazaar to get something.

When I got back home, Ramu was sitting outside my room, waiting for me with my suitcase and bag.

'Bibi Ji asked me to help you. She has given your room to someone else. Where do you want to go…? I can get you an auto.'

I didn't think that Kamlesh would do this to me. But she has given me a good week, and I had promised her that I would move.

'Ramu, get me an auto for the railway station, please.'

Halfway there, I changed my mind and asked the driver to stop at a Gurdwara instead. I needed to clear my mind and there was no better place for this than a Gurdwara. I would take sanctuary there and then decide what to do in the morning. I tried to find a corner on the women's side of the big hall.

Now I'm so tired; I cannot keep my eyes open. I've not slept properly for days. A priest had gone past me a few times. Finally, he stopped, looked at my suitcase and asked, 'Where do you want to go, Bibi? We are going to close the Gurdwara at eleven.'

'Ji, I wish to stay here tonight, and I do not have anywhere else to go.'

'But a young… single… girl… alone… no, you can't stay in the Gurdwara.'

'I don't need a bed; I will just sleep here, I won't disturb anyone.'

'Sorry, I can't allow that. What will I do if someone finds out? No, no… this is not in my hands… you have to ask a Committee member.'

'Where would I find a Committee member?'

'They will be here tomorrow, sister.'

'But I need this tonight. You have called me sister. Can't a sister ask a brother for sanctuary?'

'No… No… not for a single girl… No, this place is not safe.'

'Then, where is the safe place for a young, single girl?'

'The railway station,' he said, and then he went away.

When I got to the station, I bought a ticket to Ludhiana. There is no train tonight; the first one is at 12.50 PM tomorrow. Pushing and being pushed, I arrived in the women only waiting room to spend the rest of the night. A middle-aged woman who has half a dozen children seems to have taken control of one side of the waiting room. She stares at me as though asking, *why are you here?*

My brain has stopped functioning now, my eyes are very tired and I seem to fall in and out of sleep. Sabah had told me that she would find me a room the last time I met her. I was optimistic then and did not take much notice of Sabah's offer.

It is well past midnight. I should try to nap, but sleep does not come to me. I'm not someone who can sleep through this much noise.

MONDAY, NOVEMBER 14TH

There are still six hours to my train to Punjab, so I have decided to go to my college in Patel Nagar for the last time. There isn't much hope left of finding accommodation, perhaps I am clutching the last straw. Sabah might help. Monday is normally a full day at college, the most enjoyable day with lots of gossip and stories to share or admire each other's clothes, *'where did you get this?'* is quite a common phrase.

I went to the café near our college. This is where we usually gather between periods. I placed my suitcase and bag on the side and asked for tea and some breakfast. I knew Sabah would come here for her tea break after the second class, so this is the best place to wait for her.

I ordered a second cup of tea and kept staring at it as if all the answers to my problems were written there. It was going to be very difficult to face friends and family back in Punjab. What would I say? I would have to admit failure. I did not listen to any of them when I rushed off to Delhi.

The café owner, Harpreet, comes and sits in front of me. He is also from Punjab and is here to make living.

'Are you going home, sis?' He asked politely.

'I'm not sure yet. How do you find room in Delhi, Bhaji?' I hadn't even finished my sentence when I felt a well-known hand on my shoulder.

'You give this responsibility to your friends, then it is up to them to do it.'

'So…?' I turned to see Sabah standing there.

'I have found you a room. I've asked Ammi Jaan's permission. But you have to share it with me.'

'Yes, yes, of course! Thank you so much.' I couldn't believe it. I was so happy that I started to cry.

Staying with Sabah, I have to follow certain strict conditions:

– Other girls live there too; I cannot question or interfere in their lives.

– You never question or answer back to Ammi Jaan. You simply listen and abide.

– You're not allowed to have a boyfriend.

– Lastly, all girls who live here tend to change their names. I have decided to take the name 'Nirmal'.

I have met the other girls; they have received me with open arms and showed me a lot of warmth.

Most of what is written above has been written in my new room. I'm feeling very sleepy now. Good night, Diary.

TUESDAY, NOVEMBER 15TH

I have become *Nirmal* now; no one knows my real name except Sabah. Although the night was peaceful, I kept hearing the sound of the tabla, harmonium and filmy music. I am beginning to realise what goes on around here.

In the morning, Sabah explained it to me. 'If you mind your own business, it shouldn't make any difference to you. Everyone is busy earning their living in their own way. We are not here to judge what's right and what's wrong.'

'What about here?'

'Look, a room is a room. It could be anywhere. You have just been thrown out of a respectable house because the man of the house was not respectful. We live in a world of hypocrisy and double standards, my dear.'

'Is there anyone in this house who lives by this business?'

'There are seven other girls here. All of them are from very poor families, or they do not have any family at all. They all receive an education; in fact, Ammi Jaan encourages them to do so. When the time comes, she will get them married. What else do they want? They are all virgins, if that is what your question is. Ammi Jaan does not allow for such indiscretions.'

She looked at my partly satisfied expression and continues with the conversation. 'This is the safest house, and no one dares look this way because they all know Ammi Jaan. On the other hand, you are not living here for free. You will have to pay 250 rupees for food and rent every month. Is that all right with you?'

'That'll be fine.'

'One condition though – you have to teach me Punjabi. I love hearing you and Harnek speak.'

Sabah made sense, as usual. I did not have any other choice but to go back to my village. This accommodation had at least given me a breathing space and if it got really bad then I would have time to go somewhere else.

TUESDAY, NOVEMBER 29TH

It has been two weeks since I came here. Time is passing quickly. I have so much to do during the day – work, and college keep me busy. I am trying to get employment at the same place where Sabah works. I have learnt a lot about this place and life in general since coming here.

At last, I met Ammi Jaan today. I thought she would be a Paan chewing, big, old, middle aged woman with a whip in her hand but no, she is very different. She is about 30 or 35-years old, sleek, very smart and a beautiful, well-dressed woman. She is tough. However, in her position she has to be, to keep everyone in line. She talks freely to us all but my turn for a proper audience has not come yet. I believe she is a mistress of some rich man, who has bought her this kothi and a farmhouse as well. My initial impression of her is that she is not bad to you, as long as you obey the rules.

SUNDAY, DECEMBER 17TH 1967

Every week, Sabah buys tickets to the cinema for both of us. She has to watch every movie in its first week. She was not too well today, so I took Shamim. Shamim is completely different from Sabah. She is very brave and talks a lot. She looks after the house and collects rent from everyone for Ammi Jaan. We have become very good friends and in fact, we have a lot in common. I have opened up to her and told her about my life in Delhi.

We got home very late, and it was well past midnight by the time we went to bed.

SATURDAY, JANUARY 20ᵀᴴ 1968

May be the winds have come from that direction, for today the memories of my village have come flooding in. Mum must have become a political leader by now. I wonder if she ever thinks of me.

I try my best to keep busy, but today I miss my old life, my brother and my father. I feel terribly alone.

I know that once gone, no one comes back, but sometimes it seems as though Satbir will come through the door and ask me what I'm doing here, telling me that we need to go home.

I am trying hard to keep myself from disintegrating into pieces. I am … trying …

Whenever I feel this sad, I seek comfort in the epic story of Heer written by the great Waris Shah. I read and recite until I can no longer stay awake.

SUNDAY, JANUARY 21ˢᵀ 1968

If I had to describe three of us then, I say, I am quite practical but not as daring and out spoken as Shamim. Sabah is normally the quitter one but whatever she says always make sense. She acts as my elder sister and tries to protect me. Getting me the room could not have been easy, but she did manage to get Ammi Jaan's permission, somehow.

Shamim is different, she could be brash and forceful. She likes to control everything, everyone, and is much closer to Ammi Jaan.

She is fearless and sometimes takes unnecessary risks. Always ready for an argument with the opposite sex. I honestly feel very lucky that I have these two friends. Where will I be without them?

Everyone is in revision mood.

I have found work in the same place as Sabah, so we go together and sometimes share the auto fare. The manager of this factory is a strange man. He orders the raw material very late. There have been times when we had to come home early. Today was such a day, so instead of coming back home, we decided to watch, 'Phool Aur Pather', the Meena Kumari and Dharmendra starrer at Ajanta Cinema. I really enjoyed it. Sabah says my frizzy hair look like Meena Kumari's. It feels nice when someone says you resemble someone famous.

After the film we went to Connaught Place and had coffee at the famous India Coffee House.

I feel very sorry for Sabah's plight. She belongs to a very poor family. Her father died when she was only twelve and since then she's been the breadwinner for her family. Her mother had been ill for years. She pays for the education of her younger brother and sister. It was sheer good luck that Ammi Jaan has accepted and looked after her. She has confessed everything to me and I feel very concerned about her.

She says, 'I'm indebted to Ammi Jaan for giving me shelter when I needed it most. Therefore, I have to do whatever she asks me to.'

'But you an educated person, you should do what is right for you not what is right for Ammi Jaan. You pay rent for the room and the other expenses. I don't really understand. You hate what she does to girls and still you allow her to do what she pleases with you.'

'Let us not go there today. I will tell you everything when the time is right.'

Shamim is playing with fire these days. She has formed a very intimate relationship with Yusuf and keeps telling everyone that he is going to be the father of her children. Yusuf is a smart young man who is pursuing a degree in law. He has fallen head over heels for our Shamim. His elder brother runs a family restaurant called Roxy in Chandni Chowk. Shamim spends quite a lot of time there. Whenever Ammi Jaan goes to her farmhouse for the day, Yusuf sneaks in and spends a lot of time in Shamim's bedroom.

SATURDAY, FEBRUARY 10TH 1968

I really shouldn't be focusing on anything but my exams now. However, one thing that has upset me: the disappearance of two girls overnight. No one is allowed to say anything, not even the chatterbox Shamim. This place sometimes resembles a very high security defence establishment. All I know is that one of the girls was sold for eighteen thousand and the other for twenty, as if they are in the cattle market. Ammi Jaan gives them a couple of thousands and retains the rest. This is the value of virginity. The price drops drastically for a used girl. *Why would anyone part with money to buy a second hand item?*

The people who buy them are supposedly respectable and well to do. Whether this is their real need or just thrill seeking adventure, I do not know. Bit of both I guess. It is the lure of virginity and young flesh, which probably makes them get so low. These must be respectable, successful men to afford a mistress.

What annoys me is the fact that these girls participate in this trade happily. Or are they just too scared to say no? I do not know. I have heard that it is not easy to get a place here as there are plenty of poor girls chasing the dream of having a good life. Now I understand why they change their names as soon as they enter the house. Sabah's actual name is Shanti Behan. Now who would want to buy a girl whose name has religious connotations? I hope that Sabah has told Ammi Jaan that I am certainly not one of these girls. I am only a lodger here. Everyone considers me an outsider so no one bothers to tell me anything anyway.

SATURDAY, FEBRUARY 17ᵀᴴ

A week has gone by since the two girls were sold. I am having difficulty concentrating on my studies as I keep thinking about Ammi Jaan's business. I'm getting a bit concerned for my own self too. After my exams, I should try to find alternative accommodation.

Sabah sees the questions on my face and starts talking about this without me asking her anything. She says calmly, 'Look, my darling, every one of them has their own circumstances but they are all very poor. A few are orphans with no one to turn to. This is much better than a life in the gutter. Ammi Jaan helps them with their education. She only accepts those who have a minimum qualification, matric at the least. They don't have another choice.'

'But still… just pay Ammi Jaan a little extra for her help and then go. Slavery was abolished a long time ago, Sabah.'

'Not in India. Poverty is the worst form of slavery. Anyway, it is not as simple as that.'

'So if you plan on doing the same, why go to college at all?'

'You do have a point, Nirmal, but once you are in it, you feel trapped. You get the feeling that the only way out is to do what Ammi Jaan asks and leave the rest to your fate.'

'So when you have no real answer, God comes into it. Fate comes into it. What has God to do with becoming someone's mistress? What kind of God pushes people into prostitution?'

'I understand what you are saying, but consider my case. How am I going to return the twelve hundred rupees I borrowed from Ammi Jaan? I needed it for my mother's medication. I do not have a single rupee with me. Whatever I earn, I send it home to keep everything going. I don't want to do this. I just want to get married to a decent man, have children and a place of my own, but I can't. I'm the bread winner in my family.'

'But, Sabah, once you finish your degree, why don't you simply pay Ammi Jaan and run away?'

'What you are saying is not wrong, but Ammi Jaan is a very dangerous woman. Prostitutes form a very close-knit community. They are in all the major cities in India. They never hesitate to help each other. Last time, a girl ran away and after three days, Ammi's found her goons in Patiala. It did not take those stray dogs long to tear her apart, and I heard that she is now working in the brothel down the road.'

Sabah started to sob. I felt very bad and consoled her, saying that we will find a way out. I gave her five hundred rupees and asked her to send it to her family.

She refused to take my money, but I forced her to keep it with the promise that she could return it when she had more.

SUNDAY, MARCH 24TH 1968

Thank God! It's the last exam today. I feel ill during exams, which is normal for me. But overall, I expect to get very good grades this time.

We went to an adult movie, which had a lot of kissing scenes. We all seemed to watch very intently. We bought ice creams during the interval and tried to emulate the kissing by licking in a certain way. All this mischief is to be expected, I guess, after the exams.

A couple of the girls are just like Shamim, spending their time teasing two poor young boys. What I have learnt today is that kissing as an art. It will be interesting to try when the time comes.

WEDNESDAY, MARCH 27TH

A short, very slim man has come to see Ammi Jaan two/three times. It is not normal as she does not like people discussing business in the house. In addition, respectable people would not want to be seen loitering here. It seems as though Ammi Jaan is trying to show him a few girls. Showing is probably not the correct way of describing; it is more like a catwalk conducted without the participant's consent. Even that is not the correct description. It resembles a cattle market where you look more at the body and build than anything else. These men measure boobs with their x-ray eyes.

Dear Ammi Jaan called Sabah and me to her room on the flimsiest of excuses in the evening. The man there stared at us hesitantly, avoiding direct eye contact. It still felt as though he were measuring us, though. Sabah winked, asking me to stay under control and not say anything.

Ammi Jaan made the introduction with a big smile. 'This is Mr. Mittal, a good friend of mine.'

Once he left, she asked us to sit down and gave us a lecture about Mr. Mittal. She told us that he is a good businessman with plenty of money. He has a big factory and supplies spare parts directly to the famous Royal Enfield motorcycle company. He is single as well. If we need work, he will give us a job. In fact, she thinks that we should work for him.

Sabah says to me, 'Don't worry our turn has not come yet. As long as we continue with our studies, she will not say anything. She gets more money if the girls are educated and capable of learning a bit of sophistication.'

As I lay in bed, the questions, which I tried to avoid at exam times, arose once again. Today's meeting with Ammi Jaan has brought them up.

I wondered what questions Sabah had had to face when getting permission to share the room with me. Had she given Ammi Jaan the false impression that I have nobody and I am *one of them?* Something inside me tells me that I should disappear from here quickly but then I feel sorry for Sabah and I cannot leave Shamim either.

I need to be brave and careful. *You call yourself Nirmal, now you have to prove it,* I told to myself. I will be strong and live life the way I want to live it. I am ready to face the challenge.

SUNDAY, JUNE 22ND 1968

After the exams, there are generally a couple of weeks for relaxation. You have to recharge your batteries and get ready for the next years' struggle. Both Shamim and I tend to eat a lot and put on weight during this period. Most of what we eat is junk food. Sabah is a good girl though; she knows how to control herself.

It a very satisfying feeling when your hard work bears fruit. The exam results have been declared, and I have secured very high marks and passed with a First Division. I must go at once to my village and share the news with Bibi.

I have made up my mind and told Sabah that I won't be working in the same factory any longer. I do have enough savings to last for three months. It is also not difficult to get a job in Delhi as long as you are prepared to accept a pittance for a salary.

PART FOUR

PARTFOUR

4.1

---‹‹‹›››---

HOME COMING...

THURSDAY, JUNE 27TH 1968

There I stood, knocking at the gates of the haveli, back in my village.

I imagined that Mum would come running to hold and hug me. She would shower me with kisses and say that she has missed me a lot. A year is a long time to be away from your only child. She would not have had anyone to talk to and would be feeling very lonely.

But nothing like that happened. My mother has changed completely and seems to have lost all her warmth. She greeted me with very little emotion. She has become a leader, and there were about six people waiting for an audience in her durbar. There was a big pile of official looking papers in front of her.

She looked up at me and said, 'So you have come to us. It is nice to see you, Sharnjit. Go inside and freshen up. You must be tired from your journey.' Those were very business-like words delivered without a hint of emotion.

A servant walked in with my luggage and showed me to a room, just like in a hotel.

I looked at her with a pitiful appeal in my eyes.

'You take rest now and we'll meet at breakfast. I'm quite busy today. Let the servant know if you need anything,' she said.

I felt like ice cold water had been thrown on my dreams of a loving reunion.

I remember my mother used to say to me, 'You're like a younger sister to me.' I wanted that love. I wanted her to tell everyone to go away, to come the next day so she could spend time with me now. I wanted her to go tell the whole village that her daughter had come home from Delhi. She may be a successful politician but she is my mother first. These thoughts rushed through my mind and made me want to cry out.

The servants of the house keep coming into my room asking after my welfare and waiting for my command. They have given me a new name, 'Chhote Bibi Ji'. Someone asks, 'Shall I fill the bath tub with warm water for you?' A young girl, probably the daughter of one of the servants, asks me, 'Chhote Bibi Ji, shall I massage your feet with oil?' I smile and say 'No'.

What would you like to have, Ji... something to eat? There are many more sweet questions. They are disappointed when I say 'no'. I cannot tell them my hunger is not for food, but for my mother's love. All I need is an embrace from my Mum. Just that...

Bachno's whole family has worked solely for Sarpanch for many years. Her husband works on the farm and both her daughters-- Jeeti who is in the eleventh and Preeti, in the tenth--help her in the kitchen. Bachno is in-charge of both the kitchen and the general house keeping.

I have had my bath and now am eagerly waiting for Biji. Just to pass the time, I call Jeeti in and she starts asking me questions, which I like. At least someone is showing interest in me.

'Chhote Bibi Ji, Delhi's fashion is so nice. This lemon colour suit looks very nice on you,' she says with a lot of admiration and envy in her voice.

'This suit is yours now. Wash and wear it from tomorrow.'

She says 'No, it is yours, Bibi Ji... I can't take it,' and so on, but I can see her face brimming with happiness. I ask her about the village and if she has anything important to tell me. How is everyone? What was it like while I was away? Once Jeeti starts, she doesn't stop. She just goes on and on...

'What is this, *Chhote Bibi Ji* business? I'm only a year older; you will call me Sharn as you used to. None of this "Bibi Ji" business.'

'I will call you Didi Sharn Ji, then.'

'As you please, Jeeti.'

'Didi Ji, everyone calls your mother, *Bibi Ji* now. She has become a Panchayat member and done so much for the village. Sarpanch Ji is a leader only in name. Bibi Ji does everything. The village loves her.'

I really liked what Jeeti was telling me, so I let her carry on.

'Didi Ji, Bibi has done so much for the village in such a short time. We have really made a lot of progress. Most of our streets and water channels in the village are now re-done with bricks and the village pond has been dug deeper. Now that the water has been contained better, we don't have to worry about diseases spreading so easily.'

Jeeti had so much to say that she was losing her breath. I nodded to show my approval.

'So all that has been done by Bibi Ji, on her own?'

'Yes Didi Ji. Bibi Ji works very hard and there are so many people she has to meet with. People come to her with their problems, they don't go to Sarpanch Ji.'

Jeeti told me lot of stories, but it was just past nine o'clock, and I was feeling a little tired from the journey. Bachno brought in delicious smelling food and I tucked in. No food can match the flavour of Punjabi food cooked fresh off the farm.

I have over eaten and can't keep my eyes open any longer, so I asked Jeeti to see me at six in the morning. We may go for a morning walk.

I have to get used to calling Mum *Bibi Ji* like everyone else. She might have the time to see me tomorrow.

FRIDAY, JUNE 29TH 1968

I've been up since four o'clock because of my eagerness to see my mother. My mind keeps going backwards and forwards. I'm also cursing myself for not staying awake. I've come all the way from Delhi to share my happiness with her. She must have come into my room and found me fast asleep and did not want to wake me up.

Jeeti arrived at the agreed time.

'Did you have to get up early for me, Jeeti?'

'No, I'm always up early. What's the point of lying in bed? You waste so much time sleeping. Shall I get the bicycle out or are we going walking, Didi Ji?'

'Just because I live in Delhi, it doesn't mean I've suddenly become soft. We will walk. I love to walk and get my clothes damp with the morning dew.' We decided to take the dirt road to our farm and Jeeti started where she left off yesterday in her storytelling.

'Didi Ji, initially, Bibi Ji didn't tell anyone you had gone away to study but later she took pleasure in telling everyone that she has no problem with sending you for further studies and girls have the same right to education as boys. People really like this. You know how politicians need every vote, Didi Ji.'

'Oh, they need every vote,' I repeated to myself. I saw that Jeeti had been won over and when the public starts to feel that they are part of the achievement, then you know you have been successful and your message has been delivered.

'Does she ever say she misses me, Jeeti?' I asked more out of hope than anything else. Jeeti went into deep thoughts as if trying to find a suitable, diplomatic answer.

'Bibi Ji has a very busy schedule and a very kind heart too. People do not leave her alone; she is busy all the time, but I am sure she does miss you. Every mother misses her child.'

'Our Jeeti has learned politics very quickly,' I said. She smiled. 'What time did your Bibi Ji got home last night, Jeeti?'

'Oh, she came very late, around eleven. Sarpanch Ji and two other men were also with her. I think they went to attend a very important election meeting. Didi Ji, she cares for you. Maybe she did not want to wake you up.'

I could see that Jeeti was trying her best to make me feel good. She was trying to find justification for all Bibi Ji's actions.

We arrived at our farmhouse. At the sight of it, all my old memories have come rushing

'Didi Ji, old *Nehmetaan* has been asking about you.'

'Oh, does she really …why?' I ask eagerly. This old woman is considered the most knowledgeable person in the village. She is always very frank and fair. The people of the village admire her and listen to her words of wisdom.

'As soon as she found out about Bibi Ji moving out to the haveli, she was really concerned about you. She said that it was not right. Both you and Bibi Ji should have stayed together and shared the burden of grief.'

'We'll go later today to see her.' I had no interest in Sarpanch's son Harnek, but just to keep some conversation going I asked 'How is Sarpanch's dear son, Jeeti?'

'Oh… Didi, you don't want to know about him. He has grown like a camel but has the smallest of brains. He is shameless.'

Given the expression on Jeeti's face and disgust in her voice, I assumed I had touched a nerve there.

'Why? What has he done?'

Jeeti started apologising when she realised that it was my cousin she was criticizing.

'I'm very sorry, Didi, I know he's your cousin. I shouldn't have said what I did. I am so sorry. You must be very angry with me.'

'No, don't be silly. I don't mind at all. You can't change the fact that someone is bad. From now on, you are my younger sister and best friend too, so you can share anything and everything with me.' I put a reassuring hand on her shoulder. 'I don't like him either. He is simply a brainless beast.'

My words made her breathe again and I could see a lot of affection and gratitude in her eyes.

'Didi Ji, he's got a twisted mind. It seems like he cannot control his feelings like the rest of us can. Do you remember Kamaljit, the carpenter's daughter? She's in her first year.'

'I remember Kamaljit. What about her?'

'Didi Ji, she was standing alone outside the college canteen when he came from nowhere and grabbed her breast from behind. He is big and strong and just wouldn't let go of the poor girl. Her cries were so loud that a crowd of students gathered around and saved her. He didn't even say sorry. Oh, it was very shameful for the Sarpanch's son to behave in that way. It's not normal, Didi. She was taken to her house crying. What happened afterword you just don't want to know.'

Jeeti stopped to take a breath.

'Kamaljit ran home crying. You know Didi Ji, there are some people who snatch any opportunity to add fuel to the fire. The whole of the carpenter's mohalla got together and came running with swords and sticks to the haveli. The mob was so incensed that they wanted to kill Harnek. Luckily for him, he hid in the haveli. Then Bibi Ji managed to assert some control and pacified the crowd very tactfully. She took five old and prominent people inside the haveli. Sarpanch slapped Harnek in front of the men and apologised to them. Harnek was made to apologise to Kamaljit and were made to call her sister. It took Bibi Ji's skills to manage the situation; it could've got out of hand easily. Sarpanch Ji wouldn't have been able to deal with it. Our Bibi Ji has received more respect because of it. However, Didi Ji, as they say, you can't straighten a dog's tail. It is always bent. The next day Harnek was back to his normal self. He keeps annoying me now with his silly behaviour.' Jeeti was carefully watching the expressions on my face to see whether I was sympathetic to her.

It was nearly 10 o'clock in the morning, but I did not feel like going back to the haveli yet. Was my desire to see my mother diminishing or was this my silent protest? I resumed my conversation with Jeeti.

'Well Jeeti, you said Harnek is being silly with you, what did he do?'

'Oh Didi Ji, he starts by saying, *you are so beautiful... I dream about you... I have lost my sleep over you* and many other things like that. Initially, I tried to ignore him and told him that he is being silly but instead, he became more and more daring. Then one day, when I was here at the farm, he sneaked behind me and grabbed hold of my hand. "*You are our farmhand's daughter. Stop messing around. I can do what I like with you. No one is going to come running to help you. I am being nice because I love you. I promise I will marry you if you let me... and if you refuse then I am going to rape you anyway. It is all up to you. You know that this is nothing new; all landlords and workers' daughters have these relationships. It does not really matter to your people whether you are a virgin or not,*" he said. This really hurt me. You tell me, Didi Ji, why the workers' daughters have no self-respect now. Why can't we be treated with dignity?'

'You're right, Jeeti. Everyone ought to respect the dignity of others, regardless of their financial standing, caste or the work they do. It is diabolical to think otherwise.'

'I will not allow anyone to touch me. My purity is for my husband. I would rather die than lose my respect to him or anyone. I'm strong enough. I'll kill before dying.'

Slowly, we made our way home. It was nearly 11 o'clock and I was a little worried that Mum would be annoyed with me for taking so long at the farm. Truth be told, I would enjoy her annoyance. It would feel good to know that she cared. I would go running toward her and she would take me in her embrace and all my protests would disappear.

As I entered the big front gates, I found out that she had gone out around eight o'clock with Sarpanch Ji to canvass for votes. All my hopes of spending time with her were dashed.

No one is going to refuse to vote for a beautiful woman, I said to myself and then felt disgusted for thinking in that way. I needed to grow up and understand her responsibilities and commitments to others. She is a political leader now and the public comes first, before her own family.

Most of my time is now being spent eating, relaxing and talking to Jeeti and Bachno. Waiting for Mum is becoming unbearable.

LATER THE DAY...

It was 10.45 PM when I heard the noise of the gate opening. Bibi Ji and two others came in. They spent about fifteen minutes in deep conversation. I could not make out what they were saying. I watched as Sarpanch and Bibi Ji went to the room at the end of the hall and shut the door. I tried to force myself to go to sleep but failed. My mother seemed to have found a new life and I did not figure in her routine any longer. I could easily make out her new relationship with Sarpanch, but it upset me to see it before me nonetheless. I kept telling myself that I shouldn't have come. Then an inner voice said, *Face the reality, dear. A woman needs the strength of broad shoulders and the warmth of a man's body. She is a human being with desires and needs. Your mother is a courageous woman who has managed to not buckle under the stress of adversity.*

SATURDAY, JUNE 29TH 1968

I decided last night that come what may, I will make every effort to see Mum. Even if she is busy, I will make sure that I am in her sight so that she cannot ignore me. Although I told Jeeti to wake me up at six with a cup of tea, I have been up since five, counting the minutes.

'Good Morning, Didi Ji! I have brought your favourite Masala chai.' Jeeti walked in with a big smile, surprised to see me ready.

'Thank you, Jeeti; we won't go out today till we meet Bibi Ji.' I said with confidence.

'You are right Didi Ji, we will not let her escape today. You have tea while I get the hot water ready for your bath.'

'No, Jeeti, come and sit with me, we have plenty of time. What if she goes while I'm in the bath? Close the door and tell me, does Bibi Ji drink? She seemed quite shaky on her feet, or was that my imagination? Doesn't Sarpanch go home to Tayee Ji anymore?' I asked. Jeeti was obviously very uncomfortable with questions. Perhaps she had not expected me to be so blunt early in the morning.

'We are not supposed to question our elders, Didi Ji. Bibi Ji has a lot of responsibility and she must get tired and these are the election days, you know,' she said diplomatically.

Jeeti didn't have to say anything; her initial hesitation had already given me the answer.

As I bathed under the warm water from the hand pump, a thought crept up in my mind. Maybe I was being extremely selfish and refusing to trust my mother. Someone has to be the first to clean up the mess in this country after all, and the distrust that has been created in the minds of ordinary people for many years.

From now on, I am not going to let any negative thoughts enter my mind.

I put on my best clothes and sat down at the breakfast table. I wanted to show to Mum that her little girl has become an educated and sophisticated young woman in Delhi. I knew she would be pleased to see me like this.

The smell coming from Bachno's parathas was testing my will power. I had to wait for Mum, I told myself.

Suddenly, Jeeti announced that she was coming and there she was, sitting in front of me. She put her papers on the side of the table, looked towards me and asked, 'Are you well, Beta Sharnjit?'

She smiled at me and without waiting for my answer, started looking at papers placed in front of her by a very short, chubby, ugly man.

'Yes, Bibi Ji, I'm very well.' I said. She smiled at me again.

When breakfast was served, she put the papers away and said, 'We have to make sure that Sarpanch Sahib, your Taya Ji, wins the election. That is why I have been so busy these days. You ought to have informed me before coming from Delhi. Anyway, let Jeeti know if you need anything.'

In the meantime, Sarpanch Sahib arrived as if half-drunk, and parked himself at the far end of the table. He looked ten years younger with his hair dyed black. He must have spent the night with Tayee Ji.

'How are you, Beti Sharnjit? How is your study going?' He asked me.

'Very well, Sarpanch Taya Ji.'

'You should give advice to your *good for nothing* brother. He should stop loitering around all day.'

I could not say anything and had no desire to get into a lengthy conversation with him. I was simply lost in my own little world, waiting for the moment when Mum would hold me in her arms and say, 'I am not going anywhere, I'm staying with Sharn today.'

But Mum is in politics now. Leaders do not show emotions in public. I have heard people say that the Queen of England did not shed a tear in public when her mother passed away. Grief and happiness are a private affair. This is called dignity. Laughing, crying and showing emotions—that is for the common people, like us.

I console myself with the thought that at least she had asked me how I was. *You must understand the present... stop living in the past... if you do not walk with it, you will be left behind, unable to catch up. Let the past go... you simply cannot live in the past... you can make the present a pleasant time or sulk in the past. Your Mum has chosen her path,* the voice of wisdom spoke in my head.

The very name of the leadership chair should be changed to Chair of Miracles. It has that power, once you are attached to it, you never want to let go. You change as a person. You start seeing everyone as a 'Vote' and nothing else. Making humongous promises and breaking them is the norm. The most successful politician is the one who is able to sell these utterly false promises to the public wrapped in sweetness.

'*O people! My Mum has become Bibi Ji… O God! Please help… Please give my mum back.*'

Everyone has just about finished the breakfast and the whole procession is about to start with the *trying to look dangerous* bodyguards. After having so many Pranthas they probably have lost their voice as well now.

Bibi Ji and Sarpanch sit in one car with an adviser and the Body Guards follow in earnest. Then there is another car behind them of the honest party workers. Party workers are always honest otherwise why would someone breathe dust all day long.

All gone and what is left behind is cloud of dust… lots of dust… all my hopes have gone in the dust too.

'Jeeti… please come back after two hours and we will go to the village. I'm going to my room to clear my head,' I said.

TWO HOURS LATER…

After Jeeti had arrived, we knocked on Tayi Ji's door. Tayi Ji always lived in the house in the old house in village, never moved to the haveli.

'Who is it?'

'Sharnjit, Tayi Ji.'

'Sharnjit… Our Sharnjit… come in… why are you standing outside? … Come sit with me,' she said with real affection.

'Get her a chair, Jeeti; she is now a city person, shouldn't sit on the ground like us,' Tayi Ji said with a smile.

'What has happened to you, Sharnjit? Don't you get any food in Delhi? You look so thin. Now have a glass of milk and get some energy into you.'

As far as my Tayi Ji is concerned, nothing has changed. She is still full of affection for me. She has always been a very fair person, regardless of the situation with Mum. If anything, I was feeling a little nervous. How must she feel now that Mum has moved into the haveli?

'I am very well, Tayi Ji. I went to Delhi to study, but came to visit now. Your hot milk is going to bring me back from wherever I go. How is life treating you, Tayi Ji?'

I believe that she understood what I was hinting at. With a little prompt from me, she started to tell me her side of the story. She probably wanted to tell me any way. We all need someone to talk to from time to time.

'Initially, I was very upset about your mother moving into the haveli, but then I thought I can't keep your Taya Ji tied down in the house. If that is what he is going to do, then he is going to do it anyway. I can't be with him all the time. Therefore, I told him that he could go wherever he wanted during the day but he must be home at night. He has kept his promise so far and I can't really complain.'

Where do women get so much tolerance? I wonder about it sometimes. Would anyone ask a man to tolerate what Tayi Ji had? What if she had brought some man to stay at home with her? Taya Ji certainly would've murdered her.

Tayi Ji took a large sip of tea and said, 'I'm not educated at all. Sarpanch Ji needed someone to help him with his work. Your mother is well educated, so it was an obvious choice. The village has gone mad and is now calling her Bibi Ji; I still can't call her Bibi Ji.' She says this with distaste in her voice.

It is unbelievable that she has taken all this so philosophically. 'Oh well, one thing is, Sharnjit, Bibi Ji has changed the face of our village. All the progress and new facilities have come about because of her effort, not Sarpanch Ji's. I have no choice but to accept the situation as it is.'

I asked her without any real interest, 'How is Harnek, Tayi Ji?'

'…Jeeti, you go make some tea.' She deliberately sent Jeeti away and said with lots of sorrow in her voice, 'He has gone off the hook. He spends all day with his useless friends. He did not like your mother moving into the haveli. He and his father seem to argue about everything. The boy has lost all respect for his father. He doesn't listen to me either. He shouldn't be drinking but these days he gets drunk and doesn't get up for a couple of days.

'I have never seen him with a book in his hand. Please talk to him… he may listen to you… why don't you take him to Delhi with you? Don't worry, I will pay for his fees,' she said and started sobbing.

Tayi Ji's plight has moved me enough that I even begin to contemplate taking Harnek back to Delhi with me. After all, he is my cousin. Then the reality hits me. He has never given me any respect as his sister. But that may change. Everyone goes through tough times in their lives.

Speak of the devil… Harnek walked in and without even saying hello, rushed upstairs to his room.

He couldn't escape Tayi Ji's eyes, she shouted his name and called him back.

'O, Harnek, look who is here! Your sister Sharnjit has come to see you,' she said as he came down.

'Hello, Harnek, I've been here for three days. Why didn't you come to the haveli to see me?' I asked.

'Haveli?' he said sarcastically, 'You can walk… you could've come.' I felt that there was a lot of anger in his voice.

'Why do you have to fight with her?' Tayi Ji said.

'The truth is, Tayi Ji, I didn't like Mum moving to the haveli either, but there was nothing I could do to stop her.' I showed my sympathy for them. Tayi Ji had a tear or two in her eyes but it seemed to have no impact on Harnek. I felt so sorry for Tayi Ji who had two men in her life, both of whom had given her nothing but grief.

Jeeti made a timely intervention and said, 'Tayi Ji, aren't you going to the Gurdwara today? It is the first day of the month.'

'Oh I forgot. Let's get ready quickly. You bring a half basket of grain from the store and I'll take some milk,' she said hurriedly.

We rushed and managed to arrive just in time at the Gurdwara; the Priest was still reciting verses from the Guru Granth.

'All human beings belong to one and are equal in His eyes' are the verses by Guru Gobind Singh Ji being recited. Preacher is explaining the meaning of verses by giving historical examples. It always sounds pleasant and is not that difficult if you have the desire to understand. Message given by Guru Ji is very simple but us human being has done our best to complicate it. Colour, Cast, Creed Religion, Profession and Isms have created division between human beings.'

The Preacher is carrying on with his reciting cum advice; he probably does not fully understand the true meanings himself but carries on none the less. More money people offer him louder he carries on preaches.

In the end, 'Prasad' (sweet dish) is given to the congregation. Tayi Ji and I both belong to higher cast so we sit at front but Jeeti being a servant's daughter and lower cast have to sit outside the Gurdwara. The Preacher covers his face when giving Prasad to the untouchable. I am astonished at the pure hypocrisy of it all. A few minutes earlier, he was telling us, we are all equal in the eyes of God, but here we are doing totally the opposite. In fact, it makes me feel sick and I cannot answer the question in Jeeti eyes.

'Come on, Jeeti, let's go, it's enough for the day.'

In very emotional state, I say goodbye and take leave from Tayi Ji.

When we got back to the haveli, I took refuse in my room.

'Jeeti, please open all the windows, I'm feeling suffocated.' The suffocation is eternal though, and opening windows is not going to help.

'Didi Ji, call me if you need tea or anything else. I had better go and help my mother before she starts moaning.'

Lying on the bed, staring at the white ceiling of the room was not going to give me any answers. I still hadn't been able to meet with Mum… and I hated to see Tayi Ji in pain.

I was so mentally exhausted that I couldn't remember when I dozed off… Even diary writing was becoming a bit tedious. I wished to take out my anger on something, but what? What was I this angry for, anyway?

'Come on, Jeeti; let's go to my old house.' I said the next morning.

'Didi Ji, do you know your old house has been sold to Jagiri? Jagiri from England.'

'What do you mean, sold?'

'However, we do keep the keys Didi Ji…'

'Sold?' I repeated as if I had misheard.

'Yes, Didi Ji. He is going to demolish it and build a new house there. That's what I've heard.'

A big ugly looking lock now hangs at the front door of my old house. The story of my childhood will soon be buried beneath the rubble. Someone new will come in and new history and memories will be created in this place.

I understand that progress is inevitable. I fully understand the desire to build new things. I know that the Himalayas were conquered because of a human desire to scale new heights. I don't deny all this, but I can't forget that feelings and memories cannot be buried under rubble in the name of progress. Bibi Ji can run away from the past, but I can't and I don't want to either.

I've managed to maintain a hold on my feelings but my inner being is very badly shaken. I do have the right to that house and I'd not even been informed, let alone consulted in this decision. Can it be that my mother is trying to get rid of what is old and belongs to the past? Am I part of that too? My whole being feels frozen by the cold reception in Mum's voice. I'm no longer her priority.

I came to Punjab with high expectations and in need of motherly love. But I found nothing of it.

WEDNESDAY, JULY 3RD 1968

I returned to Delhi sad, alone and confused. I knew that the time had come for me to make my own decision and be ready for the consequences. I was no longer a little girl crying out for mummy's attention.

The wise voice spoke inside me. *Dear Sharnjit! The very first things that has become clear is that you are forever Nirmal now. The second is that you have to learn to live with your surroundings; no one else is going to help. In other words, you are on your own. And third and most importantL every woman has a basic need for a male shoulder. Your mother has done no wrong, and your time will come too. Problems, difficulties, sadness and sorrows will come in abundance and uninvited but happiness and smiles need to be sought nonetheless. You are not going to change the world's behaviour. Everyone is busy and has no time for your idealistic world.*

'Seize the opportunity when happiness knocks on your door, you may not get a second chance.'

It feels so cosy to return to one's room and bed. It's as if I've returned from a dream to reality. Both Sabah and Shamim are so happy to see me. I learnt that Yusuf has been here almost on a daily basis since Ammi Jaan has been away.

'Have a little of bit shame Shamim… you seem to have become trained in hugging. Leave me alone, I'm not your Yusuf.'

'You'll need to learn, darling!'

SATURDAY, JULY 13TH 1968

There is one good thing about Delhi – it never lets you get bored. Once you enter the rat race, you are in it forever.

Both Sabah and I have joined the yoga group that meets in the park. Shamim has joined too, but she hardly does any exercises. Her mind is always full of mischief. Sometime what she says about the positions is unprintable.

Ammi Jaan is back, and she came and chatted to us quite freely. She seems happy.

It was a strange day at work today. We ended up having an argument with the new supervisor. There was no need for him to be so nasty to Sabah. The poor girl has only two hands and cannot work any faster. She kept listening to his garbage but I could not take it anymore and called him out for his boorish behaviour. Ultimately, we both resigned.

'What happened today at the factory was not good. We shouldn't have argued, Nirmal. After all, they are our masters,' Sabah said when we reached our room.

'What you mean, masters? They have bought our labour but not us. Production had been doubled in our section and what about that that son of the factory owner? He touched your bottom. I don't think it was funny. He was lucky I didn't slap him. You are so docile, it's unbelievable.'

'My dear, Nirmal, the idealistic world we desire does not exist. They are all the same. What makes you think the next one won't be as bad? All supervisors take bribes to give overtime pay to workers; in fact, they take a percentage, which I think is totally unfair and unjust.'

'So we have to sell ourselves, not work with any dignity at all? Your bum is for everyone to touch? That's disgusting.'

'You're right. We did the right thing. It would have happened eventually. I actually fancied that owner's son,' and she burst out laughing.

'One thing I have noticed is that since you came back from Punjab, you are not the same, relaxed, Nirmal. You get edgy very quickly,' Sabah said.

'There is so much wrong happening around us and we can't

seem to do anything about it. There is no will to change anything, and that annoys me big time.'

SUNDAY, SEPTEMBER 8TH 1968

'You know that little man who comes to Ammi Jaan often, I believe he is a factory owner. Should I ask Ammi Jaan if he has any vacancies?' Shamim asked both me and Sabah today.

'Yes, I don't see any harm in that. It does not matter where we work as long as we are treated right. We will not know till we try,' Sabah said.

'Okay, we will discuss it later,' I respond.

Shamim cannot keep anything to herself for too long. Now Ammi Jaan knows that we are unemployed and looking for work. She summoned us to her durbar and announces, 'This is Mittal Sahib. He is a big businessperson and has his own factory. I have requested that he give you work,' she said as she made tea for him. 'I thought it better if you meet up here,' she explained.

The little man stretched himself, smirked and looked us up and down. His dark face had gone maroon and an uncontrollable dribble had fallen on his black shoes. He had probably not seen two beautiful girls in their prime this close before. I felt very uncomfortable and didn't like this at all. We promised to be at his factory tomorrow and then we took our leave of Ammi Jaan. She seemed to be radiating triumph.

'Sabah, I do not like the look of this man, neither do I want to work in his factory. Did you see how he was staring at our bodies?'

'Don't take this the wrong way, Nirmal. I felt very uncomfortable as well, but we do have to work to keep ourselves going. Wherever you go, they are all the same. Indian men do not have the same respect for women as their western counterparts do. Listen… we'll deal with the *silly ass* as you say.' We laughed, but we knew we were only consoling ourselves.

Enter Shamim. 'What is the matter with you both? Why such long faces – has somebody died?'

'Come, sit down, Shamim. We were waiting for you. You've put us in this situation, now tell us what we should do about this Mittal job,' Sabah said.

'I didn't like the way he was staring at us,' I said.

'Hey … who would not want to look at these two beauties? Forbidden fruit is always tempting. Poor Mittal…' Shamim said with a mischievous smile.

'Your bent brain thinks only one way these days, Shamim. We were talking about work,' I said, annoyed.

'Sweet heart, I'm talking about the job too… Listen, that Mittal has lost his heart to you two, so he is now in your palm. Just give him a bit of lift and he won't be able to give you any problem. And let this tasty brown chocolate use her magic. She always says that all she wants is someone with lots of money,' she pointed to Sabah.

Sabah was warming to her idea. She listened very intently.

'I'll do it, Shamim, if you teach me what to do,' Sabah finally said, sounding excited.

'One thing I have to tell you, Nirmal, is that the idealistic world you live in exists only in your imagination. In reality it does not exist,' Sabah said with confidence.

'One shouldn't play with fire though, it could be fatal.' I finally gave in.

TUESDAY, SEPTEMBER 10TH 1968

We'd decided to go to Mittal's factory in the afternoon. So we spent our time jaunting from one place to the next, and now we finally had to go.

We reached at 2.30 PM. We had got ourselves worked up for no reason, really. It was just work after all. Mittal Sahib had probably been waiting for us since the morning. He met us with big smile, and was very civilised, offering us tea and biscuits. He was very polite, discussed our wages, timetable and what he wants us to do. There are around ten workers in his employ. We were somewhat surprised that it is nothing more than a small cottage factory outfit that makes spare parts for motorcycles.

I'm a little relieved now, but there is still something not right about this man. I don't like the way he glares at our busts.

Sabah has already started using on the advice Shamim gave her. Her smiles have lasted a fraction of a moment too long.

TUESDAY, SEPTEMBER 24TH

It's been two weeks since we started work at Mittal's factory. Things have settled down a bit. We have both been given the responsibility of getting the orders on time. One advantage we have is that we are the only workers who can read and write.

Sabah is getting too close to Mittal for my liking. Every night, she gives Shamim the full account of the day. We have unanimously bestowed the title 'Professor of Love and Dirty Language' on Shamim.

Now, from Monday to Friday, we get up very early – go to Mittal's, then to college , walk or do yoga in the evening and then gossip with Shamim at night.

On Saturday, we study the whole day, after asking Shamim to keep her mouth shut.

On Sunday, we take in the morning show of an English movie, either in Sheila or Odeon Cinema. Then we eat gol gappa, samosa, chana kulcha and ice cream or other such junk, then catch a 6 to 9 show of a new Hindi movie.

Mittal Sahib has gone out today. This is nothing new, as he spends very little time at factory, giving orders in the morning then going for most of the day. *This order is already very late, hurry up,* is something he says all the time.

Around 11, a young, good-looking man walked in, clutching accountancy books. 'Oh, he is handsome...' Sabah winked. He said hello to everyone and went straight into the office. Sabah winked at me and told me to go in. I wanted to go anyway. All I needed was a nod from her.

'What should I say? What excuse do I use?' I asked.

'Be friendly, just ask if he wants tea or something?'

So I went and knocked on the door without hesitation.

'Hi, I'm Nirmal.'

'Hi,' he says without looking.

'Strange man,' I said.

'Did you say anything...?' He looked up.

'Yes, I'm Nirmal,' I repeated with a smile.

' Sorry... sorry, Parkash... Parkash Sohal... from Punjab.'

What a plonker, I thought. A beautiful girl is standing in front of him. Go on ask me something... make a conversation...look interested, at least. Bore. 'I'm from Punjab too,' I said excitedly. Our eyes met. Nothing was said; nothing needed to be said.

I've been in dreamland all day. Sabah must have asked me thousands of questions by now. What happened, what did he say, what did you say, and many more. 'Well, nothing was said,' was my dull reply.

The whole world seems like a pleasant place now. I remember the epic love story of Heer and Ranjha by Waris Shah. Heer, daughter of the head of the clan, learns that a stranger has been sleeping in the bed reserved for her on the boat. She goes to the boat with her mates, bursting with anger, ready to beat up this intruder and teach him a lesson. When she enters, she shouts, 'How could you dare to lie on my bed?' and the intruder turns and looks up. She instantly falls in love and they live and die for love. This is exactly what has happened to this Heer today.

Parkash... Parkash Sohal... from Punjab. The words are ringing in my ears. I keep repeating them.

I got home to find that the tables had turned. Where is

Shamim? It was now my turn to hold her tight in my arms. I wanted to shout out, 'I am in love… I have found my own Yusuf… I am so excited…'

Shamim shook me by the shoulder and I came back to earth from my dreams.

'Would you kindly tell me what's happened to my very careful Nirmal? Who has stolen her heart? What's his name?'

I held Shamim's hands. 'His name is Parkash Sohal and he's Punjabi like I am.'

'And…is that it?'

'That is it.'

'You're so excited just because his name is… If I were in your place, I wouldn't have come back without a few hugs and kisses, but you are "Nirrrr…mal".'

'You, my dear Shamim Ji, will not understand. Who even needs words? Everything that needed to be said was conveyed through our eyes. It does not take long to fall in love.'

'Yes… you are very right, and if anyone understands, I do. I can give my life for Yusuf. All I say to you is, be careful – very careful, not only of the world but yourself.'

'But you're never careful, you go boasting to the world. Why do you give me this advice?'

'To me what I'm doing is not wrong but dangerous… but I can't do anything, this is my weakness. Yusuf is my weakness… I start buckling when I'm with him.'

There was a pause. I have never seen Shamim in a serious mood before.

'I'm not too worried about myself, but I worry for you. You are different… too honest… too bloody truthful. I know, this is your strength but it can become your weakness as well, in this cruel world. Ammi Jaan is a very mean woman. She forgives no one and keeps many dangerous mad dogs – her goons. So make sure you keep it secret as much as you can – but you must tell me though,' and we had a hearty laugh.

'I'll tell Sabah to keep her gob shut as well,' she said.

Lying in my bed I recalled the conversation Shamim and I had had and the events of my momentous day. To be loved is the basic right of any person. A musical instrument lies silent till someone – someone who know how to play – comes along, touches and makes beautiful music.

That someone has touched my cords. I have come alive. Life seems worth living.

SUNDAY, SEPTEMBER 29TH 1968

I got up early to go to Gurdwara Sis Ganj to thank God for his kindness. *Look God; I am keeping my side of the bargain. Now you have to look after me and my... Well! I do not need to say. You run this world, you know everything! I wish to belong to someone... please help me, my dear God!'*

Mittal Sahib has become just *Mittal* now. He carries on with his bizarre antics and silly conversation all day long. Sabah seems to be enjoying it. However, when the owner behaves that way with his workers, he loses any respect he might have had.

Babu Ji... Parkash Ji... Babu and Parkash Sohal do not go well together. For me it is going to be 'Sardar Parkash' from now on.

I am dying to see him. I want to talk to him but have to wait until next Tuesday.

TUESDAY, OCTOBER 1ST 1968

Finally, Tuesday has arrived. I will be meeting Sardar Parkash. I spent extra time in front of the mirror this morning. This light yellow Punjabi suit looks very nice on me, Shamim told me. I hope Sardar Parkash likes it too. I have even rehearsed what I am going to say to him. I have secretly found out his routine too. He arrives at our factory at around eleven, puts in two hours of work in the office and then he goes for lunch at the nearby dhaba. That is going to be our meeting place.

LATER...

Sardar Parkash was sitting in the far corner reading a magazine, a cup of tea growing cold on the table. He has not seen us yet. Sabah and I deliberately walked in front of him to get his attention and we succeeed..

'Oh... Nirmal Ji ... Sabah Ji, please come, have a seat... what would you like to have?' He said with a polite smile.

'Thank you, Sabah is going get our lunch.' I sent Sabah away. I wanted to be alone with him. Sabah understood.

'Sorry, I did not say much that day in the office. I was just – a little overwhelmed.'

'Yes. I understand. Thank God, you are Punjabi. I have been dying to speak to someone in Punjabi.'

'There aren't many Punjabi speaking people here. I'm pleased that you're Punjabi too.'

'I don't want to call you Babu Ji. To me, you are "Sardar Parkash" henceforth. And I'm not Nirmal Ji either, just Nirmal for you.' I have no idea how I got so much courage to say all this in one breath.

He smirked and said, 'Yes Nirmal Ji, but my work is that of an accountant, or Babu Ji. You can call me whatever you like.'

'Nirmal Ji?'

'Addressing someone with due respect is not a bad thing. *Ji* is respectful word.'

'But it's impersonal between friends. I long for you to just call me Nirmal.'

'Now that we've become friends ...' I stopped him in the middle of the sentence and said, 'Our friendship started at five past eleven last Tuesday.'

'Yes …I felt those were special moments.'

'Now that we are friends, I want to know everything about you. I do have the right.'

'Yes, Nirmal, it is your right… but some things need not be said in words.'.

I remember Gurbuksh Singh Preetlari, the famous writer, once said, *Love is not possession but an understanding of feelings.*

'Well. Well, our Nirmal has an appreciation of Punjabi literature as well. I am very fond of reading too. So we will not get bored. Oh, just one more thing, this light yellow looks very nice on you.'

His appreciation filled my heart with happiness. All that time spent in front of the mirror was worth it. There is a feeling of cosiness around me. I feel very close to him; it seems like we have known each other for years. We seem to have so much in common. We had to break off our conversation because Sabah walked back and intervened. 'Mr. Parkash, has she filled your brain with her philosophy yet?'

'If you'd taken a few minutes longer, we would've had the chance to finish our conversation.' I said with a little bit of disappointment.

'…Parkash Sahib, let me tell you one thing… this girl really loves you. Your name is on her lips all the time. She is a good girl and lovely person, our Nirmal. You must look after her. I know that you love her too. Then just get together guys…'

Sabah has no full stops once she opens her mouth. This is probably the first time that I wished she were not around.

'You're right Sabah, some relationships form automatically because they are so natural. Nirmal's friendship is a godsend for me. I must have done something very good in my past life to deserve this.'

I am so happy today. I have found my true love. '*Thank you, God! Thank you very much,*' I have said many times in my mind. My prayers have been answered.

Sabah must have said many things but I do not remember any of them. I was not there; I was probably in my dreamland. The mere thought of being with Sardar Parkash fills me with joy. Suddenly, life feels so complete and worth living again. You may be beautiful – you stand in front of the mirror and adore yourself – but it is entirely different when someone else says *you look beautiful* especially the opposite sex. Then you feel you really are beautiful.

I want to be with him all the time but I have to wait for Tuesday – the day he comes to our factory. Why can't we meet somewhere else? I have started counting days. *'Oh God what is happening to me?'* I cry out loud and then feel a little embarrassed when I stand in front of the mirror and start talking to myself. I did ask Sabah to leave us alone that day. I think I am becoming a little selfish. Never mind… who cares – everything is fair in love and war.

MONDAY, OCTOBER 7TH 1968

He is a very sensible and sensitive man, that much I know. The topics of our conversation are always deep and serious. He also gets deep into conversation with Sabah and they both have strong views. Everything has to be morally right for him. He often says that Sabah is very street-smart person.

There is one thing that is bothering me a lot. How will he react if he finds out that I am living at a Twaif's house? I should move out soon. I have said that to myself so many times. My problem is that I've settled in so well here, become so much used to Shamim, my best friend and mentor. The very idea of being away from her sends shivers down my spine. She has always been there for me. In fact, I feel so lucky to have both Shamim and Sardar Parkash, the very best people, as my best friends. Sabah is a very good friend too but I don't know why I can't open up to her as I can with Shamim.

SATURDAY, OCTOBER 12TH 1968

This giving a lift to Mittal, which began as a joke, can become very dangerous. He may already have begun to think that Sabah wants to have a relationship with him. I know that she is merely playing around, but he might take her seriously. I have told her so many times, but she doesn't seem to listen and just laughs it off. Mittal has started to join us for lunch at the dhaba as well. He rarely came there before but now he comes often and insists on paying for our meals. When your boss starts to sit with you and behave cheaply, he tends to lose his respect in your eyes.

Of all the full-time factory workers, Sabah and I are the only ones who are educated. We have naturally taken a lot of responsibility for sorting out orders, packing and making sure that all orders are correct and sent on time. Production has gone up thirty percent with the same number of workers because we have now departmentalised our responsibilities. Mittal seems very happy because profits have gone up but he is so tight with money, and he has not even thanked us.

Sabah did not go to lunch with me today. So there I was, alone with Sardar Parkash with no one to disturb us. He has not hesitated even one bit to tell me about his life. The more I know, the closer I get to him. This is not a one-sided affair, I definitely know that much, but he will never say that he loves me. He is too bloody reserved. He is full of admiration for what I wear and how beautiful I look.

'Sabah is very nice person,' he said to me today.

'Yes, she's like an elder sister to me.'

'She cares a lot for you; it is good to have friends like her. You are very lucky, Nirmal.'

'I'm very lucky because I have got you as well...' and I saw him looking approvingly at me.

'But I don't like Mittal, your friend. He keeps gazing at me as if... oh I don't know, but I don't like him at all.'

'This world is full of good and bad people. As long as you believe you are being truthful to yourself and others, you shouldn't worry. Some people are the way they are. Mittal's not a bad person, he just gets carried away sometimes… everyone is attracted to beautiful flowers,' he said with a smile.

He asked me about myself, but I said, *No, your turn to ask questions hasn't come yet. I just want to talk about you, know everything about you.* I have successfully managed to fend off his questions, at least for the time being. He is a real gentle man so he doesn't insist.

I could keep writing all night long. It is well past mid night and Sabah is snoring away…

TUESDAY, OCTOBER 15TH 1968

Another week has flown by. Today's meeting with Sardar Parkash was very special. He said something special in a roundabout way. "Nirmal, you dress in a very cultured way. The yellow suit you wear really looks so nice on you. You look like a princess – a fairy tale princess – my fairy tale princess. You know… yellow is my favourite colour… No, no yellow becomes my favourite colour when you wear it. My wish is to keep looking at you for the rest of my life."

He then looked into my eyes. There was so much love in his eyes.

Now how hard is it to say *I love you?*

I'm feeling on top of the world today. Everything looks right. Oh God! You are so kind.

I must go to the Gurdwara soon and give my thanks to the Almighty. I've started to believe in Him again.

My love Sardar Parkash,

"Each one of our meetings has become a milestone in my life and every little step is taking me closer to my destination. You have taught me so much about true love and life. Even at such a young age, you talk about the deep philosophies of life and high moral values. I wish to walk the path of life with you as your partner."

A letter I never posted…

FRIDAY, NOVEMBER 1ST 1968

I met Santokh today. He is such a nice, simple young man. He is Sardar Prakash's childhood friend. They have such a strong bond and that's why he has come to see Sardar Parkash, all the way from Punjab. He complains that he wants to see more of Delhi and Sardar Parkash is very busy and has very little time. Therefore, Sabah and I promised that we would take him out one day. I have a secret motive behind this as well. I wish to know a lot more about Sardar Parkash. So, what could be a better opportunity than this?

SATURDAY, NOVEMBER 9TH

I have so much to write about this wonderful day. Sabah could not come, but I did manage to take a day off work. I spent the whole day with Santokh. We had pure ghee parathas at the Sardar Dhaba, and then we went to Sis Ganj Gurdwara. We had the best time sitting on the green lawns of the Red Fort. I kept asking him questions, and he told me everything without hesitation. I know more about my Sardar Parkash than he does himself.

One of the best things that happened was that he started to call me 'Bhabi Ji' and it felt so natural coming from him. This title is usually given after marriage. Why he pre-empted it, I do not know. Maybe Sardar Parkash has told him a lot more. Maybe he has discussed our future with him. Maybe… but whatever the reason, I like it… I love it, in fact. I have repeated the word '*Bhabi*

Ji' so many times and it feels so good. 'Yes, that is what I want, Santokh'. He is my sweet 'Dewar Ji.'

'Bhabi ji, one thing I want to tell you about Bhaji is that he really loves you but he will never say it. He wants to marry you... but he will not say it because he is so shy and reserved. Bhabi Ji sometimes you have to tell the other person how you feel, otherwise how are they going to know what is in your mind?' he asks philosophically, looking far away in the distance and immersed in deep thoughts.

'So, what are we going to do, Santokh?'

'Well, Bhabi Ji, you need to tell him... if we wait for him to say anything, it'll be years.'

'What do I say? Girls do not say it first. He has to, don't you think? And what do I say anyway?'

'Oh, Bhabi Ji, just tell him you want to marry him. Don't worry, leave the rest to me!'

SUNDAY, DECEMBER 15TH 1968

It has been well over a month since we met. We can meet any other day but waiting for Tuesday feels good. Today we met at the Dhaba. Sabah was also there. I thought I should pay for lunch but he did not like it. Perhaps he feels that a man should always pay.

We were having a good laugh when Mittal walked in. He did not say anything, but we could see from his expression that he did not like us sitting together.

'We're not slaves, it's our lunch time, and we can do whatever we like,' I said.

'But remember he still is your boss and you should not upset him,' Sardar Parkash said with a smile.

'Yes, Nirmal, let us finish our lunch on time today.' The intelligent Sabah said.

Tonight, Mittal came to our house, and we saw him in deep conversation with Ammi Jaan. It's worrying. What business could he have with Ammi Jaan? Was he there to make complaint against us? Why should he complain? We can have lunch with whomever we like.

Sabah is carrying on her playfulness with Mittal. He hardly says anything to me, in fact, he ignores me. It suits me because that is what I wished for. But he does continue to stare at me sometimes, which I really dislike.

Something is also not quite right between Sardar Parkash and Mittal. They do not say much to each other these days. Sardar Parkash just comes in, does his work and goes. Marwaha Saheb is our raw material supplier and is a very good friend of Sardar Parkash's. They have much in common. Both have a love for reading and writing poetry. Whenever Mittal falls behind on his payment and Marwaha refuses to release the raw material, it is always Sardar Parkash who has to ask him. Mittal is just a bad businessperson.

Sardar Parkash and I have not met alone for nearly four weeks now. We are both very busy at work and exams are approaching.

Good night diary, just one more thing, Ammi Jaan has been away for three days and our Shamim has had real fun, We have been listening to the details off her mischief.

TUESDAY, FEBRUARY 25TH 1969

Today, Sardar Parkash wished me good morning, smiled and went straight into the office. Mittal normally sits with him in the office for a while, but today as soon as Sardar Parkash came in, he went out of the factory without saying anything. He was out for about an hour and half. Soon after getting back, he asked everyone to stop work and listen as he had an important announcement to make. We all looked at each other thinking and guessing. Maybe he was going to announce a pay rise or a bonus because production has gone up by forty percent?

But instead he just barked, *"I am going to get married to Nirmal."*

'What nonsense! If this is a joke then it's a very bad joke!' I said. I was in an utter shock. Everyone looked astonished. I was so annoyed that I felt like slapping him, but Sabah told me to keep quiet and say nothing.

If his aim was to upset Sardar Parkash then he definitely succeeded. Sardar Parkash just looked at me, took his papers and walked out. Mittal went out soon after and didn't come back.

I was so furious that even Sabah couldn't say anything to me. I didn't understand this. Mittal knew where I lived. I wondered if he would exploit that.

We returned to our room without saying a single word to each other. Sabah could see the worry on my face and said, 'Listen, Nirmal; let him bark if that's what he wants to do. We only have two months to go to for the exams, so let's just keep our heads down, work up to that period and then say goodbye to him. Just ignore him. He is just jealous of your friendship with Parkash, and made a fool of himself in front of the workers. No one takes him seriously.'

'I know he might be jealous but this is a very silly way of behaving. I felt like slapping him there and then.'

There is so much that I don't understand. My head is spinning. Mittal has dared to say those words to me. He must have Ammi Jaan's support. Alternatively, has Ammi Jaan sold me off as well, like the others?

I keep staring at door as if someone is going to come and take me away. It's a horrible feeling. I'm unable to go to sleep. Sabah is right; I just have to put up with this until the exams and then find a room somewhere else.

TUESDAY, MARCH 4TH

I knew he wouldn't come to Mittal's factory so I went to Simon Sahib's and waited for Sardar Parkash. As soon as I entered, I couldn't control my tears and all I could ask him was whether he could meet me at the dhaba for lunch.

Later, I saw him sitting at his favourite table in the corner, looking very pensive.

'Are you annoyed with me? Mittal is a shameless idiot… he just says whatever comes into his twisted mind… how am I to blame?' I couldn't control my tears anymore.

'No, Nirmal, I can never be angry with you… I can't even bear the thought of being angry with you. I just do not wish to step into that shameless person's factory. There's not an ounce of decency left in him.'

He held my hands in his. It felt so comforting. 'Being with you has given me so much strength to carry on with my struggles,' I said, heaving a sigh of relief.

'We should try to meet somewhere else… away from these prying eyes. Let's put all this behind us and concentrate on studying. After the exams, I am going to stop doing his work. He doesn't pay me anything, so it's not a loss at all,' he said with a warm smile.

FRIDAY, MARCH 7TH 1969

My mind is filled with sadness these days. Sardar and I haven't seen each other for well over three weeks now. I really want to be with him. Something strange is happening to me. I wish to be in his arms, having him hold me tight and never let go. I wish…

'What's the matter with my dear Punjaban?' Shamim asks me. 'Why this long face? Have you not seen Sardar Parkash lately? What difference is it going to make, whether you see him or not? You are not going to touch each other. Pure love... eh...Nirrrrmal. If he's slow, then you can make him run faster... I will teach you...'

'Everyone's not shameless like you my dear Sis. All that before marriage... my God! This girl! No, not for us. When the time is right, everything will happen automatically. However, at this moment I have a big problem. I'm very confused and really don't know what to do.' I told her what had happened at the factory with Mittal.

After listening very attentively, she simply laughed and said, 'Now where's the problem...? You are both brainless, that's what the problem is. Fools, his weakness, as you tell me, are *women*. You both got the strength, use it.'

'You, dear Gujratan, come here and listen to me very carefully. You need to use a bit of your charm, widen those big black eyes of yours and open the top button of your blouse when he is around. I'm sure even you can do that much... hey, Sabah?'

'Shamim, why are you teaching her all this rubbish, we are going to be in more trouble if we do what you are saying. What if he takes the bait? What then?'

'Yep, that's it...let him take the bait. She's not going to get into his bed, is she?' Shamim said.

'I want to do it Shamim! Yes, it'll be fun,' Sabah said.

'But what if she gets into a tangle with him, Shamim? Is it not too dangerous?' I asked hesitantly.

'Hey listen, we know that he's already married. These married men just seek a bit on the side but are very worried about their respect and scared of being found out. In fact, they run scared of their wives most of the time and that's their weakness. Bloody hypocrites.'

'She listens to everything you say. Please, Shamim, don't encourage her. It's very dangerous path. We should just ignore him.'

I thought about what Shamim said as I lay in bed. Her way of saying things might be direct and rude at times, but she is right. Most men, given the slightest of chance, will be tempted to go after other women.

My diary is becoming more like a novel. I want to become a writer in the future. I must come out of my dream world and go to sleep. I have exams coming up and that silly Mittal to face.

FRIDAY, JUNE 13TH 1969

Finally, the time has arrived. The results have come out and all three of us have done better than expected. Both Shamim and I can now call ourselves graduates. Sardar Parkash becomes a little resentful sometimes because he has lost a year of study at the start.

To get him into a better mood, I suggested that we celebrate our achievement.

'That's a brilliant idea… yes, let us celebrate,' Sabah said excitedly.

'What do you think, Mr Boring?' I said with a little mischief in my voice.

'I think, we must… yes, it is time to celebrate… I'm with you on this.'

'However, you have to suggest where to go because I'm not good at that,' Sardar Parkash said with a smirk. This is rather reassuring because I haven't seen him smile for a long time.

'We should tell Mittal' Sabah said.

This astonished me, and I said in firm voice, 'Why? He has not written any exams.'

'I am sorry; I just thought… it may be taken as a goodwill gesture.'

'It is okay, Nirmal; anyone can join in celebrating our happiness. He is our friend, not an enemy. It will be a good opportunity to forget about our differences and be friends again,' Sardar Parkash said calmly.

I like this about him. He does not walk with a chip on his shoulder. He is prepared to forgive even an evil person like Mittal. We know that Mittal takes advantage of this niceness.

I also know that Mittal, given the slightest of opportunity, will turn up.

SATURDAY, JUNE 14TH 1969

Sabah, Sardar Parkash and I arrived at Connaught Place as planned. As we were a bit early, we decided to sit in Central Park for a while. A few minutes later Mittal walked up to us. On seeing him, I was bursting with anger but Sardar Parkash calmed me down by saying, 'It is okay, let's enjoy today'. It felt strange though. Sabah had recognised her folly of inviting Mittal as he kept staring at our boobs. She begged me to stay calm and apologised to me.

We finished our meal. Sabah and Mittal had not stopped talking for a second. Sardar and I were mere spectators. I felt suffocated, so I got up, and went to the ice cream counter. Mittal followed me and stood behind, almost touching me. I could see that Sardar was also getting irritated now. When we got back, I said, 'Sardar Parkash, can we meet up next week on Tuesday? Not for an hour, but the whole day.'

I did not even wait for his answer to say 'That's fixed.'

Mittal's face went pale. He was clearly very upset, but he can't stop me.

WEDNESDAY, JUNE 18TH 1969

For the next three four days, apart from a mere hello, we haven't said much to Mittal. He, in fact, finds excuses to calls Sabah into his office. He tells her how bad Sardar Parkash is. He says things like 'Parkash has stabbed me in the back. I helped him so much when he first came from Punjab. He is a villager and a farmer's son. Nirmal is best advised to stay away from him.' He does not say anything to me and in fact, since that day, he has stayed away from me.

Shamim has been clever; we have deliberately misled him into believing that we are meeting on Tuesday. I came to work as normal but changed my meeting with Sardar to Saturday instead. You never know with evil men, and I don't wish to take any chances on our first date. I went with Shamim to visit Sardar Prakash's landlady a few days ago to let her know of our plan. Initially, Shamim tried to lie to her and introduced me as Sardar Prakash's fiancée, but a lie is a lie. She saw through us and I could not keep up with more lies and said, 'Have we been caught?'

'Yes, I'm afraid so, a woman cannot lie to another woman in these matters. We all have gone through this . If you want to surprise Parkash then I'm with you all the way. I must tell you that your choice is good. He's a very nice young man, well spoken but reserved. So you have to handle him with care, my dear.'

SATURDAY, JUNE 28TH 1969

When you want to get somewhere on time, it seems as though everyone sets out to delay you. My usual auto driver came exactly ten minutes late. Ultimatley, this led to me knocking at the door of Sardar Prakash's house at ten minutes to seven in the morning.

His landlady winked at me while he looked astonished. He was standing in front of me in his Punjabi night clothes. Oh, he looked so cute and confused! I said in a slightly high tone of voice, 'Are you going to help me or stand there staring?'

He really did not know how to handle the situation. I was having difficulty keeping a straight face.

His landlady deliberately asked, 'Who is this girl, Parkash?'

He said, 'She is …I …I …me… me… mine…'

'What is this...I ...I...me, me...?' She said firmly, trying to hold her laugh back.

'She is... Nirr ..r..mal' was all he could muster in a very low apologetic voice.

I knew he was not expecting to see me this early, but I did not wish to waste any time. I wanted to spend the whole day and I meant the whole day with him.

The area he lives in is quite poor but it is clean and feels very nice and open. Just few yards away there are open fields. There is also a small canal nearby where he goes every day for his morning walk. I am going to follow that routine.

'Shall we go for a morning walk, and then have our breakfast?' I asked him.

'I'm in your hands today, Nirmal. Yes, I'm sure you will enjoy the morning walk. Let me take you to a special place.'

We were walking along the grassy canal bank, when I saw a board that read 'J. S. Farm'. When we came closer, a dog ran towards us, barking. I clung to his shoulder. It felt so good. I wished it would keep barking.

Sardar gave me lecture on how the dog is the best servant and friend of his master. As we went further, we met a young, well-built man who I understood to be the owner of the farm and a good friend of Sardar Parkash's.

At the farm, I met Jaswinder's beautiful wife – Satwinder. She is lovely and we bonded quickly. Her children are very fond of their Uncle Parkash.

'Nirmal, do you want to be my sister or sister in law?'

'Both – it will be very enjoyable to be your sister in law and you are an elder sister to me anyway, so you can be my teacher as well.'

'When are you getting married?'

'Oh, we haven't decided yet.'

'My darling, hold on to him tight. Never let him go... he is such a nice young man. You both make a lovely couple.'

'Ji, Bhabi Ji, you will guide me.'

'You haven't arrived at the point where you need my advice…' she teased me.

We went back to a lovely breakfast served by his landlady, Kulwinder Ji, who had cooked all Sardar's favourites. At about half past eleven we are ready to go on our date. Shamim had told me a lot about Okhla; she had called it a lover's paradise. While we made our way there, I wondered why he hadn't asked me about the suitcase I had brought to his room. Could it be that he is so absent minded that he hadn't even noticed it?

After the Chaat, we head towards Yamuna River. On most popular side, there are a couple of families enjoying picnics but on the opposite side, it is all deserted. So we keep walking towards this almost barren side. Our conversation is all bits and pieces, nothing important really, when he suddenly asks, 'What's your life plan, Nirmal.'

'To be with you for the rest of my life.' I say without hesitation.

'I mean what you want to become in life?'

'Your wife, mother and a teacher…Yeh that's it. I will live where we chose to live, of course. What is yours?'

'I do not know the answer as for as work is concerned. I certainly do not wish to work as an accountant for the rest of my life. I want to be with you always… want to earn sufficient money to provide you with a good life,' he said. I just love what he said… it is so nice to hear that he cares for me so much.

We must have walked a mile along the shore, holding hands, until we saw a tree with a little shade. He sat there while I kept walking alongside the bank. I walked a long way away. I wrote both our names in the sand and a few minutes later, a big wave came and washed it away. I was frightened. A debate began to rage in my head.

'You are lying to him by not telling him where you live.'

'No,' the other voice in my head spoke up. 'I'm not lying, I just haven't told him yet.'

'Waiting for the right moment, are we? Why not now?'

'I will tell him. I will not hide it from him.'

'What if someone else tells him first, what then? You will lose your respect and credibility. How can he trust you then?'

'I will not let anything ruin our day today, I will not…'

Another big wave arrived and washed away the little sand castle I had built. 'What if Mittal tells him where I live?' I started sobbing. My whole body was trembling with fear when I ran back to him for comfort.

I was out of breath when I fell helplessly into his lap. I felt so secure here.

'What is the matter? You look frightened… what happened, Nirmal?' He stroked my hair. I felt safe. This was where I belonged.

'Nothing… please do not ask me. Let our hearts do the talking, you'll have your answers then…'

His hands were caressing my face and his fingers ran through my hair. His touch felt divine. There was so much love, affection and warmth in his hands. I felt his warm breath on my neck, the cosy togetherness of our bodies… It had an intoxicating effect on my being. I wanted to behave like Shamim today. I did not care about the world any more. I just wanted him to give me everything right here, right now. I wanted him to feel my burning lips. I wanted us to cross all limits. I wanted to so badly…

I don't know when we fell asleep. One thing I do know is that when I woke up, I found my hand firmly and securely in his. I wished time had stopped for us.

'Time never stops, my love. We need to make a move now,' he said, and we came back to earth.

We did not want to leave but reluctantly made our way back, hand in hand.

After lunch, we made our way to Natraj Cinema, where we were going to watch a movie. As soon as we were seated in the hall, he held my hand and I leaned against his shoulder. It felt heavenly. I generally get very emotionally attached to films, but this one was special. Both of us are great fans of Asha Parekh, the heroine of this movie, who is treated very badly by her villainous husband. She has been forced to marry him instead of the man she really loves.

The film has a very sad ending, in which both the hero and heroine die. I cried, and he held me in his arms. Suddenly, our lips were touching. For a moment or two, we were in seventh heaven, oblivious to anyone looking at us. We kissed...

Then it was time to go to the auto stand. My turn came and I sat down in one. The driver probably asked me where I wanted to go but I couldn't remember telling him...

Everything went so quiet. 'Please,' I wanted to tell Sardar, 'do not let me go... please...' My cries touched the sky but never reached him. I had hoped he would stop me, but he didn't. I do not know why. Though my body came home, my mind stayed behind with him.

Shamim was waiting for me in my room and her first question was, 'Did you do it?' I answered 'Yes'. She asked me many questions and I believe I made up some of the answers just to keep her happy. This most certainly had been the best day of my life. I went to sleep feeling fulfilled with love, affection and warmth.

It has taken me two days to write this entry. I enjoyed every moment of reliving it. I have read it so many times... this is how the journey of my love begins.

WEDNESDAY, JULY 2ND 1969

I have taken a few days off from work. This morning, I told Sabah that I would not be working for Mittal any longer. So we went for an interview for the position of trainee managers in a clothes shop in Connaught Place and to our surprise, we both got the job! We will start in three weeks' time.

FRIDAY,, JULY 4TH 1969

Hurray! Today is our last day with Mittal. We are going to resign. He came to the factory around midday. We requested a meeting with him.

After about an hour, he summoned me alone to his office and waved me towards a chair without looking at me. I sat down reluctantly.

'Yes, what's your problem?' He barked at me.

'Sabah and I are resigning and won't be coming to work from tomorrow. Thank you very much for giving us the job. We are owed two months' salary so it would be wonderful if you clear our account as well.' I said it all in one breath. As I tried to get up, he came around and stood in front of me and put both his hands on my shoulders. I jumped from my chair, very angry at his behaviour. He held my arm and tried to pull me towards him. I tried to get my hands free and pushed him back with force.

'How dare you touch me…?' I shouted. He started swearing at me and tried to slap me. But I'm no longer a weak helpless woman who can be pushed around by this little man. I have become the true 'Jatti of Punjab'. I slapped him with so much force that he fell and his face hit the corner of the table. His nose started bleeding. We were both shouting at each other when other workers came rushing in and saved him from me.

I went out of the office shouting, 'Bastard wants to buy me… what about the wedded one sitting in his house?' Sabah walked in with Simon Sahib who took control of the situation and asked Mittal, 'You want me to call the police? You will be put away for a few years for messing with the girls. Is that what you want?'

Mittal saw his folly and paid all our dues. We walked out of the factory for good.

When I got back home, Mittal's words, 'I *will buy you*' kept ringing in my ears. Had Ammi Jaan made a deal with him about me? I consoled myself, telling myself that he was lying.

SATURDAY, JULY 12TH 1969

Today, I have decided to spend the day with Shamim. There is a rumour going around in the house that Sabah has been sold to a rich seth. He is said to be between 35 to 40 years old, and a widower. His wife left a six-year-old daughter behind, so Sabah will become a mother right away. Most of the girls are bought, but this Seth is needy and will conduct a proper marriage once he test-drives her and finds her to his liking. You wouldn't buy a car without driving it first or would you? The only difference here is that in this case virginity the real value is at stake.

I'm disgusted with all this and with Sabah too. But why am I getting so worked up? It is a brothel after all. They don't sell spare parts, they sell the whole body in this house.

It is always fun to spend time with Shamim. She is not keen on going to shops for no reason. We normally sit in the park, eat a lot and gossip – yep, that is our perfect day.

'What happened on the date, Punjaban?' she asked with a smirk.

'Oh, he held my hand without hesitation,' I said.

'And? After holding hands…?'

'Well, I sat very close to him and he touched my hair and said very beautiful things.'

'I really don't know what you two are made of. Nothing happens between you. If it were Yousef and me, we would have done it on the sand bank. Ooo…it would've been lovely. You two are boring farts…' She took a breath and asked me, 'Why did you not go back to his room? You had an excuse--getting the suitcase.'

I very much wanted to go further that day. My whole body was burning with desire but we did not do anything. He said *Nirmal* means "pure, untouched, a virgin". I will stay Nirmal till our first night together as a married couple.'

As I lay in bed, this conversation kept playing in my mind. I wonder what Sardar will want to call me after we get married:

Nirmal or Sharnjit? But the cards need to be printed in the name of Sharnjit. But he loves the name Nirmal. Where would we live, in Punjab or Delhi? I would like to live with his parents, they need someone to look after them. Well! When you have so much land why work for others for a pitiful sum of money. No, I will not be a housewife like my mum was. I must share my knowledge with others. I will be a teacher!

SUNDAY, JULY 13TH 1969.

My happy dreams have turned into a real nightmare. I'm having difficulty writing this in my diary. I feel very upset. I think my diary has become a very good companion. I feel as though, by writing, I'm getting things off my chest, and might even find a solution to my problems.

I went out this morning for few hours – I had few urgent things to sort out before I join my new job. When I got home, everything seemed to have turned upside down. It would've been nice if I'd shifted to another room, but it is too late now. Mittal was at our house with Ammi Jaan for a couple of hours, probably trying to buy me from her. He's a real bastard. I thought it would be sufficient for him to learn a lesson. But no, he is waiting for revenge.

Sardar Parkash has gone to Punjab to see his parents. Even if he were here, I couldn't have involved him in my mess.

When I stepped into my room, Shamim was already there, looking very worried. She put her arms around me and started sobbing. I'd never seen her this way.

'Nirmal, it has all gone wrong here, very wrong… just get out of here, if you can.'

MONDAY, JULY 14TH 1969 AT 9.40 AM
NEW DELHI RAILWAY STATION

I've said goodbye to Delhi forever and my train is moving towards Punjab. What happened yesterday keeps playing before my eyes: Ammi Jaan entering our room without knocking. Shamim and I sitting on my bed, worrying about what is happening around us.

'Nirmal, Mittal came see me yesterday. He was telling me that you had a wage dispute with him. You shouldn't fight with him on such trivial matters. He's a nice and well to do businessman. I'm sure he will keep you happy,' Ammi Jaan said.

Shamim tried to distract Ammi Jaan and said, 'Ammi Jaan, how much is Mittal paying for Nirmal?'

'Oh… we've agreed on twenty-five thousand, and he has even paid two thousand as deposit. He will do a proper wedding with her. He really loves Nirmal. She's very lucky girl.'

I stayed out all day, just wandering aimlessly. Shamim didn't go out and was in house all day. She reported what had happened.

'You must get out of here without delay. You don't have time. That bitch is not going to leave you alone,' she said.

'But I'm just her lodger, not her girl for sale. I haven't come here to be traded like a cow. I'm not living in the jungle, and there are laws and rules. I'll go to the police,' I said.

'What they are going to do? They are all bent. Most of them are on her payroll. Who is going to listen to you?'

I'm a brave person generally and can take a lot but today I was unable to control my emotions and I started sobbing uncontrollably like a child. *'I have not come here to be sold by this bitch…* if I had known earlier…' I keep on repeating this to myself. It was my own folly.

'You have no idea what Sabah might have said to Ammi Jaan to get you the room. Anyway, it doesn't matter now, that woman is only interested in money – by hook or crook she would've got her way. She is a Twaif after all.'

'I won't be able to see Sardar Parkash; he has run to Punjab, now that I need him so desperately.' I cried.

'Listen, Nirmal, we don't have much time for thinking. We must face this with courage. The very first thing we need to do is to keep control over our emotions and make sure no one else gets wind of what we are doing. If her dogs find out, they will tear you apart. '

'I'm worried about you too, Shamim. She knows we are close. She is definitely going to interrogate you. I can't get you in trouble.'

'Don't worry about me… and don't tell me where you are going either. If I don't know, then I can't tell, can I? Anyway I have Yusuf and his gangster brothers to look after me.'

I looked out of the train window just now. A thought entered my head, and I started sobbing uncontrollably. An old woman sitting opposite me asked, 'Have you parted with someone very close?'

I nodded and my crying became even louder. She put her hands on mine. 'You will be with him soon, just trust God,' she said. Someone gave me a glass of water.

But if I were to go back to Delhi, Ammi Jaan would get to know. She must have found out everything about Sardar Parkash from Mittal, including where he lives. But does Mittal know where he lives…? I cannot take the chance. I cannot put Sardar Parkash in harm's way… no, I can't. And how is he going to find me? He does not know, no one knows my village address because I haven't given it to anyone and even Nirmal is not my real name. Oh God! What should I do?

Our train halted at Ambala Cant and I got two cups of hot tea – one for me and one for the old woman. She just looks at me with graciousness and warmth in her eyes and did not say anything. Perhaps she'd loved someone the same mad way as I love Sardar Parkash… and knows the deep hurt parting causes.

PART FIVE

5.1

—/\/\/—

BACK TO SQUARE ONE...

I have arrived in my village and it looks so different. Even my mother's attitude seems to have changed. She met me with new enthusiasm this time. I've learnt that our village has made a lot of progress in the past two years – a library has been built in the Panchayat Ghar. A wooden bridge has been erected for the schoolchildren so that can get school even during heavy rains. Our Panchayat Ghar also has radio given by the Soviet Union as a goodwill gesture and the elders of the village gather there every evening to listen to programmes on agriculture, news and folk music. There is also a new sewing school for the ladies and above all, there is a hope that our primary school will soon become a middle school. All these achievements are because of Bibi Ji – my Mum--and I feel very happy and proud of her. Jeeti has told me all this with pride in her voice.

A MONTH LATER...

It has been a month since I left Delhi. I miss Sardar Parkash a lot. I cannot think of a way to get in touch with him. I feel that it will be best if I can tell him everything of myself. He will get annoyed and has the right to do so because I've kept so many secrets from him. I will apologise wholeheartedly. He has a big heart and I'm confident that he'll understand and forgive me. I can't afford to lose him and I can't imagine life without him. All the promises and programmes we made keep coming back to me.

I cannot go back to Delhi yet. It is too soon. When I think of Delhi, I see a big mad dog running towards me and biting me around the neck and another one biting into my virgin body. Everything and all the purity that I managed to keep safe will go to waste. I start shivering with fear and anguish.

5.2

AS A SCHOOL TEACHER...

MONDAY, SEPTEMBER 1ST 1969

Mum's political influence has made some difference and I now have a job as an English teacher in the middle school in a nearby village. I'm more than qualified for the job but it will do for the time being. It is keeping my mind occupied at least. Trying to resolve small problems for students reminds of my own school days. Me and my co-teacher, Saroj, have become good friends. We talk a lot and have a lot in common as well.

Mum holds a darbar every day and people come to her with their problems. She routinely asks everyone, *'How are you today?'* without even looking at them. I believe that if I was dead she would still ask me, 'How are you today?' This phrase has become so impersonal that it has lost its true meaning, for me at least.

I've told Saroj about Sardar Parkash. Apart from why I left, I've told her everything. She's a very sympathetic person and cares for me a lot.

I'm so desperate to see Sardar Parkash. He's been on my mind a lot. I miss him so much that I do not have the words to express it. It is easy to get to Delhi by train but then where would I stay? I've never stayed in a hotel before. It's not safe for a young woman to stay alone in a cheap hotel. I can't afford the more expensive ones. Even Gurdwaras aren't keen to give a young girl sanctuary.

He often goes away on business for a few days. Saroj suggests that if I go to Delhi, I should take Santokh with me. I'm sure he won't refuse me. In fact, he'll do everything to facilitate my meeting with Sardar Parkash. Why did I not think of this before?

Santokh is also capable of pacifying Sardar if he gets annoyed with me. Sardar Parkash respects him a lot. Saroj has promised to go with me to their village and to Delhi if need be. I feel a new hope rise within me.

***

Following words in italic are mine (Parkash's).

"I found that she'd not written in the diary for a long time and most of the pages are blank. However, I found another three pages folded neatly between the dates November 14 and 15th. On the page, 14 November is written, then crossed out. They have been torn from a different note pad and I can see that they are folded in such a way that shows they may have been in an envelope. Whether November 14 or 15 has any significance, I do not know. It's also difficult to figure out whether she wanted these pages included in her book.

After reading them, my whole being has been shaken. I am ashamed at my weakness and inability to help her, of not being there when she needed me most. She had been fighting single handedly with the man-dominated world and she never gave up.

It has been very difficult for me to decide whether I was wise to include these pages. I have not written a single word for the past two months. In fact, this has been a torturous decision. I wondered if I should not write this book after all, but I figured that if she did not want them to be included, she would not have given them to me.

So here they are, with no amendment from me."

5.3

SO... HERE IT IS...

AROUND FRIDAY, 14TH NOVEMBER

There is a lot happening in our village today. People are dressed up as it is the anniversary of the death of Sarpanch's mother and the whole village is invited to the memorial. There is *Akhand Path* at the Gurdwara for the departed soul and langer food for everyone. The Sarpanch is also using this opportunity to woo his supporters.

I need to go to the service as well, otherwise Bibi Ji will be angry. The truth is, I have no interest in Sarpanch or his show business. But because it is my *Dadi Ji's* function, I need to help with the Langer. Harnek is also here. He keeps staring at me and it reminds me of Mittal. They have the same lustful stare. He is my brother, for God's sake!

LATER...

Some time ago, Harnek was passing by me and deliberately pressed against my bust. His breath smelled of alcohol. I can't believe he would be drunk in a Gurudwara. What's wrong with him? I thought it best to sneak out of the Gurdwara and go to my room.

I've been feeling suffocated and have developed a headache as well, so I opened all the windows as soon I reached my room in the haveli. Harnek probably saw me leaving the Gurdwara and sneakily followed me to my room. I was standing next to the window, looking at the green fields when he came from behind and grabbed hold of my breast. I tried my best to get away from him, I shouted but there was no one there to hear my cries.

'What are you doing, Harnek? Get off me! I'm your sister! I tie a rakhi on your wrist every year!'

'Shut up…you are not my sister!' He held me even tighter and threw me on the bed.

I couldn't free myself as he was much stronger than me. I begged him once again, 'Please let me go. You are my own brother. Please, I won't tell Tayee Ji… I promise …look, you are drunk! Please, let me go!'

But he spoke right over my please. 'I'm not going to let you go …not today…I'm going to take revenge – your mother hasn't done any less …bitch …bitch …bitch…'

I was doing everything I could to get free but was not succeeding. He slapped my face very hard and my ears started to hurt. 'Please, let me go…'

I saw someone else enter the room. He had covered his face, so I couldn't recognise him. One of them now held my arms while the other sat on my legs. A strange stink entered my nostrils and I don't know what happened next.

My brain seemed to have frozen. I was trying to feel myself with my hands. My whole body was aching and I felt as if all my energy had been sapped. My clothes had been ripped and I was completely naked. My breast had teeth marks, as though I had been bitten by a dog. My private parts were burning. My privacy, dignity, self-respect, everything has been ripped apart. The unthinkable had happened.

What a luck!, I managed to keep myself safe and 'Nirmal' at the Twaif's Kotha but in my own village, in my own room and from my own brother – could not keep safe… lost the most precious thing a woman has – my virginity.

Nothing seems real any more… nothing.

On seeing fresh blood on the white sheet and her very naked daughter, it would not have taken long for my mother to guess what had happened. Sarpanch walked in behind her and began to swear. Then he ran out.

Nothing has sunk in yet. It all feels so unreal. I can't see or hear anyone anymore. I'm not crying either… no tears are coming out. I've either run out of them or they've been frozen. Crying is not going help me.

Sarpanch entered and dragged the dog in with him. He carried on with the drama of slapping him, calling him every name under the sun. He took his shoe and pretended to hit him. When I looked up, all I saw was a face infested with maggots. I felt the stink coming towards me and probably fainted again.

Mum has cried and screamed, but now she has put on her practical hat.

'We have no alternative but to get them married now,' she said.

'Have you gone mad, Bibi Ji? If the opposition finds out, all our political ambition will be dead and buried forever. The newspapers will have a field day. They are brother and sister!'

'Your beloved son has ruined Sharn's life. Now he has to pay for it. I think we should take them somewhere else, get them married and send them away to another country. No one will ever know.'

'People will find out sooner or later. That will be political suicide. I'm dreaming of becoming the Block Chairman.'

They both went on for a while, thinking of their careers, how best they could limit the damage. What was best for them politically? I was completely forgotten and the dog escaped.

An announcement has been made: 'Let us bury this as nothing has happened. Thank God the servants are not here. It is only the four of us who know. It is best keep quiet until we find a solution. Children do make mistakes, it's for the elders to sort them out,' Sarpanch said to Bibi Ji.

A silent cry asks, *'what is my mistake Sarpanch Sahib…? Is it that I grew up in this village and I am your brother's daughter? Is growing up a sin? My brother… my cousin brother who was supposed to look after me, rapes me… destroy my dignity. Is that my fault, Bibi Ji and Sarpanch Sahib? Is it my fault that my own mother is more worried about her own political career than her daughter's life? Sarpanch Sahib, only woman loses out, it makes no difference what so ever to the man. He, in fact, has one more medal up his arc. I am the one who has become second hand… used Sarpanch Sahib… USED. Man can go to a different woman every day it will make no difference. A used woman loses her value straight away. All men desire virgin."*

They both suddenly remembered that I was still there. Sarpanch shouted, 'I'll take of care of that bastard Harnek…you get Sharnjit washed and dressed properly as though nothing has happened. Give me these soiled clothes, it is best to burn them.'

'Listen Bibi Ji, Jagir Singh has just returned from England. I think he's come to get married. He is the one who bought your old house.'

Suddenly Bibi Ji also perked up. 'He has got some land as well. He will be good for our Sharnjit…she'll be happy to go abroad.'

'Let's finish with Mother's Anniversary first. You leave it to me…I'll invite him one evening in the next few days and we'll discuss it with him. All NRIs are fond of meat and drink, so I'll get some English Scotch, chicken and some other meat. He's going to be okay, you look after Sharn,' he walks off as if nothing has happened, what's all this fuss about.

LATEST NEWS:

There have been a few deaths at the haveli.

One: Nirmal died today.

Two: My mother must have felt her daughter's pain and is

probably heart broken, but she is a political leader and must sweep these things under the carpet. Votes, bhai, votes!

My mother died today.

Three: My cousin, on whose wrist I've been tying rakhi for years and who was supposed to look after my honour, has taken away my dignity.

My cousin died today.

Four: My Taya Ji, my dad's elder brother, who calls me his own beti and says he loves me so much, is worried about his political career. This is nothing – children do make mistakes.

My Taya Ji died today.

Five: I had many dreams…dreams of spending my life with the one I loved so much, my Sardar Parkash.

A dream died today.

Six: He was not there when I needed him most. What is God…?

My faith died today.

God died today.

***

("There are no more entries. Nirmal stopped writing her diary a while ago. Whatever she wrote after this was on loose pages. There are no dates or numbers on them. I've tried to piece the story together after looking at the events. Another thought that keeps coming into my mind is that she wanted to publish her story. Most of her writing resembles a novel. It has taken me over twenty years to pluck up my courage and face her words. I am heartbroken after reading this. But her story must go on.")

5.4

ENGAGEMENT... HOORAY!

Mr NRI has been invited and they're really going over the top to look after him. Sarpanch does not wait long, so he got right into it and asked, 'Jagir Singh, I understand that you've decided to get married. Now you have everything but a wife, and we happen to be looking for someone for our Sharn. She's just finished her degree from Delhi University. Top class marks, Ji. We think you're the most suitable person for her.' After the opening speech, he was waiting for the response from our guest and poured a bit more whiskey in his glass.

'Sarpanch Sahib, how can I refuse you... whatever you say is Ow-rat (all right)...but let me have a little look at the girl.'

'Bibi Ji, ask Sharnjit to bring us some water.' Bibi Ji understood the message.

What good luck I had. I'd been raped just two days ago and today a suitable boy (or a middle-aged man, rather) had been found for me. No one is asking me how I feel. I'm supposed say nothing, get married and be whisked away to a foreign country. My opinion doesn't matter anymore.

Mr NRI stared at me as if he had seen a ghost or could not believe his luck and said, 'Ow-rat, Ow-rat'. In addition, he put an extra size bite of chicken in his mouth. He has a strange way of eating. He puts the whole drumstick in his mouth, takes a bite, brings it out, and repeats it until only the bare bone is left. It looks bad, but he does have a British passport.

The deal has been struck and the big burden that was hanging over Bibi Ji's head has been taken away. I will be someone else's responsibility now, and far away too.

I'm having difficulty sleeping these days. I've been put in the same room where the deed was done…there is no other room available so I have to put up with it. It was nothing anyway – just a small mistake done by children. It will happen to someone else again. It will be swept under the carpet in a hush-hush manner. In this proud, male dominated country of ours, a woman is treated like a shoe.

Bibi Ji entered my room and showed a lot of affection as she asked, 'What do you think, Sharn? He is a very nice boy…he will look after you like a queen.'

A thirty six year old with oversized belly being called a boy makes me smile.

'Yes, Bibi Ji. But I think Mr Jagir Singh should know what happened to me a few days ago. I will not lie or cheat. If he accepts me as I am, then I have no objection.'

'You don't worry, Sharnjit. Of course, I'll tell him everything. You leave that to me.'

At my insistence, it was decided that Jagir Singh and I would meet again. So there we were, two days later.

'Sharnjit, your Mum said you're very educated, BA pass. But I'm totally not educated. I can speak a little bit. If you work with white people you pick up a little bit of English…Ow-rat eh…?'

'Yes, Ji' I said.

'I have my own house, no mortgage. I think free house first… marriage after. Ow-rat.'

'It's all okay…but has Bibi Ji told you everything about me?' I said hesitatingly.

'Yeh, Yeh…Ow-rat, Ow-rat.' He was smiling without any reason. The meeting was over. A life partner had been chosen. It must be a fashionable to drink so early in the morning, because his breath stank when he said Ow-rat, Ow-rat.

I told Saroj everything, except for the rape. Everything about Ammi Jaan as well.

'Sharnjit, you can't give up so quickly. We must try to find Sardar Parkash,' she said.

'But what can I do? Where would I find him? What would he say when he finds out about me?'

'It may be that he is also trying to find you, but how can he? You haven't given him your address or even your real name. He knows you as Nirmal, doesn't he? If he truly loves you then I'm sure he will understand your predicament. You're such a strong person; I don't know why you're being so negative. Mr NRI is no match for him. You're marrying him because he lives in the UK. He needs an Aunty Ji, not a twenty four year old girl. From what you've said, he sounds more like an uncle than a husband.'

'Saroj, you're right, but I've seen so many failures that I've given up now.'

'No, my darling sis, you have to give it a last try. You won't be able to forgive yourself if you don't.'

How do I tell Saroj that I have nothing left to give? I can't go to Sardar Parkash and say, here's your 'Nirmal'. Used flowers are not presented at the devta's feet. Half-heartedly I've made a plan with Saroj to go to Sardar Parkash's village. Our Head Mistress has written a letter to her peer at his village school to facilitate our visit. Our programme is to see Santokh and ask him to come with us to Delhi. I hope he agrees.

Saroj's Vespa found it a little difficult to cope with the mud roads, but somehow we managed and we met with the Head Mistress of the Sohal Jagir school. She is really looking after us well and at our request has sent some boys to inform Santokh that he has guests waiting for him at the school. He came towards us ten minutes later.

'Oh, hello, Bhabi Ji. How are you? What are you doing here?

We've spent so many days trying to find you. We went everywhere.'
He looked surprised to see us there. 'You didn't tell him your real
name and where you lived. Bhaji went to Delhi to find you but
your friend said you had gone and were not coming back.'.

'I've come to see your brother, where is he?' I said with
helplessness and sorrow in my voice.

'Bhabi Ji, he has gone now.'

'Gone where?'

'Where else? To England. He has gone to England. Only last
week I went to Delhi Airport to see him off. Bhabi Ji, he was
very sad. He'd tears in his eyes. He was so desperate to see you.
It pained him a lot and he kept saying to me, "Nirmal wasn't like
that. Maybe she had no faith in me – in my ability to look after
her."'

*"He kept saying that your Bhabi did not trust me. That she treated
me like a child,"* he said. It is okay. I will write to him – either
come back or call Bhabi Ji to England. Bhabi ji he hasn't gone
to England for money either, he just wanted to get out of here.
I think he ran away from his disappointment, but he'll be back
soon. I know. He promised me. Let's go to my house. We'll have
tea and you can meet your mother in law, our Biji. She is very nice.
She will like you very much. I know that. Let's go.'

'No, Santokh, my brother, we already had tea; we'll come
some other time. Definitely.'

I can't tell Santokh that his Bhabi is no longer Nirmal and
going to wed someone else in few days' time.

We got back home quite late. I have decided to leave myself in
hands of my destiny.

I have spent the whole night awake. I can hear the emptiness
in my head. I feel my solitary anchor has broken and I am now
rudderless and directionless, slapped on the face by waves of
cruelty, pain and sorrow. Wherever I look, I see darkness. My
life has become a bleak house. A single moment in my life has
traumatised me forever. I cannot get over the nightmares. Every

night I see a face infested with maggots…I cry a lot when I'm alone. I get up in the middle of the night and start debating various way of committing suicide. A voice inside me says, *"Do it, there is nothing left for you…no one wants you…even your own mother is doing everything to get rid of you."* Then again, another, calmer voice says, *"Don't be silly, life is precious…it is a severe test of your character, your resilience…you are not the first or the last woman to be raped. It happens every day in India and will continue to happen. You need to fight and begin to live again. What has Sardar Parkash done wrong? What if he could have supported you unconditionally? There is always a ray of hope…there is always light at the end of every tunnel. The only thing that you have to do is to keep going – keep fighting – keep searching for the light."*

My life may have halted for a while but everything else carries on as usual. Routines will continue unabated.

'Please send me to England.'

'But to study further, you need a lot of money and sponsorship. Why don't you get married to Jagir Singh and study while you're there?'

Bibi Ji had a point.

'Have you told him about my past, Bibi Ji? What did he say?'

'Oh, yes…he said, 'Ow-rite'. In western countries, everyone has a relationship before marriage. He is westernized.'

'No, Bibi Ji, that is insulting. There is a vast difference between rape and relationship. And what has happened to that mad dog?'

'Oh, he is very sorry for what he's done. Sarpanch Sahib has given him a real hard time. 'Okay, now tell me what you want to do. Jagir Singh is waiting for your decision.' Bibi Ji said with a slight harshness in her voice.

'As you please.'

'I'm not your enemy, Sharn, I'm your mother.'

' Bibi Ji, whatever you decide is okay with me. It doesn't make any difference to me.'

5.5

ENGLAND...EH, LUCKY ME...

Two weeks have passed and everything has gone with military precision. I've got my passport and am ready to go to England.

As I lay in bed, many thoughts lingered in my mind. One prominent one was that we have such a beautiful country, a cultured nation where so many gurus and mahatmas have been born. So why can't we get rid of the curses that plague us – the mistreatment of women, rape, child labour and bribery?'

I wondered whether I should go to the police and register an FIR, but then I knew that the Indian police is the most corrupt in the world. If a woman were to enter a police station even to register a complaint, it would be a miracle if came out unscathed. Few of them will celebrate an early Diwali at the woman's expense. Moreover, the society will never accept a woman who has ever been to a police station.

Another cancer is the double standard of Indian Man's thinking. Our Constitution provides equal rights for woman but it has not changed the way Indian men think She is treated like a second-class citizen, will remain so to eternity. Man never allows her to be equal whether at home or outside. From the day she is born, the second-class treatment starts. If a boy comes out of the womb, then the news will spread in seconds and so will the celebrations, even if the woman is still in labour but if a girl was born, then it's a failure on the part of the woman who has given birth. Her schooling, growing up and everything will come second to the boys. I'm talking of double standards here – she is worshipped as Mata, Maha-Laxmi or Durga, Deity and so by many other names. A mother is the highest pedestal a woman can reach. Nothing higher than that – not even God. However, if she has the misfortune of getting raped, the blame is entirely hers. Society looks down on her, male gets away scot-free. Now how pathetic is that? There can't be any bigger hypocrisy than that. There can't be any double standard than that. This may be the extreme but even in daily life, her treatment in any field of life needs a lot to be desired. Nothing will change till the Indian Man's mentality is changed especially of those on high echelon.

Above all, it seems like a sin, curse or just sheer bad luck to be a young beautiful woman in India. In buses, trains, walking on roads, in colleges and offices and at every other place, all you see is, men, grown up men staring at you, raping your dignity with their dirty looks. Wherever you go that stare follows you. Single woman alone in her own house is not safe either. If a woman touches a man's bottom, people will call her cheap but what about men who are always busy raping in their thoughts. This is what I call double standard – jumbled up thinking.

To the Male gender of my beloved Country, I respectfully say, *'I fully understand that the steering wheel is in your hands, but a car needs front and back wheel too. So please stop this oppression of one-half of the population.'*

Stop making this noise Sharn, who is going to listen to you. No one is interested in your idealist views. Face the immediate problem. Okay you have got it off your chest...and well said too... now move on ...get ready to face a bit of realism.

5.6

LAWFULLY WEDDED WIFE...

Everything was ready. The Akhand Path for Mr Jagir Singh's father, who had passed away two years ago, had just finished. My wedding ceremony had taken place in my old house which now belonged to my new husband. Most of the village were saying things like, *Bibi Ji was intelligent, we thought, so why marry an educated girl to an illiterate man who is old enough to be her father? Oh, UK passport! That has value. God bless the poor girl* and so on. My husband had been drinking on a daily basis. In fact, he seems to be happy eating and drinking most of the day. A lot of chicken and an unmeasured amount of alcohol is being consumed.

Oh, our honeymoon has been postponed till we're in the UK. That suits me to the tee.

PART SIX

6.1

---∿---

'WELCOME TO UNITED KINGDOM'

HEATHROW – TERMINAL 3 – FLIGHT – AIR INDIA WEDNESDAY, MARCH 4TH 1970

Mr Jagir Singh has been drinking throughout the flight. Now that I am his wife, we've found a novel way of getting the free whiskey twice. I do not drink, but he orders one for me as well. Guess in whose big belly it all ends up?

I'm dressed up almost like a Christmas tree, which is embarrassing in itself, and it does not help that he looks more like my father than my husband. Is it just me or are these Indian people staring at us? There is a vast difference between the two cultures. Indian people stare and ask questions…Westerners seem to have a 'do not care' attitude.

I am in Handsworth, Birmingham in my husband's house – no, in our house. Why do I keep forgetting it? I am now Mrs Singh.

All NRI Punjabi women in this neighbourhood look very similar. They carry out their welcoming ritual of putting a drop or two of incense oil on the doorframe of the front door and putting a tiny bit of sweet in my mouth before I'm allowed in. It's considered good luck for the newlyweds. More than anything, they are surprised at Jagir Singh's luck. How did he manage to get such a beautiful, well-educated young wife? Some of them have called me lucky because I am now in the UK, which is a big thing. People pay a lot of money to get into England by hook or by crook. We have a long relationship of love and hate with this country, since the days of the Raj. I remember my father saying, *It was better under the British, because of the security, discipline and nonexistence of small bribery. Since independence, all these diseases have mushroomed.*

Some say, *Oh, she will definitely take care of his drinking.* Then they burst into uncontrollable laughter. There was a lot of dirty talk about the first night, all done in the name of womanly fun. It seems vulgar and absurd that middle-aged women should talk like that. I feel I am more cultured than they are.

On my first morning as his lawfully wedded wife, Jagir Singh started lecturing me about what to do and what not to do. *"In the morning, I've three sosey (sausages) for breakfast, five sosey in four bread lunchtime; put in container…I take…Ow-rat. Two glass beer in the morning, two lunchtime and two when work finish. Hot work – need cold beer…Ow-rat… don't mind! Ow-rat."*

My dear husband speaks strange English but I'm trying to understand and cooperate with him. Our honeymoon is still pending. Don't get excited. Thank God Shamim is not here to ask me what happened. I don't have to make up stories.

WEDNESDAY, MARCH 11TH 1970

It's been a week since I came to England. I'm bored. There's nothing much to do here. I'm a surprised, how little and cramped houses are here in the UK.

Our house is a three bedroom, terraced house. You judge the size and price of the house by the number of bedrooms. Only a few well to do people have four bedrooms. All rooms including the bedrooms are similar in shape and size in most houses. There is a double bed in the middle of the master bedroom, a chair, a second hand dresser and cheap rickety wardrobe. On top of wardrobe there are two old suitcases which haven't been moved in ages. There is an A4 size framed picture of Jagir Singh when he was a handsome young man, probably in his early twenties, without the beer belly. There are two calendars hanging opposite, one of half-naked white women and the other with more beautiful women scantily dressed.

In the front room (lounge), there is a cheap leather type sofa set and a shining gold colour drinks cabinet with glass door. On top shelf, there are lots of different types of wine and whisky tumblers. Second shelf has small prizes and trophies probably bought from the sale –not won. …Oh and two real medals from some Dart Competition. My Husband has been a dart player at some point in his life. There is also a black and white photograph of him with his parent when he was a young boy. He looks cute there. In the bottom shelf, there are two bottles of Bell Whiskey and one-half finished Captain Morgan Rum bottle.

There's marble fireplace, in the middle of the room, which probably started its life as coal fire, now houses an electric heater with two rods. You only switch one on when you have guests coming if you switch both on at the same time then it may cause overheating and blow the fuse. So… at least one good thing that the electricity in our house is as temperamental as in Punjab. And on the mantelpiece; there's collection of random little porcelain and gold metal items bought from the sales. We do not have a car yet but have little model which children play with on our mantelpiece too. Jagir Singh said he hasn't learnt driving but I can later. One more thing, there a three-year-old calendar of some grocery store with Guru Nanak Ji's photo, hanging in the far corner.

Then there is of course a tiny kitchen, enough you can swing a cat but no bigger. Three wall hung units full of unused utensils etc. and a white cooker – I say white because that is how it started its life, now looks more rusty black. It hasn't been cleaned for some time and I think it has seen better days. I've spent a whole day trying to clean it but some of the burnt food mixed with rust is refusing to shift.

My husband and I hardly see each other. He leaves for work at six in the morning as his shifts starts at seven. I have learned to cook eight sausages very quickly and six slices of bread. I leave them in the kitchen and go back to sleep. At night, he comes home late because he goes directly to the pub and stays there till closing time, which I believe is 11 pm. He comes home and drinks again before going to bed on his own in the spare room.

Mr Jagir Singh's lifestyle is amazing. Is he the dirtiest man ever or do all Punjabi NRIs live this way, I wonder? He works five and half days a week, washes only his hands and face on a daily basis, has a bath once a week and wears the same clothes to work every day– an oversized grey-brown jumper, a dark brown cap, a black anorak and large shoulder bag. He drinks every day. He stinks of coal from the foundry he works in. I do not know why he got married, and am dreading the moment we consummate our marriage.

I have already realised that marrying Jagir Singh was the biggest mistake of my life. This was the first time I allowed others to decide what happens to me. We have nothing in common. He swears and abuses me a lot. I wonder if it makes him feel manly.

The only reason I agreed to come here was the knowledge that I would be in the same country, breathing the same air as Sardar Parkash. But maybe I am clutching desperately at straws here.

It is not Jagir Singh's fault. He is what he is. For him eating massive quantities of lamb, drinking lots of whiskey and beer and swearing is his way of life.

There is a big challenge in front of me. How do I change him even slightly regarding his personal hygiene and his drinking habits? I will beg if he can come home a little earlier even once or twice in a week and have to make a mental adjustment too that whatever he is, he is my husband and I've to do my wife's duty in the bed. I will… I will try my very best. The biggest problem is his hygiene. He is not a baby, I can't put him under the tap.

6.2

—*w*—

HONEYMOON...

SATURDAY, MARCH 14TH 1970

Yes, it is a Saturday, but a couple of Jagir Singh's friends has decided to drop in uninvited. I say uninvited because Mr Jagir Singh only issued the order in the morning, saying that there are two chickens in the fridge – make one dry and one with gravy dish and put extra chillies in both, otherwise people tend to eat too much. Oh, I also received instructions to use washing powder sparingly as it is very expensive.

What a stupid day. Friends and their wives and truckload of kids have come too. The women were helping me in the kitchen but their dirty talk annoyed me. They kept asking me questions about our time in the bedroom. When I told them nothing had happened yet, they thought I was lying. Then the same stupid questions started up again and again.

One man had too much to drink, and vomited in the garden. The mess is visible from the kitchen window. In Jagir Singh's words, 'Fuckin bastard'. This is the life Asian people lead here, which surprises me.

FINALLY... HONEYMOON TIME.

I feel that I'm not doing my duty as his wife, so have to face the situation. The time for the honeymoon has finally arrived. I asked him in the nicest manner to come home early and not drink in the pub. I planned to cook his favourite Bhuna meat and let him have a little drink here at home. He plans to come home by ten.

When he came home, he tried to get me to drink with him. He grabbed hold of my hand, pulled me towards himself. He tried to put his whiskey glass to my lips. I managed to get free and said apologetically, 'I'm sorry, I don't drink.'

'Bitch'…he said while he poured a little bit more in his glass. 'Bitch…fuckin' bitch.'

He'd one too many and knocked off completely. He fell asleep on the sofa, and snored while I threw an old blanket over him.

The honeymoon is cancelled. I went back to my bed and slept like a log.

TUESDAY, MARCH 17ᵀᴴ 1970

I was in the garden, trying to hang clothes on the line when the neighbour wished me good morning. I was a little surprised to hear a cultured voice. It was my neighbour's daughter. Her name is Surinder, or Sandy for the English. She came around to or house and an instant friendship was formed between us. She is such a nice person, well educated, well spoken and beautiful – she is just about my age. We have a lot in common. It will be easy to pass the time as I can go out to shops with her and don't have to rely on my husband.

SECOND, ATTEMPT…
SATURDAY, MARCH 21ˢᵀ 1970

Frankly, I'm so fed up with life that I am trying to find some comfort by laughing at myself. So here, we go…

He came home early, around eleven o'clock. He seemed to

have controlled his drinking. I served him food and sat with him for a while. He was quite nice to me and didn't shout or say any swear words. Maybe he was not that drunk yet.

He came to my room with a bottle of whiskey in his hand. He took off his clothes and stood naked before me. Oh, he is so ugly; his belly hangs down like a pregnant woman's. He has hair all over his body like a bear and he stinks like a toilet. God! I did not know what to do. I kept telling myself, *Be brave Sharnjit, you have to keep calm, you have to cope. You are his wife after all.*

Now the real him returned with another sip of whiskey and the swearing started. "Joo bitch, have drink...joo fucking bitch, take cloth off."

He had probably gone blind too, since I'd taken my clothes off and was in bed. He jumped into bed. The foreplay had begun. His hands were like sandpaper. He ran them all over my body, squeezing me with all his strength. What Goddamn enjoyment did he find in hurting a woman? I was doing my best to cooperate. What else could I do?

He swore again and again until he completely passed out. I had the strength to drag him to his bed where he lay face down and snored.

I was stinking, so I took a hot shower. So ended my second honeymoon night.

MONDAY, MARCH 23ᴿᴰ 1970

Today I found out he has a sister. I got her telephone number from the address book and called her for courtesy's sake. She lives in Telford.

'Hello, Sister Ji, I am Sharnjit, your brother's wife, your Bhabi.' I started the conversation politely.

'Oh, has Jagiri got another one. Have you both got married?'

'We got properly married in a Gurdwara in India.'

'The first one only lasted two months. She ran away with jewellery and all his money.'

'Sorry, I called you,' I said and put the phone down. So he was married before. Why did she run away? Oh, I know why she left. A woman can live in extreme poverty with a loving husband but she cannot live with an impotent man.

One good that has happened is that Sandy and her mother have become good friends of mine, and they look after me. Sandy and I talk a lot. She is in her final year of graduation. She is finding it difficult to decide whether she wants to study further or take up a job. One decision she has taken that she will not get married for another two or three years, although her mother has started to look for a suitable boy. I have asked her to speak only in English with me. As a result, my English has improved so much and I am losing my Indian accent.

Time is passing quickly, days are turning into weeks. My husband and I have tried two or three times to enter into proper married life, but each time he has been confronted by a big failure. The only thing that has changed is that he now blames me for his impotence. He says that I do not excite him and he may be right. I am not an expert in seduction. I have no clue how to make love. He ends up calling me bitch, lies face down, and snores.

I have tried so hard to please him, even taking a sip of whiskey that burned my throat as it went down. His problem is that he is never sober. How do they allow him to work in the foundry? There must be some health and safety laws.

A BOMBSHELL...
FRIDAY, APRIL 3RD 1970

It has been four weeks since I came to England. I do not feel well these days, and constantly have headaches and a sense of nausea. Sandy has registered me with her doctor. They've done so many tests on me. Blood test, urine test, blood pressure, this test, that test. In India, they don't do that many tests even if a patient is dying. Finally, the doctor shook my head and said, 'Congratulations, Mrs. Singh! You're pregnant.'

'Pregnant? What?' I shook my head in disbelief.

'Yes, you are pregnant.'

'Thank you, doctor,' is all I could muster. Sandy was very happy for me and kept hugging and kissing me. 'Beautiful, my Bhabi ji is pregnant!' I asked her to keep it a secret for now.

We got home and I went straight to bed. Questions kept pelting through my mind. What can I do? If Jagir Singh had some life in him, I might have managed. Our marriage has not been consummated, which means I am in a real trouble. I won't be able to hide my condition much longer and it may be too late for abortion. At the mere mention of abortion, my whole body shivers.

What is wrong with me? Why don't I trust my friends? Why don't I open up to them as they do to me? Sandy has told me everything about herself, even about her love life. However, here I am with a million secrets hidden first from Sardar Parkash and now my best friend.

I have little choice left but to tell Jagir Singh about the pregnancy and wait for his reaction. Alternatively, I could try to consummate our marriage. However, even if that were to happen, he may still know that child is not his. I am stuck. No man will accept someone else's child, especially one conceived from rape. Additionally, when can I speak to him? He is always drunk!

6.3

MOUNT EVEREST ...
THE FINAL ATTEMPT

SATURDAY, APRIL 4TH 1970

This Saturday, history repeated itself. I pleaded with him not to drink and to come home early, tried to be extra nice to him and told him I would try sip of whiskey with lots of water in it. This seemed to have worked for a while. He saw it as a triumph and that made him happy. I left him downstairs as he takes ages to finish his food. To my surprise, he took all his clothes off and jumped into my bed the moment he came upstairs. I tried everything he asked me to do but he was trying to fire a gun with bent nozzle. There is no life left in him. I couldn't do anything, and it's all a big disappointment once again. I tried to make it out to be my fault, but he got angry and swore at me as usual. He called me bitch countless times. I'm truly fed up now. I think I'm going to blow up but I understand that I'm the guilty party here. It's not his problem, it's mine. I actually feel sorry for him.

NEXT DAY... WE ARE PREGNANT ...

Yep... we are pregnant. Although our marriage is not consummated yet, we are pregnant. These days I feel rotten with morning sickness. If this is how pregnancies are than I don't want one. I feel so tired and dizzy all the time. I have completely lost my appetite.

I've taken the boldest of decisions to tell him tonight. Therefore, I told him to come home early and not drink excessively, I have something very important to discuss with you and it cannot wait,' I said.

But there is some good news too. Sandy and I have gotten jobs in a private school as assistant teachers. We will start in two weeks with a month's training and will be paid a very good salary from the very first day.

SATURDAY, APRIL 11TH

He came home drunk at eleven o'clock, despite my request. I did not try for any niceties and said to him, 'Jagir Singh, please sit down and listen. I went to see my doctor last week and he told me that I'm pregnant.'

'Joo What…? Fuckin' bitch, what joo say… pregnant… whose… not mine …whose baby… fuckin' bitch.'

'Bibi Ji told you everything about the rape. And you said, "Ow rat".'

'Don't remember… I drunk… don't remember… joo fuckin bitch… get out… my house… now.'

'Where can I go, please…? I have no one here…and stop calling me bitch.' I pleaded. I went back to my bedroom but he came after me shouting 'Joo bitch…Joo fuckin bitch'. He slapped me very hard and then took his belt out and started to beat me with it. Something was triggered inside me. 'I will not take this anymore!' I screamed and snatched his belt, pushed him onto the bed and beat him with his own belt. He was crying and I kept hitting him until he begged me to stop. His drunkenness had disappeared by now. I told him my conditions:

'You and I are finished. You have married me under false pretences. You didn't tell me you were married before and it didn't last even two months, or that you were impotent. Therefore, you have to agree to a divorce with immediate effect.

'I will stay in this house until I find myself alternative accommodation.

'If you swear at me ever again I will beat you with the same belt or I'll cut your tongue up into small pieces.

'We can live as friends, if you wish. I will still do the cooking, and all the other housework for you. If you agree, tell me right now.'

He wept and said he was sorry. I helped him stand on his feet and said, 'Let us find a solution together.'

6.4

SEPARATE WAYS...

Things have improved massively at home. However, I am feeling rotten for having behaved the way I did. It was completely out of character for me, but I also know that if I hadn't stood up to Jagir Singh, the violence would have continued because he got a kick from swearing and hitting me. Two wrongs do not make right, though. My behaviour was not lady-like.

I can also see that Bibi Ji and Sarpanch used his weakness as tool to get rid of me. They saw me as problem for their political careers. Jagir remembers no discussion of the rape, but Bibi Ji said that she told him. I don't know who to trust.

He also recognises his folly of marrying me when he knew that he was incapable of making love – the basic requirement of a marriage.

My health is not good and crying doesn't help. I feel very alone and lost in a foreign country with very little money. I have borrowed some from Sandy and promised Jagir Singh that I will pay him back for my airfare when I have money. The entire expenditure for the wedding was borne by Bibi Ji anyway.

I keep on thinking about my pregnancy, and now I've told Sandy everything about the rape too. I did not tell her that the culprit was my cousin, though. She has become even more sympathetic. I am now worried about what is happening inside me. Should I abort or not? This is the question knocking in my mind. So there I was, sitting with Sandy in the reception room of a Councillor/Advisor, Liz Worthing.

I went into a plush looking office and Liz introduced herself with a smile.

'Your friend has told me about you and your situation. You can tell me a lot more about yourself. Please do not hesitate, I'm your friend and here to help you as much I can.'

I could not tell her about the rape. I feel ashamed. I'd made up a story about my husband not wanting this baby. She did not believe me. Sandy had told her differently.

We spoke for an hour and Liz now knows almost everything about me. Her approach is very gentle. She allowed me to talk freely and did not lead me on with questions. She said, 'Mrs Singh, I can only put the available options before you, but I cannot decide for you. You must make your own decisions. We've established that you will not live with your husband but instead have decided to be a single mother. There are many single mothers in our country and there's a support network that I can arrange for you. You will also get help from the government. I'm a single mother myself and proud of it.'

She then took a deep breath and became professional again. 'As far as termination is concerned, it probably is too late. It is dangerous to abort now and doctors will be very reluctant unless there is a medical need to do so, something that poses a threat to you or your baby.'

This was the first time the foetus had been called my baby, and it had the desired effect. I would carry on with my pregnancy, come what may. Life had thrown me a new challenge.

My biggest problem was going be my mental state. How was I going to cope with the thought that this was the child of the person I loathed the most, and not someone I truly loved? It would be a constant reminder of what had happened. But then I realized that a drop of semen did not make someone a father---there is so much more to it than that.

6.5

New Pastures...

So much has changed in two months. I have said my final goodbyes to Jagir Singh. I have rented a small room in a friendly house and I have a job I like. My pay is good but I have also started to hold private tuitions, which pay me even better. My colleagues are very friendly and helpful. I feel that this is a country where people are very nice, honest and helpful overall, especially the middle and the educated class. Because I am pregnant, they take extra care of me. The headmaster told me that I could take work home because I am assistant and not a full-fledged teacher yet. I've not taken a day off though and am working very hard.

I very much want to see Sardar Parkash but at the same time, I've resigned myself to the fact that I may never see him again. I sometimes wonder what would happen if I were to suddenly meet him, what I would say. I know I cannot turn the clock back. There is one thing though: whenever his name comes to mind, a whiff of the same fresh air we breathed together and the warmth of his hands surrounds me. I feel so cosy and comfortable. I feel as if I'm with him. That will keep me going throughout my life.

I've written to Santokh and asked for his address. It was a mad moment. Now I've posted the letter and I keep wondering if I should have done it. I've no right to upset his life.

6.6

SIX YEARS LATER...

Sandy and I both work in the same school. She has lost her first love and understands the pain and says, 'It hurts'. Something inside me says silently, *It really hurts.*

I've been living in Birmingham for a long time. We have celebrated the fifth birthday of my darling daughter, Simran. She is brilliant girl and cute too. She talks a lot – I call her chatterbox. I earn a lot more than I need so I have bought a freehold house for myself.

Either Santokh has not received my letter or the reply has gone astray. In any case, I could not trace Sardar Parkash. I remember him almost on a daily basis. He is always with me in my thoughts. When I left for the UK, I thought I would find him, but now I know how impossible it is to trace someone without an address. He must be married by now. Would he still recognise me if he saw me?

Sandy has just gotten married to a very good-looking doctor. He is based in Harlow near London so she told me, 'Look, I've to be where my husband is, but I can't live so far away from you. You've to shift to London. You always said that you wanted to live in London – the cultural centre of England. Here's your chance.'

She said it in such a way that I couldn't refuse.

I've bought a house in Harlow as well and luckily, we both have found new, better-paid jobs in the same school. I've joined as deputy head for much better pay. This is my final move as I can't keep moving. It will have a detrimental effect on Simran's schooling.

6.7

Life Goes on...

My life has seen many changes and I've been very busy. Apart from teaching at school, conducting tuitions and looking after Simran, I've continued with my studies in Child Psychology as well as doing my job. Another opportunity has come my way. Our head mistress had a freak accident while skiing and hurt her back. The injury was quite bad and she could not continue with her job. Her misfortune became an opportunity for me. It is sad in a way but here I am, the head mistress of the school and earning a considerable amount of money.

Now I wear western clothes and only don salwar kameezes to go to the Gurudwara. Every Sunday, Simran and I go to Southall, our mini Punjab, to shop. We also go to the Gurdwara without fail and eat Langar. Simran has learned Punjabi as a subject in school. She is very fond of reading. I am, in fact, surprised by her knowledge of Punjabi. I think the reason is that she is a bookworm like me; our house is full of books and broadsheet newspapers. I also go to Virdi Book Store and buy a Punjabi book or two every week.

As I get older, I miss Sardar Parkash even more. I share my good memories with Simran. She asks me many questions as I read my diaries to her.

I feel envious, especially on Monday, when the other teachers talk about their weekends and the good times they had with their partners. Sometimes, I long for someone to hold me tight in his strong arms.

6.8

<center>~~~~</center>

ENTER PAUL...

Time is flying by and another year has gone. This year I met Paul, a Chemistry teacher who works under me. He is six feet tall, well-built and very handsome. He loves his sports, and teaches cricket in his spare time. He seems a very dedicated teacher. We talk and discuss many subjects aside from the curriculum and have enjoyed each other's company. In short, I seem to be attracted towards him. But I've told my colleagues that Paul and I are just good friends not lovers.

Paul's ex-wife, Jenny, has two sons. One of them is Paul's, the other one's father is unknown. Jenny is now a single parent and lives with Richard. Paul introduced me to Jenny and we have become very close friends. We meet regularly for coffee or a meal and her children come to my home and vice versa.

Jenny and Paul's divorce was very amicable, and they have stayed friends. They share the duty of looking after the children. When Jenny wants to go out with friends, Paul does the baby-sitting. Their arrangement works well. Besides sleeping in the same bed, they do most things together. Jenny does not mind my friendship with Paul; in fact, she is the one who encourages me to go further with it.

When I asked Jenny about the reason behind their divorce, she said, 'Oh, we got bored. There was no spark left with Paul. We had the same old routine – getting drunk, getting into bed and ten minutes later we would be snoring with our backs turned. It did not matter to Paul, but I get bored quickly. Then Richard came along… and he is magical! He knows how to keep me happy. Paul was okay with the divorce. He never lingers, he gets on with life. He is a lovely person and frankly I think you are both made for each other. You're both boring,' she said, and laughed.

'But what if you get bored with Richard? What then?'

'Oh no, you can't get bored with Richard. He always has a trick or two up his sleeves. He treats me both like a princess and like shit at same time and I love it…I just love it!'

Dangerous Liaisons…

I'm re-starting my life by trying to get closer to Paul, if that makes sense. Our conversations have changed from politics and education to more personal things. We now talk openly about having a full-blown relationship.

Yesterday, he came to my office and closed the door. With no hesitation, he came and stood close and said, 'I'm dying to kiss you…please.' I lost control, and that was my first long kiss with him. But then I realized where I was and pulled away.

'Paul, this is not the right place. Don't forget, I'm your boss and we cannot afford to lose our jobs, can we?' Once he had gone, I closed my eyes and relived the memory.

He came back after an hour and said, 'Let's go to India together. I always wanted to visit it and you can show me your home.'

'Yes, that is be a good idea, Paul,' I said without thinking about it too much.

Paul's coming to my office and showing affection has rekindled a fire inside me. As I get home from work, I go straight into my shower. I look at my beautiful body and its curves. Doing yoga regularly has kept me in shape. I touch my lips. Paul has made me feel like a woman again. If I'm honest, I really want to move on, I want to enjoy my life again and need to face reality and stop living in the past.

6.9

A FRESH START...

Jenny had come to see me and after a cup of coffee, our conversation started.

'Paul is such a nice guy,' she said. 'He's better than most of the rest. He loves, he cares and more than that, he is a very genuine guy.'

'Then why…? Why did you let him go…? I don't understand.'

'As I told you before, making love with him was becoming too predictable and I couldn't handle it. I say don't let him go; he is worth holding on to. He loves you a lot.'

'How do you know?'

'We are still best friends; he told me he really fancies you. And I have told him you are not run of the mill stuff. You are special and he has to treat you special if he wants to come near you. Do you like him?'

'Of course I like him. He might have told you already. We kissed in my office and it felt good. But would you mind if he is with me?'

'Don't be silly. He is a free man. He can see whoever he likes. I would love it if he were with you.'

We kept on talking about him for ages and she said, 'He is a very shy person, so you will have to take the initiative and ask him out.'

The conversation with Jenny has certainly made me think.

For the past few days, I seem to be looking at myself in the mirror for a lot longer.

I met Paul on the school grounds today. Remembering Jenny's advice, I have, without hesitation, told him, 'Paul, I'm ready for full blown relationship with you.'

'That's great! I wanted to ask you myself,' he smiled shyly.

'Good. We should make some programme soon.'

'Sure…I'm going away to Africa for two weeks and as soon as I return we'll get together…'

I really feel overjoyed today now that I've spoken to Paul and decided to start afresh. I've had enough of sadness. Jenny lives for today and so will I from now on. I can't take the burdens imposed by society for the rest of my life.

I'm counting days like a sixteen-year-old girl waiting for her first date. What to wear, what make up to put on, nails, hairs and body cleansing, all of this is coming into my head. A school teacher is behaving like a teenager!

GETTING SORTED...
SATURDAY, MARCH 15TH 1980

I've left Simran with my neighbour and made a date with Jenny to go to spa.

This time the reason for going to spa is that I'm making a special effort because of meeting with Paul. I really want to leave a very good first impression on him. Jenny is getting me ready and does everything to make sure that Paul and I get into not a one-night stand but a long lasting relationship. She still cares for Paul a lot and wants him to be happy. There may be a guilty feeling that is driving her. She is also training me what to do, Paul likes and dislikes. She will probably do the same with Paul.

TUESDAY, MARCH 25TH 1980

After his holiday, Paul came to my house. 'Sharon, you have ruined my holidays,' he said cheekily.

'How come?'

'Well you have been on my mind all this time. All I did was think about you.' He came near and held my hands and said, 'I really missed you. Let's get together soon.'

'So what are you proposing and where?'

'This Saturday, come to my place around seven.'

I agreed. He kissed me on my cheek and left.

A FRESH START...OR IS IT?
SATURDAY, MARCH 29TH

The day of reckoning has arrived. It is Saturday. The day I turn a page and put away the past for good. A fresh start...

Try to sleep well. Do not get up too early, otherwise you will have bags under your eyes, Jenny had said to me.

But I can't help but be anxious. I try to rush through everything so I am on time.

'Why are you rushing me mum? There is still half an hour to my piano lesson!' Even Simran could tell that something was going on. I smiled and said, 'I have to go to the hair dresser and run some errands. I'm going on a date tonight. You need to stay with Brenda till I get back.'

She jumped up and down on the bed and said, 'My Mom has a date...wow!'

I try not to hide anything from Simran. She is not only my daughter but my best friend as well.

LATER...

I can't decide what to wear. Should I wear a saree and look like an Indian princess or a gown and be an English Cinderella? I bought a dress yesterday with Jenny. It has such a low neck and tiny strings to hold up my beautiful bust.

I feel you can't beat an Indian silk saree and a pure pashmina Shawl, but for tonight, I've decided to wear the black low-neck dress and wrap myself in my most expensive Kashmiri shawl. I've put on a little extra perfume. I'm really behaving like a young girl going on her first date. Oh, I'm so nervous today; I hope all goes well. I am deliberately trying not to think of my past.

It was seven o'clock on the dot and I hesitantly pressed my fingers on the bell. He opened the door and greeted me with a beautiful bunch of red roses. We did the customary hug and he took my coat, leading me to his lounge. I kept my shawl on for the time being, pretending to be cold..

Paul knows that I do not drink but he still offered me wine. I refused with a smile and he said, 'Do you mind if I've some?'

'No, no, not at all. You go ahead.'

Paul put in a lot of effort to make it an Indian themed night. He'd lit several agarbattis, and was playing Pundit Ravi Shankar's sitar music in the background. He kept asking me what music I like, what food I like and so on.

I loved how much effort he put into it. It was just past nine o'clock and in those two hours our conversation had raged non-stop .

He'd hired two waiters from an Indian restaurant. They had laid out a beautiful meal for us. Paul had had about four of five glasss of wine already. After dinner, we started dancing to the music. His chest was caressing my half-naked breast. It feels so nice. I closed my eyes as I do not want to come out of the dream.

At just past eleven, he took me to his bedroom. He pulled me towards himself. There seemed to be steam coming out of bodies.

Our desire was burning at its peak. He unzipped my dress and it fell to the floor. He took off his shirt and our bodies touched.

I got into bed, covering myself with the white sheet. He had probably not seen such a beautiful body before and seemed to be in a daze. I blushed, overcome by his praise.

As he began to kiss my breasts, his face turned and all I could see was a face full of maggots. I saw his teeth going into my breast. A cry ripped from my lungs and I jumped out of bed. 'I can't do it, I can't!' I gasped, and ran from the room.

Simran was already asleep when I got home. I threw away my dress and sat naked on the floor, crying. I opened the window and a whiff of fresh air rushed as if it were waiting for me. A fragrance, my fragrance, that has been with me since the day at the Yamuna comes in and fills my nostrils. I am reassured. This is mine... this is ours. It will always be mine. Sardar Parkash is here with me and always will be. I have lived with this fragrance and will live with it for the rest of my life. My sweet memories are enough to keep me going.

The next day I apologised to Paul, and he said 'he understands'.

Five Years have passed. Jenny and Paul are back together. They now have a beautiful daughter as well. The three of us have remained good friends. Paul left our school some time ago and is now a Deputy Head in another school.

PART SEVEN

7.1

---~~~---

DOCTOR SHARNJIT
THIRTEEN YEARS LATER...

FRIDAY, MARCH 4TH 1983

I've now become Doctor Sharnjit and once again, I'm writing my story after so many years of hiatus. When I read what I've written in the past, it makes me laugh and cry at the same time. Some of it makes me feel sorry for myself.

Simran is now eighteen and she is beautiful. She is always at the top of her class. She remains a very good friend to me. She is planning to become a doctor.

Simran's friend and my teaching colleagues and friends had booked the whole of an Indian restaurant for her nineteenth birthday party. Satinder, my friend's handsome son, was also at the party and I saw that Simran seems to have an interest in him. Their eyes kept meeting. This is the first step towards falling in love. It reminds me of Sardar Parkash – how that was a case of love at first sight. We recognised there was something special between us before saying a single word.

We really had a good time at the party. On our way back, Simran suddenly said, 'Mom, let's go to India for the holidays.'

'Why India?' I was surprised at her suggestion.

'You were born there, Mom...don't you want to visit your birthplace?'

'I've never refused you before and am not going to refuse you now. We can go, but I don't think anyone will recognise me. It's been too long and Bibi Ji and I haven't been in touch for years. But anyway, if you wish to go then we will go.'

Although I'd said yes to the trip, I'm concerned that things might have changed. How will Bibi Ji react to seeing her daughter after nearly twenty years? Also, would it be safe to take my beautiful daughter to the same village where that bastard Harnek lives? Then another voice whispers, giving me reassurance, and says, *Sharnjit, the world is not all hate. There are good people who live in it too.*

MONDAY, 14 MARCH 1983

We've gotten ready to go to India and I've booked tickets. *I need to stay positive,* I keep telling myself.

7.2

—◦◦◦—

WELCOME TO INCREDIBLE INDIA...

I'm a British citizen and I love the UK, but when my feet touch Indian soil, I feel I've come home. The air, dust and heat--yes, the heat--they all have a certain smell. The very second you step out of the air-conditioned Airport, it hits you as if someone were blowing a hairdryer in your face. It's very warm today but thankfully a wind is blowing and it's amusing to see Simran trying to manage her handbag and her floppy hat.

We're staying in the five star Intercontinental Hotel and it seems that the standards and the ambiance are much superior to that of European hotels.

Most of the past two and half days have been spent shopping. We were going crazy – there is so much beautiful stuff here and Indian suits of the latest fashion. I went into a shop and saw a beautiful yellow suit. It was so lovely and reminded me of Sardar Parkash.

Next day Simran say, 'I don't want to go out today, Mom – will just sit round and relax. I'll go to the gym and then do a bit of swimming. But you go and see your old places.'

'We both can stay...have a relaxing day.'

'No, Mom, I want you to go, just on your on and see the old places, just by yourself.'

'Oh, okay… you look after yourself. I'll be back soon.'

'No, Mom, take your time, your Simran is a grown up woman and can take care of herself.'

I can't tell her that my worries increase because she is now a beautiful young woman and there are plenty of preying eyes here.

I came out of the hotel and looked around with no specific plan of where to go. An auto driver approached me, asking me for my destination. Without even thinking, the first name that came to mind was Okhla. So I was dropped off at Okhla where, nearly twenty years ago, I had spent the day with Sardar Parkash.

I walked along the banks of the Yamuna, the laziest of rivers. Memories of yester years came flooding in. I felt his presence and smelled the same fragrance that has been with me ever since that day. The tree under which we sat is still there, but it is now half-dry and struggling for life. Perhaps it is waiting for us to come back and sit under it again. *We promised we would be back.* I got up and kept walking along the bank.

Finally, when my feet were extremely tired, I sat on a bench, struggling with emotion.

The same driver was waiting for me. I asked him, 'How did you know I would be going back so soon?'

'Sister, there is nothing much left to see at Okhla, and not many people come here anymore. So where do you want to go now?'

'Oh, let's go to GB Road.'

He looked at me in astonishment and repeated, 'GB Road?'

'Don't worry, Bhai; I'm not going there for the wrong reasons.'

Everything has changed in twenty years. India has changed. Ammi Jaan's house has been redeveloped and in its place are beautiful apartments and shops. Roxy Restaurant is no longer there but I found out where Shamim and her solicitor husband now live.

Shamim has not changed. 'Oh, hello Punjabney, how are you? Still looking so young. You haven't changed one bit. How is Sardar Parkash? Is he with you?'

'You tell me about yourself first. How is Ammi Jaan?' I asked hesitantly.

'I'm fine. I have four kids –two sons and two daughters. A balanced family! My solicitor is still going strong in both his practice and his practice with me. And Ammi Jaan passed away a few years ago. Had a dog's life in the end. You know the Seth – her lover--died. Once his sons took over, they chucked her out and redeveloped the whole area. She was very mean in last few years. You were very lucky to escape when you did. Oh, she gave us so much trouble. Anyway where is your Sardar Parkash...has he come to India as well?'

I told her my whole story. She offered me the use of her car and driver whilst I was in Delhi.

I left and returned to the hotel.

When I walked towards the hotel bar, I saw Simran in deep conversation with a good-looking young man. I went straight to them.

'Hi, Mom, this is Doctor Avinash Singh,' she said without hesitation.

I put my hand out and said, 'Simran's Mum – Sharnjit.'

'Sat Siri Akaal Ji,' he said shyly. 'Aunty Ji, my village is near Ludhiana and I belong to a Jat Sikh family. Our main occupation, or my parents' main occupation, is farming. I'm a doctor and I've come here to attend a seminar. Simran has told me a lot about you. You've a very intelligent daughter,' he smiled.

'Mom, he's promised to show us his village and I've invited him to London. Is that okay, Mom?'

'Yes, Beta Ji, definitely.'

'We've exchanged addresses, Aunty Ji. Please come, my whole family will be delighted to meet you.'

Simran asked me later that night, 'Do you really like him, Mom?'

'Oh, he seems like a very nice, handsome, young man.'

'I like him very much, Mom.' She hugged me tight. 'Where did you go today?'

I told her the whole story, including meeting Shamim and her offering her car and driver.

'Oh, that's very generous of her; perhaps we should take her up on that offer.'

We have decided to use the room service and eat in the room.

Simran's face has become very serious as she asks me, 'Mom, I want to talk to about something very serious. Please give an honest and frank answer.'

I wait in anticipation, 'Yes...okay...go ahead. What is it?'

'Mom, there are two well-educated, intelligent people who love each other so much, promise to live life together but circumstances do not allow that to happen and they live separate lives. Then my question is – do they suddenly become bad people? And my supplementary question is, 'Do they become enemies and the love between them just ends?'

'Your question is right. I've thought about it many times myself. Those people do not become bad neither the love between diminishes. Yes, someone else comes in between them who have the right to that love, affection and the care.'

'Then, by someone else joining in, does the fist love diminish? You say yourself that love is a feeling. Do the feelings become any lesser?'

'Then what is it that keeps those two people apart? Can't they be friends...just good friends without physical contact?'

'I can't give the answer you are looking for, but... can tell you, I still love Sardar Parkash, more than ever. In addition, the reason I've been able to manage life is because of that love not in spite of. One single dose was enough for my whole life.'

'Now that you're in mood to listen, let me also say this, Mom, I've been thinking,' Simran began. 'How was Sardar Parkash supposed to find you? You didn't try hard enough to find him either. I've always found it difficult to understand why. Why this sacrifice? I'm sorry Mom, I shouldn't talk like this. You've gone through hell and here I'm, blaming you. Bringing me up as a single parent couldn't have been easy.'

'No, you need not feel sorry. What you've said is the truth… I've not tried myself, nor have I given him a chance, but I had my reasons at that time.'

'I'm going to find him, whatever it takes. I shall find him, Mom… I'm going to find him for us.'

Simran just lay there in my lap and as I ran my fingers through her beautiful hair, a thought entered in my head. My daughter has grown up. She understands my feelings and pain.

It is now six in the morning. I always enjoyed my early morning walk, so we both set off on foot and walked to Bangla Sahib Gurdwara. There we met Avinash.

'It's my last day at the seminar, so I thought I'd better go to Gurdwara. I request you, Aunty Ji, please visit us and let me show Simran our village. My Biji will be very pleased to meet you. As soon as you get to your hotel in Ludhiana, do call me. I'll come and collect you.'

'Please say yes Mom…please!'

'Yes, Avinash, we'll certainly come.'

He seems a very nice boy.

'Aunty Ji, with your permission, may I ask Simran for a cup of coffee?'

'Yes, yes, sure!'

7.3

MY SHINING PUNJAB...

Ludhiana seems to have made a lot of progress in the last twenty years – there are lots of new shops and bazaars. But here, unlike in Delhi, people keep staring at us as if we are aliens. I think it is the big floppy hat that Simran is wearing.

Our intention is to go to my village first and then to visit Avinash if we have the time. I'm very apprehensive about this trip. I don't think we should stay the night in the village; instead we should get back to our hotel but Simran seems to be keen on staying at the haveli. I tell her that I haven't been in touch with Bibi Ji for years, so I'm not sure what sort of reception we'll get.

'We won't know till we get there, Mom.'

The village seems to have changed completely. So many new houses have come up. We have to ask people in order to find the haveli. It looks very impressive, with big steel gates.

Preeti, Bachno's younger daughter, opened the gate and recognised me straightaway. She came running towards me with her hands folded to show her respect. She was so excited and shouted to everyone, *Didi Sharnjit Ji from London is here.* Soon after, we went in and she brought out a couple of chairs. She brought us water and tea.

'Preeti, how are you and your family?'

'Very good, Didi Ji. I have two children now, a boy and a girl. I live here permanently. I'll tell you my story later. How are you Didi Ji? Is this your daughter?'

'Yes, this is Simran, my daughter. We're very well, by the grace of God. Where are Bibi Ji and Sarpanch Ji?'

She took me to a room. At the far end was Sarpanch Sahib, looking very pale and weak and lying in a bed. Preeti told me that he has had a stroke and has lost the use of one side of his body. I feel so sorry for him.

'Where is Bibi Ji, Preeti? When is she coming home?'

'Bibi Ji had a very important meeting. She'll probably be late.'

Nothing has changed, I said to myself. Since we arrived early, we still have a long day ahead of us. I suggested that we go into the village to see our old house.

'Oh, there is nothing left of your old house, Didi Ji.' Someone else had built a beautiful house in its place. That is what happens, I suppose. Progress finds a way.

I went to Tayi Ji who has grown old but still loves me the same. She gave me a big hug. We talked for about an hour and she filled me in on all the information. Harnek has gotten married and has three children. His wife, I'm told, is a very obedient and respectful girl. He has taken over from Sarpanch Ji and works very closely with Bibi Ji. They both are very successful in politics. In fact, Bibi Ji has become a seasoned politician who wields a lot of power in the area.

Our meeting was a much more sober affair. I would rather have an uneducated, simple mother with a big heart.

'Who is she?' Bibi Ji asked, pointing towards Simran.

'She is Simran, Jagir Singh's daughter,' I said sarcastically.

'We heard that Jagir was…'

'You probably heard wrong,' I said sharply.

'It's been so long. You sent no letters, nothing. Did you forget about us?'

'You didn't bother to ask if I was dead or alive either. You did well to dispatch me to Jagir Singh.'

Simran noticed that our conversation was getting ugly, so she made a timely intervention. 'Mom, Grandma still looks so young. I think it runs in our family. I'll be a doctor, Grandma.' A few minutes later, we were all laughing and joking.

And then the dreaded moment I was so anxious to avoid arrived. Harnek walked in. He has the same gait as his father. 'Hello, Sharnjit, when did you come?' He said without blinking an eyelid, as if he had done nothing wrong... as if nothing had ever happened between us... as if it was indeed a little mistake done by children that ought to have been forgotten.

On seeing his face, a shiver ran down my spine. A stink I'd faced twenty years ago filled my nostrils again. I felt as though I were unable to breathe and I struggled for air. For a moment, all I could see was maggots falling out of his face. Then suddenly, Simran touched me and woke me up by saying, 'Mom, Uncle Ji has asked you a question.'

'We came this morning,' was all I could muster.

'Who is she?' He asked, pointing at Simran.

'She is my daughter, Simran.' I deliberately put more emphasis on 'my'. As he talked to her, I wondered whether they could tell that they are father and daughter. They were deep into conversation, as though they had known each other for years. This is why they say that blood is thicker than water.

In the course of our conversation, Preeti had deliberately passed a remark earlier that day. 'You cannot hide stink...he is lucky to have a very obedient wife who does not ask questions. But Didi Ji, there is no smoke without a fire.'

Preeti's daughters are the same age as Simran, so she has been spending time with them. We all went to my old school, which had just finished for the day. Simran was surrounded by large group of young girls wanting to know about England. I met with the teachers; they were all extremely friendly and welcoming.

'Preeti, lets leave Simran here with your daughter. I want see our farm,' I said.

As we walked on the side of dusty road, so many memories came flooding in. I spent a lot of time studying under it.

'How is Jeeti? Does she come often to see you?' The very second I mention Jeeti's name, Preeti started to sob.

'What's the matter? Is something wrong?'

'Sorry, Didi Ji, I'll tell you in a minute, just follow me,' and she takes me to a disused well.

'Now tell me yourself, Didi Ji, how can someone just fall into this well? They can't unless someone pushes them or they want to commit suicide. And one thing I don't understand is what she was doing here. I know everything Didi Ji. You know Harnek used to upset her a lot. He was always after her. I believe my mother and father both know, and when I say something about Jeeti, they tell me to keep my mouth shut. Sarpanch and the police said it was an accidental death But how, Didi Ji? After this happened, Sarpanch helped us build a small brick house for ourselves. My parents' silence was bought. I knew it, and it stank to me.'

'Let us go home, Preeti. I'm feeling suffocated in the open air.' I did not need to see anymore to guess what must have happened to that brave girl. The very words she uttered some twenty years ago suddenly sprang to mind. *I will not compromise my honour ever and if I have to die for it, I will.* I shivered. I couldn't decide whether ending one's own life is bravery or weakness, but one thing I did understand was the mental torture she must have gone through.

And the bastard who had done the deed was still roaming the streets.

LATER...

Preeti always has a lot in store to talk about. So just for conversation's sake and to take my mind off what I just been reminded, I ask her, 'How has life treated you Preeti?'

'Didi Ji, so much has happened with me, I don't know where

to begin.' Then she told me her life story and I just listened. 'It must been a year after you left for England...I had just finished my first years exams. After Jeeti was out of the way, Harnek messed round with me. He kept on saying, *"you are so beautiful... I have fallen in love with you... one day I will marry you. I will not hide our love and whatever price I had to pay, I will pay"* and so on. He also threatened me and said that if I say anything to anyone then I have to bear the consequences. I was freighted, didn't like it one bit... actually I hated it also knew that Jeeti committed suicide, and it was no accident. I didn't want to go that way... didn't want him to harm me, so played his game. I thought, I'd two more years and sooner I pass my exams I'll get married. There will plenty of people who will be interested because there are not many educated girls in the poor classes. My scheme worked for the first year. I played around with him – giving him smile, occasionally letting him hold me and once or twice let him kiss me. In the final year he behaved badly again. He wanted more and more.

Then one day I was alone at the farm and he followed me. He was a bit drunk and did not let me go. He forced me against my will. I kept on saying no, but then something happened, I did not remember anything but I got up to find, I was no longer a virgin. I simply wanted to kill myself and walked towards the disused well. He came after me, cried so much and apologised. He said he would marry me in a proper way. I felt half-guilty by leading him on.

I was desperate for help so I told Bachno. However, she said, 'he is young will understand one day. Do not worry, just mange it. It is nothing new, she said. Poverty is a curse. We do not have the same dignity or respect as rich people. Look at Sarpanch ...me first then Bibi Ji. You just have to take as it comes. You are not the first one by any means.' She told me to take advantage and blackmail him – ask him for money and favours. So I did... I let him have what he wanted and got what I needed. He bought me gifts. Something inside me liked him and I found the courage to forgive him.

We used to meet up at least once a month if not sooner. A few months later, I got pregnant, and that really created a lot of problem for both of us. We had to tell Bhajno who in turn told Bibi and Sarpanch Ji. To cut the long story short, I got married to someone Sarpanch's introduction. He paid the entire expense of the wedding. It all happened within less than two weeks. A few months later Harnek got married too, but we kept our relationship going.

'After my first child, my mother in law found out, I was still having an affair with Harnek. She then told my husband who got very aggressive towards me. He beat me up, calling me names. I cannot blame him because no one told him; I was pregnant when he got married. Bastard could not even count the months. I was pregnant again and even this time with Harnek. I was sure of that I told him about the beating and everything else. He asked to leave him so I did. So he is father of both my daughters.'

I'm listening to her in utter disbelief. He has raped three of us and escaped scot-free, living a respectable man's life.

Suddenly I'm tired and exhausted. I never felt this foolish and low in my life. '*Why did I come here? Why…?*' I keep repeating these questions to myself. I can't even face Preeti now and don't know what to do. I can't understand that this bastard has two children with Preeti, one with me and three his wife has produced. They are not aware that they are real brother and sisters.

Whatever Preeti says about Harnek, I can do nothing but hate him. I cannot bear to look at his face. He is still a bloody rapist of the worst kind who does not forgive even his own sister.

At home, I have been feeling sad and have developed a headache. Simran and Bibi Ji had lengthy discussions on various topics. Simran seems to relish the experience of village life.

We had been given the same old room to sleep in, but Simran said, 'Mom, I'm not going to sleep as yet. I have a lot to talk about with Preeti's daughters and don't want to disturb you. You take rest.' So there I was, on my own in that room.

I was so tired that I dozed off, but my mind hadn't switched off after all. My dreams were horrific, terrible, filled with images of blood and maggots and the trauma that had visited me in this room. But then I cried, 'He's dead! I killed him! I killed him!

I awoke screaming and sobbing and Simran came running from the next room. 'Are you okay, Mum?' She asks.

'Yes dear, the same nightmare I been having every night is finished now. It will not upset me anymore. I have killed the bastard…forever. No, he won't be back, not now.' A loud cry turned into intermitting sobbing. I had shot my past dead. I would be free.

From now on, I will try my best to live again. I will introduce colours to this bleak canvas. I will definitely try to find Sardar Parkash. I have punished myself enough.

A NEW DAWN…

It was around eight thirty in the morning and the telephone rings in our hotel room. 'You have a visitor, Ma'am. His name is Doctor Avinash.'

'Oh, please tell him to wait in the lobby; we'll be down there in half an hour.'

We both are very excited and panicking as well.

'Come on, Simran, get ready quick, we can't make him wait too long.'

'Oh, Mom, what shall I wear? I cannot decide, please help me, Mom.'

It reminds me of the morning of my first date with Sardar Parkash. I was panicking the same way as my daughter is now.

'Wear that yellow Punjabi suit we bought from Ludhiana.'

About twenty minutes later Simran was still not ready, so I went to Lobby and see Avinash.

He and his younger sister Kamaljit were waiting for us. They both stood up and greeted me with Sat Siri Akaal and with folded hands, the traditional Punjabi way.

'Simran will be in another few minutes yet. Are you okay to wait,' I asked.

'It is perfectly okay, Aunty Ji; we have come to collect you. My Biji is waiting for you. She is getting the breakfast ready otherwise she was going to come.'

Oh, my God! Simran looks like a princess in the yellow Punjabi suit. So beautiful, I should look away.

About half an hour later we are travelling on the dust roads, Avinash's Ambassador Car has finally arrived in front of their house. Their house is massive Haveli type about four times bigger than that of Sarpanch. They got cows and buffalos on one side and all the agricultural heavy machinery on the other. Avinash's mum, dad, grandma, granddad and quite a few other women from the neighbourhood are also there waiting to greet us. They make us feel as if we are some kind of celebrities. A drop of oil has been poured on the side of doorframes and a plate full of Laddoos (Indian Sweet) has been brought to us. We are supposed to eat a little bit of it at least before they distribute to everyone. It is called Shagun (good omen).

I have been advising Simran to touch the feet of elders as mark of respect. Therefore, Simran bends down to touch Gran's feet but is stopped by her saying, 'unmarried daughters don't touch feet. They only do it when they become brides.' What a beautiful tradition. So much, respect for daughters. I whisper in Simran's ear, 'this is what a true mother is like, mountain of love and affection.'

Breakfast started soon after we arrived. It is freshly prepared Pranthey and Curd, Corn Chapaaties, Mango chutney, Indian sweets and a lot more. I jokingly suggested to Simran who was trying having everything to be careful with her western stomach. Simran's love for Punjabi culture and living is growing very quickly.

I took Simran aside and asked her a blunt question, what were her expectations from this visit? Is it merely to see the village life or is she falling in love with Avinash? It's always best to know the pros and cons before getting too serious about it. 'Here I am, being very hypocritical. You do not do assessment before you fall in love. When it happens, it happens. It is God's gift to humankind as they say.'

'Mom, I really like him. I'll be honest with you, I think I'm already in love with him', Simran said.

'History is repeating itself, Mom. Just as you fell in love with uncle Sardar Parkash at the first sight. It all started at the breakfast in the hotel back in Delhi. There were not many seats left, and he asked me if he could sit on my table. Then we got talking. You told me not to talk to strangers, but with Avinash, it felt as if I knew him. I think we've a lot in common. Just give us some time, let me see where he stands and I'll let you know straight afterwards.' Simran looked in my eyes and said with a smile.

Avinash wanted to show Simran his farm so we decided to have lunch cum tea there. He had already made this programme and had people cooking there already.

Having lunch in the open air was such a wonderful experience. A breeze was blowing to keeps us little cool. Tube-well running, Simran and Avinash both sitting on the edge of the water channel with their feet dangling in it.. They both will make a lovely couple, I thought. I discussed everything with Avinash's parents very openly.

After an hour or so, they both came to us and said, "We wanted all of you to know that we have taken an important decision. We like each other very much and want to spend our lives together. We need your blessings."

That was it. I agreed with Avinash parents to do a simple engagement ceremony now and we can sort out marriage dates later.

Simran and I, both are over the moon. It's been the most successful holiday ever.

We did a lot more shopping and Simran spent a whole 'getting to know day' with Avinash.

Overall, our holidays to India were a great success. I got rid of my fear and nightmares. Simran had grown into a beautiful and wise woman.

7.4

---~w~---

Six Months Later...

A lot has happened in the last six months. Avinash and Simran have gotten married here in UK. His parents and sister came from India to attend the wedding. It went very well and everyone loved it. Avinash inclusion in the family has made a lot of difference. Being a doctor, he's very positive and polite person and both Simran and I've learned a lot from him. He has much calmer approach to life. He has a very good job working at the London Hospital too. ... I've become much calmer in my personal life, although the urge to meet Sardar Parkash is getting stronger.

One day, Simran came running towards me, out of breath.

'What's happened? Is everything okay?' I asked.

'Oh, Mom, I've found him...I've found him!' She cried and embraced me.

'Will you stop and tell me what have you found? Why are you so excited?'

She was jumping up and down running round like a monkey. Finally she said, 'My sweet mother, we've found him! We know where he lives. I'm talking about Uncle Sardar Parkash. I'm so happy that we've found him.'

My first reaction was disbelief. I've been longing to see him for years. This does not feel real yet.

'Mom, aren't you happy?'

'I'm very happy, Beta Ji! I'm thankful to you, but our lives have been led so far apart from one another…'

The truth is, I've wrapped myself in my own little bubble. Perhaps I'm too protective of it and any change now feels like an intrusion. It's true that there were times when I wished to come out of this state and wanted to face reality, but then the mere mention of the name Sardar Parkash would wake something inside me

'Do you remember your promise to me, Mom? You said that you would make a new start in life. You would allow new shoots of hope to grow while holding on to your very dear memories. My sweetest Mom, I'd very high hopes that you would try to make a new start. I confess that going to India was part of the plan. The second part was to find Sardar Parkash and have a grown up discussion with him, or at least find out whether he still has feelings for you.'

'I will keep my promise to you, but what if he says no and does not recognise me? I'll be completely shattered,' I said.

'You be okay, Mom… You're still so beautiful… He'll be so happy to see you. I just know.' 'It would be very difficult for me to exist. I've loved him with my heart and soul and I still do. Beta ji, please give me a bit of time. Let me get myself mentally ready. I'll have to make some adjustments to my thinking,' I said.

TUESDAY, MAY 2ND 1989

It has been quite a testing night for me. Now that I know where Sardar Parkash lives, my world has turned upside down. The desire to be with him, to be able to talk him is getting stronger by the minute. I've been able to safeguard my memories so far, but Simran has rekindled the fire that had lain asleep for almost twenty years.

7.5

---ᄿᄿᄿ---

OH MY GOD! NO...

MONDAY, MAY 27ᵀᴴ 1989

I was sitting in my office when a strange thing happened. As I got up from my chair, I couldn't see anything for a few moments. Darkness swam before my eyes, my legs were shaking and I fell down on the floor. My colleague came running and helped me get up. They said it must have happened because of tiredness from excessive work. However, I feel there's something not right with me. I very rarely use the lift but now I avoid using the stairs.

If Simran finds out then she will be unduly worried, so I have not told her anything.

A WEEK LATER...

The same thing happened again and this time it was in the main library. The students were also there when I fell and it was extremely embarrassing. Several students came running and helped me and gave me water.

I'm faced with a big dilemma. I need to consult a doctor. Maybe I'm weak and stressed out. I 've started to take Vitamin B Complex.

TWO WEEKS LATER...

I'm now in a hospital bed. I've been told that I collapsed in the kitchen and an ambulance had to be called. The doctors have carried out many tests. The signs do not look good.

Simran was sobbing uncontrollably when she came near me. 'How is this possible?' She asked. 'I can't believe it…' she clutched at my hands.

'Please stop crying. Tell me, what's wrong. Say something, Beti ji.'

'Look, Mum you are not well, but it is curable… we'll soon get you better,' she said and started sobbing again.

The doctors told me I have breast cancer.

For a few moments, the dreaded word shook me to the bone. But then, I gathered courage.

'I'm not going anywhere, Simran Beta. You know your mother is a fighter.'

After spending a week in the hospital, I've come home with a truckload of medication. I would rather die at home, in my own bed, than in a hospital. They insist that that I undergo chemotherapy, but I have no desire to lose my hair. Sardar Parkash once loved it. Neither will I allow them to remove my breasts.

Simran has been very busy for the past two days. A nurse stays with me all day. I'm being looked after well.

7.6

---~w~---

Silver Lining...

MONDAY, AUGUST 21ST 1989

Something is happening today. Simran seems to be doing spring-cleaning. There is a spring in her step and it's been a long time since I saw smile on her face. My Simran has forgotten to smile since she found out about my illness.

'Hi Mom, you have to wear this tomorrow. I want you to look your best. The hairdresser will be here in the morning to do your hair.'

She brought out my favourite suit and the yellow dupatta. I'd left this in Sardar Prakash's room in Delhi more than twenty years ago. 'Oh my God…!' was all I could say.

PART EIGHT

8.1

THE FINAL...

TUESDAY, 29 AUGUST 1989

Jinder and I'd gone through our usual drill quite a few times by now. 'Have you got your passport, ticket, wallet...?'

'Yes... how many times are you going to ask me?'

'Better to check! Now make sure Behan Ji gets the best treatment. Look after her properly, don't worry about the work here. Getting her better comes first. You have ten days. If it takes longer, you come back and I'll go.' Jinder refuses to wait for my answer.

She will carry on saying what she needs to say. I'm wondering just how much faith she has in my ability to find a cure for Nirmal's illness. Her positive thinking certainly has the desired effect on me as I've started to believe that when we come back from New York, Nirmal will be fit and healthy and this dreaded cancer will have disappeared.

Last night, Jinder and I went to the Gurdwara to pray for Nirmal's health. She has a nearly blind faith in God's ability to perform miracles. She's given me Prasad from the Gurdwara to give to Nirmal for good luck.

'Everything is going to be alright,' I keep saying to myself as I park my car at Airport car park. When we come back, we all will go on holidays together. It will be so nice. I'm choosing holiday destinations as I sit in the Shuttle Bus to the Terminal.

I've been waiting for Simran and Nirmal at the terminal for the past two hours. I'm sure this is where we were supposed to meet. Why haven't they come? They were only coming from Harlow, and it shouldn't take them too long. I take my ticket out and check the date, then buy today's newspaper and match the date with my ticket… I'm acting naive. How many times am I going to ask the airline staff if they've checked in? They don't normally tell you, but anyone can see the anxiety pasted all over my face and this helps. Check in for BA flight 321 to New York has just closed. They are still not here!

Something is not right, but I do not wish to think about anything bad. I must stay positive. I rush to the nearest phone booth, but no one is picking up the phone either. They must be on their way. But no, something inside me is panicking. I jump into a taxi and rush to Nirmal's house.

'Please answer!' I keep pressing the bell and knocking on the door. I go to the front lounge and peep inside. There seemed to no one in the house. I stand there utterly confused until the neighbour opens her door and tells me what I don't want to hear.

'Sharon collapsed earlier and was taken by ambulance to the Main Hospital in Harlow,' she says.

'Oh, my God!' I exclaim.

My world seems to have collapsed. My hopes were right at the top of Mount Everest and in a second, they've come plummeting down right at the bottom.

Half an hour later, I get to the hospital. My body is trembling with fear as I approach Nirmal.

'Oh you're here!' she says, lying in the hospital bed, smiling as though nothing has happened. She simply looks at me. Despite the internal pain and anguish, she seems to be calm and at peace. I hold both her hands in mine, caressing and kissing them. A huge warm tear that I've been holding back for so long falls on our hands. She smiles…

A few moments later, she lets go of her last breath. 'Rest in Peace, Darling,' won't be written on any stone but my heart.

8.2

——∿——

NOT THE FINAL CHAPTER...

There can *never* be a final chapter until I breathe my last, Nirmal. Yes, I was part of the funeral procession, all dressed up in white, ready to say my final farewell to you, but I couldn't. There are no goodbyes in love. You are not here in body but your soul lives on. It has taken permanent residence in a special corner of my heart. When I look up at the sky, I see you wearing the same yellow dupatta and playing hide and seek behind the clouds. I gaze at a rainbow and try to find the colours of your dupattas. I do remember you calling me *half-mad;* it wasn't true then, but I'm certainly completely mad now. Why would someone talk to the vacant passenger seat of the car? Why would someone end up a hundred miles away from his intended destination?

It has been 24 years since you left us for your heavenly abode. Today is the anniversary. Jinder reminds me of a promise that I made to you – to write your story. She brings your diaries carefully wrapped and puts them on the table in front of me. We stare at them in complete silence for a moment or two. These moments seems like an eternity. Are we ready to trespass? I don't know. Will we ever be?

'It can't be that difficult to copy them, and you promised Nirmal that you would. I'm sure you can,' she says with confidence.

I do not answer, but my fear is getting the better of me. *What if they contain something I wish I hadn't known.*

'Will you help read these while I write?' I ask.

'No, no… that will be trespassing. This story belongs to you and Nirmal. Just promise that the first book will be presented to me as a gift, and I will receive it on Nirmal's behalf. That will be the most fitting tribute,' she says.

'Yes, that will be the most fitting tribute,' I agree.

We are mortals, and we will meet up there one day, but our story will remain immortal for generations thereafter to read.

GOODBYE FOR NOW MY LOVE, REST IN PEACE

ACKNOWLEDGEMENTS

Many people have helped me in writing this book, but none more than Achala Upendran and Alison Taft, my two editors who has been wonderful and wise. My special thanks to Diane Perry for helping me choose the title and much more. Huge thanks also to Vic Uppal and Pam Dhaliwal for encouraging me along the way. Pam has very graciously created and managed my Website. Thanks Pam! Sarabjit my elder sister has acted as my critic, never shy to have a forthright view. It all helped. Since my father's departure, my brother Baldev Krishan and his son Shiv Sohal have been my pillars of strength. My departed Mum who never departed – lives in my heart and will always live. I'm a writer today because of her.

I am grateful to my elder daughter Anu Johar for being my beta reader and giving me extremely important feedback and my other two daughters Seema Sandhu and Sharan Dhami for believing in me and putting up with my ever-changing moods and mini tantrums. My special thanks goes to my son Karn Sohal for his unstinting support and looking after the business so efficiently and for giving me so much time to write and my Bahu Beti Rakhee for the respect, affection and joy she has given us all.

My true supporters are my grandchildren, Kiran, Amman, Viren, Rohan, Deeya, Amara and Sianna. They provide with me with much comfort cum distraction when I needed it most.

Finally, what can I say – 'thank you' is a small word for what you do for me – Jinder, my soulmate, my wife.

GLOSSARY

AMMI JAAN: Used for mother as a mark of respect in Muslims.

AUTO: Auto Rickshaw: World famous Three-wheeler yellow/ green scooter – a popular mode of commuting in Delhi.

BABU: A white-collar office worker.

BARSATI: A small room on the roof of the house – to escape from rain and for oddments/storage.

BETA JI: To call your son or daughter with affection.

BEHAN JI: Sister.

BEEJI: Mother.

BHAJI: Brother.

BHABI: Brother's wife.

CHHOTE BABU: A younger ranked officer/Babu.

CA SAHIB: Chartered Accountant.

DHABA: A popular roadside Cafe serving basic Punjabi Food.

DUPATTA: A thin cotton shawl.

DTU: Delhi Transport Undertaking.

GIDDA: Punjabi Folk Dance performed by women.

GULSHAN NANDA: A famous Hindi Novelist.

HAVELI: A large Farm house which has living quarters and as well room for animals etc.

JOO: You.

KABBADI: National game of Punjab – originated from villages.

KOTHA: Brothel.

KURTA: A long shirt.

MUNDU: A boy waiter.

PRASAD: A material substance of food that is religious offering given to devotees/worshippers.

SAHIB: calling someone with mark of respect.

SARPANCH: Leader of the village PANCHAYAT – Committee.

SAT SIRI AKAL: used in Sikh religion to greet someone – Meaning God is immortal.

SARDAR: Mostly used in front of the name of a Sikh or Jat Farmers as mark of respect in Punjab.

TWAIF: A prostitute.

ZIMIDAR: A farmer.

PUBLICATIONS OF THE

ARMY RECORDS SOCIETY

VOL. 41

THE FIRST WORLD WAR DIARY OF NOËL DRURY, 6TH ROYAL DUBLIN FUSILIERS

Captain Noël Drury at Hastière sur Meuse, December 1918.